The Assassin's Riddle

Paul Doherty was born in Middlesbrough in 1946. He was admitted to Liverpool University where he gained a First Class Honours Degree in History and won a state scholarship to Exeter College, Oxford. While there he met his wife, Carla.

Paul worked in Ascot, Newark and Crawley, before being appointed as Headmaster to Trinity Catholic High School, Essex, in 1981. The school has been described as one of the leading comprehensives in the U.K. and has been awarded 'Outstanding' in four consecutive OFSTED inspections. All seven of Paul and Carla's children have been educated at Trinity.

Paul has written over 100 books and has published a series of outstanding historical mysteries set in the Middle Ages, Classical Greece, Ancient Egypt and elsewhere. His books have been translated into more than twenty languages.

Also by Paul Doherty

The Brother Athelstan Mysteries

The Nightingale Gallery
The House of the Red Slayer
Murder Most Holy
The Anger of God
By Murder's Bright Light
The House of Crows
The Assassin's Riddle
The Devil's Domain
The Field of Blood
The House of Shadows
Bloodstone
The Straw Men
Candle Flame
The Book of Fires
The Herald of Hell
The Great Revolt
A Pilgrimage to Murder

PAUL DOHERTY

The Assassin's Riddle

CANELO

First published in the United Kingdom in 1996 by Headline Book
Publishing, a division of Hodder Headline PLC, under the pseudonym of
Paul Harding

This edition published in the United Kingdom in 2022 by

Canelo
Unit 9, 5th Floor
Cargo Works, 1–2 Hatfields
London, SE1 9PG
United Kingdom

A CIP catalogue record for this book is available from the British Library.

Print ISBN 978 1 80032 871 6
Ebook ISBN 978 1 78863 894 4

Look for more great books at www.canelo.co

Printed and bound in Great Britain by Clays Ltd, Elcograf S.p.A.

1

To Kathie and Peter Gosling of Chingford. Many thanks for all your help.

Prologue

Edwin Chapler, clerk of the Chancery of the Green Wax, sat in the small, musty chapel built in the centre of London Bridge. Outside the sun had set, though the sky was still gashed with red, dulling the stars and giving the inhabitants of London further excuse to trade, play, or stroll arm in arm along the riverside. The taverns and hostelries were full. The jumbled streets echoed with songs from the alehouses. The pains and hunger of winter were now forgotten, the harvest had been good and so the markets were busy. Edwin Chapler, however, had a heaviness of heart, as any man would, who had to face the truth but couldn't tell it. He looked round the small chapel. At the far end was the small sanctuary, on the left the Lady Shrine and, to the right, a huge statue of St Thomas à Becket with a sword grotesquely driven into his head.

'I should be in the Baker's Dozen,' Chapler whispered. 'Listening to a fiddler and wondering if Alison could dance to his tune.'

He had come here, as he often did, to seek guidance, but he couldn't pray. He opened his mouth but no words came out. He glanced up at the painted window. In the fast-fading light of the day, the tortured Christ still writhed on His cross.

Chapler looked away. In here it was cold and he was all alone; it might be days before he finally decided. Silent terror gripped him. What if he did nothing and it was discovered? Chapler swallowed hard. Two summers ago, he had seen a man executed for treason: a clerk who'd sold secrets to the Spanish. Chapler closed his eyes but he couldn't remove the grisly scene: the high black platform, the butcher's table underneath the soaring gallows at Tyburn. The unfortunate clerk had been cut down and sliced from gullet to crotch as a housewife would a chicken. His head was then cut off and his body quartered to be boiled in pitch and placed above the city gates.

Chapler shivered as he peered through the gloom. The two candles he had lit before the statue of St Thomas glowed like fiery eyes. The darkness pressed in. Chapler felt some evil force was lurking near, ready to jump like a monstrous cat. Outside, the thundering hooves of a horse made him jump. Chapler recalled why he was here. He had been given sufficient warning to stay silent. He'd gone to his stable and found his horse writhing in pain. A sympathetic ostler had agreed to put the animal out of its misery. When the horse's corpse had been dragged to the slaughterhouse and its belly slit open, instead of hay and straw, fish hooks and sharp thistle leaves had been found. Chapler had protested but the greasy-faced landlord who owned the stable just shrugged.

'Don't blame me!' he'd snapped. 'The horses are well looked after here. Look around, master, look around!

Why, in heaven's name, should we feed some poor horse fish hooks and thistles?'

Chapler had agreed and walked away: an enemy had done that. He closed his eyes again, clenching his hands as he knelt beside the pillar. A sound above made him start. He opened his eyes in terror at the black form which hovered under the heavy beamed roof. Chapler moaned in fear. A demon? Some dark soul hunting him? The black shadow turned, feathery wings gently beating the air. Chapler relaxed: it was only a raven, one of those great black birds which haunted London Bridge, hunting for carrion on the starlings beneath or, even better, waiting for the severed heads of criminals and traitors to be hoisted on poles. The raven must have flown in and been trapped. Chapler watched curiously: the bird didn't caw but flew up to a window ledge, its yellow beak tapping at the horned glass, then it turned on its perch. Chapler suspected it was studying him. A portent? A devil? He wondered whether to open the door and see if the bird would fly out but he couldn't move. He really couldn't be bothered; at least the bird was a companion. The raven cawed as if it could read his thoughts; its head turned, looking at the door. Chapler sighed and struggled to his feet just as the door crashed open. The raven cawed in triumph as it floated down and out into the fading light. Chapler ignored it, more intent on the shadowy figure shuffling into the church.

'Who are you?' he called.

The cowled figure didn't answer. Instead it stopped before the altar of St Christopher, just within the porch. A coin fell into the box; a tinder was struck, a candle fit and placed upon an iron spigot before the statue of the patron saint of travellers. The figure turned. It was a woman. Her coarse hair fell from under the brim of her pointed hat and lay about her shoulders in untidy coils. She shuffled closer. Chapler glimpsed a wizened face, bright beady eyes, lips tightly pursed, almost hidden by the furrows of her cheeks. He heaved a sigh of relief. It was only old Harrowtooth. A witch, a wise woman, who lived in a shabby tenement further down the bridge. She was called that because her one protruding tooth hung down like the iron tip of a plough.

'I'd like to pray above the water,' old Harrowtooth declared, forcing a smile. 'A good place to pray says I. Always quiet. God's water beneath, God's sky above.' Her clawed hand seized Chapler's wrist. 'And it's always good to see a bonny young man attending to his orisons. Many a young man I've seen in my life,' she gabbled on. 'I remember one here, drove me away with curses he did when I asked for a coin.' She pushed her ugly face closer. 'Fell ill of a fever he did: a terrible thirst raged in his throat. Yet he was afraid to moisten his lips because he could not stand the sound or touch of water.'

Chapler pulled his hand away, dipped into his purse and handed across a penny.

'God bless you, sir.' She held the coin up. 'God bless you. I come in and spend a farthing for a candle and looks I leave the richer. Who says God does not answer prayers?' The old woman's narrow shoulders shook with laughter. She opened the door and turned. 'A word of caution, young man.' Her voice was harsh, surprisingly strong. 'The raven is a harbinger of doom!' She slammed the door behind her.

Chapler went back and crouched by the pillar. Despite old Harrowtooth's appearance he felt more serene, as if his mind was made up. If he did what was right, if he did what was proper, then he'd be safe and all would be well. He stayed awhile, thinking through what he would do. He dropped to his knees. Now his soul was calm he could pray, perhaps light another candle before he left? Immersed in his devotions, Chapler didn't hear the door quietly open.

The shadowy figure came up fast like some spider, moving across the flagstones, not a sound till the iron-tipped mace cracked the back of Chapler's skull and the young man, blood pouring through his mouth, collapsed to the floor. The figure stooped and dragged him out on to the steps of the church. The assassin paused. There was no one around. Darkness had fallen, the day's business was done. He picked up Chapler, as if his victim was a friend who had drunk too much, and hurried along the side of the church to the parapet of the bridge. He couldn't be seen here. The buttress of the chapel came out to shield him from view on either side. He hoisted Chapler's body up on the rails before dropping him like a sack into the river frothing below.

Three evenings later, as the river ran strong and full to the sea, a long barge slipped out from St Paul's Wharf and made its way across the bobbing tide. The barge was poled by hooded figures. In the prow and stern stood others, garbed in a similar fashion, holding torches. In the centre of the barge sat the Fisher of Men, his cowl pulled back, lidless eyes staring across the river. He was hunting for corpses: he and his beloveds, the outcasts of London, were paid by the Corporation according to a set list of fees for every corpse they plucked from the water. One rate for an accident, another for a suicide. The highest, of course, was for any murder victim. The Fisher of Men, his eerie, bulbous face carefully oiled against the river wind, crooned a lullaby even as he studied the water.

'There'll be bodies,' he murmured. 'Look hard and long, my lovelies!'

The few barges and wherries which plied the river steered well clear. The Fisher of Men was not liked: he held special terrors for those who worked along the Thames. Rumours were rife in the taverns and alehouses that the Fisher of Men and his companions were not above arranging for their own victims to be found in the Thames. Every boatman between Southwark and Westminster prayed constantly to their patron saints that their corpse would not be found by the Fisher of Men and taken to his strange chapel where it would lie in a makeshift coffin until identified. Tonight the Fisher was hopeful. Two days ago, they'd plucked the body of a drunk and that of a Brabantine sailor who had been killed in a tavern brawl. Sir John Cranston, the portly coroner of the city, had paid them well. Now the Fisher of Men was hunting again.

'Ah yes, my lovelies!' he whispered, misquoting from the Office for the Dead. 'Remember that terrible day when the earth shall give up the dead and the rivers of God their secrets.'

He then rapped out an order and the barge turned to avoid a dung cart which stood off the Fleet dumping the ordure and offal of the city into midstream. The dung-collectors cursed and made a sign to ward off the evil eye as the ghoulish barge of the Fisher of Men swept by.

'Pole towards the bank,' the Fisher of Men ordered. He pointed to where the river turned before sweeping down to Westminster.

'Are you sure, master?' Icthus, the Fisher of Men's principal swimmer, spoke up. 'Shouldn't we stay in midstream?'

'No, no,' the Fisher replied. 'I knows the river: it runs too fast. Any corpses from Southwark or London Bridge will be swept into the reeds.'

The barge turned, the pitch torches flickering and snapping in the evening breeze. The Fisher picked up his handbell and clanged it, the sound ringing ominously across the river, telling others to stay clear. The barge moved in closer to the bank.

'I see one!' a lookout cried. 'Master, I see it! There amongst the reeds!'

The Fisher peered through the gloom. There was enough light. He studied the reeds and he, too, saw it, the glint of a buckle belt and something else.

'Go in closer!'

The barge did so. Icthus jumped over the side. He swam like the fish after which he was named. He caught the bobbing, water-soaked corpse of Edwin Chapler; he stared at the bloated face, staring eyes and blood-encrusted mouth.

'A corpse!' Icthus screeched. 'Master, we have found a corpse!'

In Ratcat Alley, just off Watling Street under the towering mass of St Paul's Cathedral, Bartholomew Drayton, a moneylender with a reputation as evil as Satan, was also preparing to meet death. Drayton lay on the floor of his vaulted counting chamber. He moaned in agony at the barbed crossbow quarrel embedded deep in his chest. He turned on his side and looked towards the door; he could not possibly pull back the different bolts or turn the keys in the three great locks. Drayton closed his eyes and groaned. He had always prided himself on that door. Six inches thick, steel-hinged, the outside protected by great brass bolts, it had proved to be his death. He'd always thought himself secure, down here in his counting house; here no thieves could break in nor could one of his greedy clerks help themselves to what he had gathered over the years. No windows, not even an arrow slit. In the end it had proved useless. Drayton, an old soldier from the King's wars in France, knew he was going to die. So strange, here in this vaulted chamber. He gazed across to the wall at the far end. Perhaps it was only right. Justice had caught up with him. He closed his eyes. His feet and legs were so cold.

Drayton, like Chapler, tried to pray but all he could think of were the words from the Gospel about the rich man who had filled his barns and looked forward to a life of feasting and merriment. 'Fool!' God had thundered back, 'Dost thou not know that the demand has been made for thy soul?' Drayton murmured a prayer. He had time to ask God's forgiveness but what about the other crime? Drayton moved to one side. With all his failing strength he tried to crawl to the far wall, to touch it. Yes, if he could touch it, he could ask forgiveness. He had moved only a few paces before the pain became too much. A coldness swept up his body and Bartholomew Drayton gave up his soul.

Chapter 1

Sir John Cranston, coroner of the city of London, perched his portly frame on a stool, pushed back his beaver hat and mopped his red, glistening face. He would have loved to draw out the miraculous wineskin from beneath his cloak, but he was not too sure about the mood of his secretarius, the Dominican, Brother Athelstan, who sat across the chamber. Athelstan was quiet, even more so than usual. His narrow, olive-skinned face under the black tonsured hair was impassive, his usually smiling eyes were now rather stern. He sat, hands up the sleeves of his white gown, chewing on the corner of his lip.

He doesn't want to be here, Cranston thought. He wants to be back across the river at St Erconwald's with his bloody parishioners. He studied his friend's face carefully. Athelstan had not even had time to shave or break his fast. He'd just finished morning Mass when Cranston had called.

'You've got to come, Brother,' the coroner had insisted. He pointed to the huge tom cat which followed Athelstan in and out of church. 'Leave Bonaventure to guard St Erconwald's. Throw some hay at old Philomel. I want to reveal a mystery which will tax even your brain: it certainly baffles mine.'

Athelstan had followed quick and quiet. They strode across London Bridge up through the crowd to the house of the usurer, Bartholomew Drayton, in Ratcat Lane.

'Tell us again.' Cranston gestured at Henry Flaxwith, his principal bailiff.

The fellow breathed out noisily.

'I know, I know,' Cranston added sweetly. 'But Brother Athelstan needs to be told all the facts. We could all be elsewhere. However, Drayton is murdered and a great deal of silver is gone.'

'It's like this, Sir John,' Flaxwith began. 'This morning, long before the bells for Matins rang, I and Samson...'

'Bugger him!' Cranston intervened. 'I don't want to hear about your bloody dog!'

'I and my dog,' Flaxwith continued remorselessly, 'were doing my tour of duty. Now Samson,' he winked at Athelstan, 'now Samson,' he intoned, ignoring Cranston's sigh of exasperation, 'always walks slowly, he likes to stop, sniff and cock his leg. I'd bought an eel pie because I hadn't broken my fast.'

Cranston closed his eyes. O God, give me patience, he prayed. Flaxwith was as lugubrious as he looked but he was honest and meticulous, with a sharp eye for detail.

'I had just finished the pie,' Flaxwith continued, 'when we came into Ratcat Lane. Two young men, Drayton's clerks, Philip Stablegate and James Flinstead, stood pounding on the door of their master's house.'

'These are the two lovelies upstairs?'

'Precisely, Sir John. Anyway, I asked what the matter was.' Flaxwith lifted his podgy face. 'I really should see how Samson is doing...'

'Samson's fine,' Cranston cooed. 'I found a sausage in the scullery, he's eating it as if there's no tomorrow.'

'Anyway, I ask them what the matter be. They told me they had rung the bell and pounded on the door but Master Drayton had not answered. Now, you have seen the front door, Sir John, thick as a Frenchman's head. So we went round the outside. All the windows were boarded and shuttered up.'

'Is there a back entrance?' Athelstan asked.

'Oh yes, but the door's like that at the front, hard as oak. We would have needed a siege machine from the Tower to break them both down.'

Cranston could stand it no longer but helped himself to a quick mouthful of claret from his wineskin. He offered it to Athelstan, who just shook his head.

'So, we break in. Master Philip climbs on Master James's shoulders. He uses a knife and prises open the shutters. Behind them is one of those small gate windows. He breaks the glass and lifts the handle.'

'You are sure of that?' Athelstan interrupted.

'Of course I am,' Flaxwith replied. 'You could see it yourself, the wood's all broken, the bars scored. Indeed, it looks as if it hasn't been opened for years. In gets Master Stablegate. He unbolts the front door, turns the lock and we enter the house.'

'How was it?' Cranston asked.

'Dark as night. Smelly and musty. No candles, no torchlight.' Flaxwith's voice fell to a whisper. 'Quiet as a tomb, Sir John, it was.'

'Go on!' Cranston barked.

'Well, all the rooms were empty. Just like this one.'

Athelstan broke from his reverie and stared round. He thought of the verse from the Gospels: *What does it profit a man to gain the whole world if he suffers the loss of his immortal soul?* Drayton, though one of the city's principal moneylenders, must have also been a miser. The chamber was shabby, with only a few sticks of furniture, whilst the rushes on the floor looked as if they hadn't been changed for years. The walls were greasy, the whitewash blotchy and peeling. Athelstan was sure he'd heard the squeak of rats along the passageway.

'Am I going too fast?' Flaxwith asked.

Cranston just smiled.

'We reached the strongroom,' the bailiff gabbled on. 'We knocked and we knocked, fair to raise the dead. There was no sound.'

'You checked the upstairs chambers?' Athelstan asked.

'Oh yes, nothing, so we knew Master Drayton must be in his counting house. Now you've seen the door, Sir John, heavy oak, steel hinges, embossed with steel bolts on the outside. By now I was afeared. I went out to the street. I paid a penny to four dung-collectors to come in. We found a chopping block in the garden and used that to smash the door down.'

'That would be impossible,' Athelstan asked, 'if you say the door was as heavy as it was?'

'You are right, Father,' Flaxwith replied. 'But one of the dung-collectors had served as a soldier, knocking down doors in France. He told us to concentrate on the hinges, so we did. Fair smashed them loose and the door gave way. Inside we found Drayton on the floor. We haven't moved the corpse, a crossbow bolt is deep in his chest and the silver's gone.'

'How much silver?'

'According to the ledger, at least five thousand good pounds sterling.'

Cranston whistled through his teeth. 'Good Lord, what else have you learnt?'

'Well, the two clerks, Stablegate and Flinstead, left the house, as they always did, just before Vespers last night. Once they had gone, Master Drayton locked and bolted the doors: that was well known, Sir John. He let no one in and no one ever came out.'

Athelstan rose and played with the wooden cross hanging on a cord round his neck.

'So, Master Flaxwith.' He smiled at the bailiff. 'According to you, here is a man who bolted and locked himself in his treasure house but he never went out and would allow no one in. In the morning the doors and windows are still bolted and shuttered. Downstairs the strongroom is still locked and secure but, inside, our moneylender is dead and his silver gone.'

'In a word, yes.'

'And there are no secret entrances, passageways or postern gates?'

'None whatsoever, Father. You've seen the house. It's built of stone, one of the few houses round here that are: that's why Drayton bought it.'

'And the strongroom?'

'See for yourself, Father,' Flaxwith retorted. 'It's a square of stone. The ceilings are plaster but that's unbroken, the walls are of pure stone as is the floor. If Drayton wanted fresh air, he'd simply open the door. Father, I know house-breakers. They go through a window as quickly as a priest into a brothel—' He abruptly stopped. 'I mean a ferret down a hole: it would take a nightwalker hours to break into that strongroom.'

'Then let's see it.'

Flaxwith rose and led them out of the chamber. Cranston grasped Athelstan by the arm. 'Brother, you are well?'

'Why, of course, Sir John. Rather sleepy, I...'

'You never slept last night, did you?' Cranston accused. 'You were on that tower studying your bloody stars again, weren't you?'

Athelstan smiled apologetically. 'Yes, Sir John, I was.'

'It's nothing else, is it?' Cranston asked. 'I mean Father Prior has not written to you about relieving you of your duties at St Erconwald's and sending you to the Halls of Oxford?'

Athelstan seized Cranston's huge podgy hand and squeezed it. 'Sir John, Father Prior asked me a month ago if I would like such a move. I replied I would not.'

Cranston hid his relief. He loved his wife, Lady Maude, his twin sons, the 'poppets', and his dogs Gog and Magog, but especially this gentle friar with his sharp brain and dry sense of humour. Cranston had served as a soldier, as well as a coroner, for many a year. He'd met many men but, as he told the Lady Maude, 'I can number my friends on one hand and still have enough fingers left to make a rude gesture at the Regent. Athelstan's my friend.' Cranston stared mournfully at the friar.

'You won't go to Oxford, will you, Brother?'

'No, Sir John. I am going down to the strongroom.' Athelstan stared round the paltry parlour. 'This is a subtle murder, Sir John, but why are you here?' He added, 'Why are you so anxious about it?'

'Drayton usually kept his money with the Lombards,' Cranston replied. 'The Frescobaldi and the Bardi brothers in Leadenhall Street. He drew most of it out: he was about to give our most noble Regent, John of Gaunt, Duke of Lancaster, a loan of five thousand pounds silver.'

Athelstan sighed.

'So you see, Brother, Gaunt couldn't give a fig if Drayton is in heaven or hell. He wants that silver, particularly now as Drayton has no heirs and he won't have to pay it back. He also wants the thief captured. As you know, my dear monk—'

'Friar, Sir John!'

'As you know, my dear friar, no one upsets our Regent and walks away scot-free.' Cranston paused as he heard Flaxwith calling. 'We'd best go, Brother.'

They went out into the passageway, dingy and gloomy, smelling of tallow fat, boiled oil and other unsavoury odours.

'Flaxwith found the chamber pot upstairs full of stools,' Cranston whispered. 'Drayton was as dirty as he was mean.'

At the top of the steps Flaxwith was waiting with a cresset torch. 'Sir John, what about Samson?' the bailiff pleaded.

'Bugger that!' Cranston retorted. 'Henry, your dog will live for eternity, which is more than I can say for myself if we don't get this silver back.'

Flaxwith shrugged and led them down the narrow stone steps. At the bottom, the huge door he had described was leaning against the wall. Flaxwith led them into the counting house and put the torch in a cresset holder.

Athelstan stared down at the corpse sprawled on the stone floor. A pool of blood had seeped out, and now ran in rivulets down the paving stones. He crouched down and stared pityingly at Drayton's scrawny features: the eyes closed in death, the blood-encrusted mouth sagging. He felt the neck; the skin was cold and clammy. Athelstan closed his eyes. He prayed that Christ, in His infinite compassion, would have mercy on this man who had lived beneath his dignity and died like a dog. He turned the body over. Drayton was dressed in a shabby jerkin and hose. The battered boots looked rather pathetic on his spindly legs; he had no chain round his neck nor rings on his fingers. Athelstan wondered what pleasure this man had ever found in life.

'Was he a bachelor?' he asked.

'He was married once,' Flaxwith replied. 'But many years ago, after the peace of Bretigny with France, his wife upped and left him. Who can blame her? He had no other family or kinsfolk.'

Athelstan examined the wound inflicted by the crossbow bolt: the quarrel had entered deep into Drayton's skinny, narrow chest. He then sat back and studied the bloodstain further down the room near the door. He hitched his robe and edged along the paving stones.

'What's the matter, brother?'

Athelstan pointed to the doorway. 'The blood begins at least a foot from that: this is where Drayton first fell.' He turned and pointed to the far wall. 'Now, here's a man who is dying, the door is bolted and locked, yes?'

Flaxwith agreed.

'Over there,' Athelstan pointed, 'is Drayton's desk, the place where he did all his business. Where he'd sit and marvel at the wealth he had amassed.'

'Yes, of course,' Cranston breathed. 'But he doesn't try and go towards the door or his desk but to the far wall. Why?'

He walked across and, pulling out his dagger, tapped at the whitewashed bricks. 'They sound solid enough to me,' he declared. 'Listen, Athelstan.'

Cranston tapped the wall again, up and down; the only response was a dull thud. 'There's no secret passageway,' he asserted, resheathing his dagger.

'Perhaps Drayton was delirious?' Flaxwith commented.

'It does prove one thing,' Athelstan remarked. 'The door must have been still locked and bolted, otherwise the poor man would have crawled towards it.' He got up, wiping his hand on the black mantle over his white robe. He stared round the chamber. 'You are correct, Master Flaxwith, a square of pure stone and plaster.'

Athelstan walked around: there was the counting desk against one wall and a boxed chair with cushions. On the desk were weighing scales, scraps of parchment, quills, inkhorns and a coffer, its clasp broken. Athelstan studied this and realised it must have been so for years. Inside there was nothing but strips of wax and more quills. The rest of the room was bare and gaunt.

'Not even a crucifix,' Athelstan whispered. 'Drayton must have been a very close and narrow soul.'

For a while all three searched the square musty chamber.

'Not even a rat could break in here,' Cranston declared, mopping his brow and taking another swig from his miraculous wineskin.

'Except through the door,' Athelstan pronounced. 'It's time we examined it.'

They took the torch from the wall and scrutinised the door. Athelstan's curiosity grew. The wood was at least nine inches thick, and the hinges were of steel. He could tell from the three bolts and two locks, with keys still inside, that the door must have been secure when it was broken down. He studied the metal bosses. On the outside these were conical-shaped, fitting into the wood with a clasp on the inside. He felt some of these but they were all tightly secure. The only opening was a small grille high in the door, about six inches across and six inches high. He pulled at the wooden flap which covered it.

'Was this up or down?'

'I'm not sure,' Flaxwith replied. 'It's hanging down now. Perhaps all the force we used knocked it loose?'

Athelstan stared at the small grille. It was broad enough for a man to see out but the bars were so close together it would be difficult to slip even a dagger through, let alone a crossbow bolt. Athelstan went back to the great steel bosses and began testing each of these.

'What are you doing?' Cranston asked curiously.

'I want to see if any are loose,' Athelstan replied. 'They are fitted into the door by clasps.'

'I did that myself,' Flaxwith declared triumphantly. 'Father, there's none loose.'

'And if there was,' Cranston intervened, 'surely it would have shaken free when Master Flaxwith and his colleagues were hammering at the door?'

Athelstan grudgingly conceded and scratched his head. 'Therefore, the problem still remains,' he said. He walked back into the counting house. 'Master Drayton would have his silver here, yes?'

Cranston agreed.

'What puzzles me,' Athelstan continued, 'is that the assassin had to kill our moneylender, take the money and escape. Yes? In the ordinary course of events the door should have been left open but, instead, Drayton is inside, the door barred and secured. So, if the robbers struck first and took the silver from the room, why is the door closed?'

'And if it is closed,' Cranston finished, 'how did the robbers enter in the first place, kill Drayton, steal his silver and get out, leaving the door barred and locked from the inside?'

'Precisely, Sir John, the perfect conundrum.'

'What is more,' Flaxwith added, 'they not only stole the silver but also any loose coins. Moreover, Drayton's clerks claim two silver candlesticks and a gold pendant are missing.'

Athelstan sat down on the stool and stared at the corpse.

'How?' he murmured. 'In or out?'

'What do you mean?' Cranston took a swig from his wineskin.

'Well, I can understand them killing Drayton and taking the silver but how did they get in and out? That door is better than a wall of steel. There are no gaps or breaks. If they'd approached the door, Drayton would have left the flap down. He was safe behind the grille. He would have refused to open the door. Now I could understand a man like Drayton letting in a clerk or a friend.' He glanced at Flaxwith. 'You are sure the key was in the lock and the bolts were drawn?'

'It's the first thing I checked,' the bailiff retorted, jumping from foot to foot. 'Oh please, Sir John, may I see my dog? Samson begins to pine if he's away from me.'

'Oh, go and see the bloody animal!' Cranston breathed. 'Give it my best regards!'

Flaxwith almost ran from the room.

'And there's another problem,' Athelstan went on. 'How did the assassin get in and out of the house without forcing a door or window?'

'Bloody mysterious!' Cranston took another slurp from the miraculous wineskin.

'The clerks are still here?' Athelstan asked.

'Oh yes, Brother. They are waiting upstairs.'

They left the chamber and went up to meet them. Athelstan took an immediate dislike to Master Philip Stablegate and his colleague James Flinstead. Oh, they were pleasant enough. They rose politely as he entered. They were of personable appearance, hair neatly cropped, their faces clean-shaven and washed. They were dressed in sober apparel, dark tunics and hose. Stablegate was fair-haired, pleasant-faced, ever ready to smile. Flinstead was darker, rather dour. Nevertheless, Athelstan felt repelled. Clever men, he thought, full of mockery. Both clerks made little attempt to hide their amusement at what they considered the coroner's antics. Cranston waved at them to sit down, then he helped Athelstan pull a rather shabby bench across to sit opposite them. Athelstan placed his writing bag between his sandalled feet and waited patiently as Sir John took another swig from the miraculous wineskin. The coroner closed his eyes and burped with pleasure. Stablegate dropped his head and sniggered. Cranston, wobbling on the bench, put the stopper back in. He must have caught the mockery.

'You are Master Drayton's clerks?' he began harshly. 'You were the last to see him alive?'

'We left just before Vespers,' Flinstead replied.

'Tell me what happened,' Athelstan asked.

'Same as always,' Flinstead said pointedly. 'You are…?'

'Brother Athelstan, priest of St Erconwald's in Southwark.'

'And my secretarius,' Cranston boomed.

'Do you suspect us of this crime?'

'Why should I?' Athelstan replied.

Flinstead seemed a little nonplussed.

'Please,' Athelstan said. 'Answer my question. What happened last night?'

'We finished the day as usual,' Stablegate answered. 'We were in our writing office, a small chamber, no more than a garret, further down the passageway. Master Drayton came up as usual to usher us out. And before you ask, Brother, no, he didn't trust us, he didn't trust anyone. We went out into the street. Master Drayton bade us goodnight, as surly as ever. Then he slammed the door shut, we heard the bolts being drawn and the locks turned.'

'And then what?'

'As usual, we went drinking at the Dancing Pig, a tavern in St Martin's Lane just near the Shambles.'

'And after that?'

'When the curfew bell rang from St Mary Le Bow, we left for our lodgings in Grubb Street off Cripplegate. We share a chamber there.'

'Mistress Aldous, our landlady, will confirm that we came home much the worse for wear. We slept till dawn, rose and came back here.'

'And?' Athelstan asked.

'The same as every morning, Father. We'd knock, pull the bell. Master Drayton would come shuffling down the passageway and let us in.'

'But this morning was different?'

'Yes it was, Father. We hammered and rang the bell to raise the dead.' He smiled thinly. 'Then Flaxwith came along. The rest you know.'

'What do I know?' Athelstan asked sharply.

'Well, we tried the shutters at the windows. The front and back doors were locked and barred as usual.'

'And so you broke in?'

'Yes,' Stablegate replied. 'I climbed on James's shoulders.'

He tapped the hilt of his dagger. 'I pushed this through a crack in the shutters and lifted the bar.'

Sir John was falling asleep now, head nodding forward, mouth open. Stablegate hid his smirk behind his hand.

'In which case...' Athelstan's voice rose as he stood up.

Sir John, startled, also staggered to his feet. The coroner stood, feet apart, and blinked, breathing in noisily through his nose. He saw the two clerks laughing. Athelstan closed his eyes.

'Do you find me amusing, sirs?' Cranston's hand fell to the dagger in his belt. He took a step forward, white moustache and whiskers bristling, fierce blue eyes popping. 'Do you find old Jack amusing? Because my poppets woke me before dawn? And old Jack has had a few mouthfuls of wine? Now, let me tell you, sirs,' he continued, breathing wine fumes into their now frightened faces. 'Old Jack is not the fool he appears to be: "Jack be nimble, Jack be quick". The poet was thinking of old Jack Cranston when he wrote that.' He lifted a finger. 'You say you live with Mistress Aldous in Grubb Street near Cripplegate?'

'Yes,' Flinstead replied, rather surprised that Sir John, who'd apparently been asleep, had still heard this.

'I know Mistress Aldous,' Cranston continued. 'Five times she has appeared before my bench on charges of soliciting, of keeping a bawdyhouse, a molly shop.'

'There's no one there now,' Stablegate retorted.

'Just you two lovely boys and Mistress Aldous, eh?'

'Yes.'

'Yes, Sir John.'

'Yes, Sir John.'

'Now let me tell you,' the coroner went on threateningly. 'Don't laugh at old Jack. A horrible murder has been done and the Crown's silver has been stolen.'

'We don't know about that.'

'No, boyo, you don't. Five thousand pounds intended for the Regent's coffers. Now it's gone.' Cranston brought a large paw down on each of their shoulders and made them wince. 'Well, my lovelies, let's see this bloody window.'

Athelstan, quietly pleased at Cranston's assertion of his authority, abruptly turned at the door.

'I am sorry.' He came back. 'You didn't know Master Drayton had five thousand pounds in silver at his counting house?'

'He'd never let us handle monies,' Stablegate retorted. 'It was one rule he always insisted on. We do know,' Stablegate continued quickly, 'that envoys from the Frescobaldi bank visited the house yesterday, though Master Drayton told us to stay in our chamber. He answered the door. We heard a murmur of voices and then they left.'

Athelstan nodded. 'And what would happen then?'

'If the bankers brought the money,' Stablegate replied, 'knowing Master Drayton, he'd count every coin, sign a receipt and keep the money in his strongroom.'

'Did you like Master Drayton?' Cranston asked.

'No!' They both answered together.

'He was the devil's own skinflint,' Flinstead declared. 'He made us work from dawn till dusk. At the Angelus time he'd give us some ale, bread and cheese, then it was back to work.' He tugged at his tunic. 'At Christmas and Easter we'd get new robes and a silver piece at midsummer. He hardly spoke to us, only visiting us every so often, as quiet as a shadow, to make sure we weren't wasting his time and money.'

'Did he ever talk about friends or family?'

'Never,' Stablegate replied. 'On one occasion I asked him if he had been married and he flew into a terrible rage.'

'Then what?'

'He went down the stairs, muttering to himself. We learnt our lesson: we never asked him again.'

'We had no choice but to work for him,' Flinstead added. 'He'd often remind us that London was full of clerks seeking employment. Beggars have no choice, Father.'

Athelstan nodded and opened the door. 'Then, sirs, let us see this window.'

The two clerks went out before him. They led them down the stairs. Flaxwith was at the bottom, stroking and talking softly to what Athelstan secretly considered the ugliest bull mastiff he'd ever clapped eyes on. As they passed, the dog lifted his head and growled.

'Now, now,' Flaxwith whispered. 'You know Sir John loves you.'

'I can't stand the bloody animal!' Cranston breathed. 'He's tried to have my leg on at least three occasions.'

The clerks led them into a small hall, full of jumble and clutter. The wooden wainscoting was cracked and covered in dust; the air stank of rotting rushes. The musicians' gallery at the far end was beginning to sag, whilst huge cobwebs hung like banners in the corners. Rats squeaked and squealed in protest and slithered across the floor, angry at this intrusion. The room was dark except for the light which poured through the thrown-back shutters of a broken window.

Athelstan pulled across a stool, told Sir John to hold him steady and climbed up to examine the window. Even a cursory glance told him that the shutters had been forced, the bar gouged by a knife: the flyblown window had been cracked so that the clerk who had entered could put his hand in to pull up the handle of the square door window. Athelstan climbed down.

'It's as you say,' he said. 'Both window and shutter have been recently forced.'

'I did that,' Stablegate declared. His voice took on a desperate plea. 'Sir John, Father, we know nothing of Bartholomew Drayton's death or the theft of his silver.'

'And you have nothing to add?' Athelstan asked.

'No, Father, we have not.'

'And what plans do you have for the future?'

Stablegate shrugged, then coughed at the dust swirling from the chamber. 'Father, what can we do? It will be back to St Paul's, walking in the middle aisle waiting for some rich merchant to hire us.'

'Have you applied for any licence to travel either here or beyond the seas?' Cranston asked.

He was not impressed by the puzzlement in their faces.

'You know full well what I mean.' He added, 'Have you applied to the office of the Chancery of the Green Wax for permission to travel? Yes or no?'

'No, Sir John.'

Cranston pushed his face closer. 'Good,' he purred. 'Then keep it that way until this matter is finished. You are to stay in your lodgings. You are not to leave London without my written permission.' He nodded. 'You may go.'

The two clerks walked out of the room, slamming the door behind them, raising fresh puffs of dust.

'What do you think, Brother?' Cranston took the wineskin out. 'Devil's futtocks, this is a dry place!'

'Every place is too dry for you, Sir John.'

Cranston winked, took a swig from the wineskin and patted his stomach. 'It's time we had refreshments, Brother, something to soak up the wine. You didn't answer my questions.'

'I think they are as guilty as Pilate and Herod,' Athelstan replied. 'In my view, Sir John, those two are evil young men who believe they have carried out the perfect crime.' He sighed. 'And they may well have.'

'They killed Drayton?' Cranston asked.

'As God made little apples, Sir John, I believe they are guilty but how they did it is a mystery.'

'Flaxwith!' Cranston roared.

The bailiff hurried into the room, Samson trotting behind him, tongue hanging out. He took one look at Sir John's juicy leg and would have launched himself forward. Flaxwith had the good sense to grab him by the leather collar and scoop him up into his arms.

'Sir John, Samson and I are at your service.'

'Bugger him!' Cranston growled. 'I want you to do three things. First, visit the bankers, the Frescobaldi, in Leadenhall Street. Seek confirmation that they made a delivery of silver here yesterday. Secondly, go to my host at the Dancing Pig: did those two beauties spend last night there? Finally, I want them and their lodgings in Grubb Street watched; if they try to leave London, arrest them!'

'For what, Sir John?'

Cranston closed his eyes. 'For cruelty to your dog.'

Chapter 2

As Athelstan and Cranston arrived in Ratcat Lane, Luke Peslep, clerk in the Chancery of the Green Wax, swaggered into the Ink and Pot tavern on the corner of Chancery Lane to break his fast. Peslep, a young man of good family and even better prospects, felt all was well with the world. Three nights ago, he had dined well and been entertained by the most delicious whore. He was still elated by it all. This morning he had risen, washed and put on new robes ready for another day in the office of the Green Wax. He stood in the taproom of the Ink and Pot and beamed round. He looked through into the back, so happy and contented he did not see the animals: a mongrel dog, a mangy cat, or the scraps of food and stable manure piled high in the midden. Nor did he notice the smell from the privies at the far end of the yard behind a hedge of scrawny bushes. Peslep only saw the sunshine reflected in the puddles, heard the clack of geese and, closing his eyes, savoured the appetising odours from the buttery. He took his usual seat in the far corner and, when Meg the slattern came up, he ordered his usual pot of ale and trencher of sliced bread, apple and cheese. Peslep, as always, put his hand down Meg's low-cut bodice and clutched one of her breasts, squeezing it gently.

'Riper every day, eh, Meg? Soon fresh for the plucking?'

Meg wiped her hair from her grease-stained face and forced a smile. She could not object. Peslep always paid in good silver and, if she protested, the landlord would only cuff her ears until they burnt. Peslep sat munching his apple, listening to the sounds drifting through the tavern. A choir carolling from a nearby church, women gossiping in the street, children shrieking, a lazy cock crowing to greet the dawn, a pedlar crying his wares. From the open workshops near the Fleet prison came a medley of sounds: planing and hammering, clanging and forging, seething and hissing. Peslep closed his eyes. This was the London he loved.

A guild of beggars entered the tavern and gathered round a table to count the coins they had collected from the crowds coming out of morning Mass. Their leader ordered jugs of wine and hot dishes. Peslep knew they would stay there until all their money was gone and they fell to the floor blind drunk to be fleeced by the wily landlord. One of the beggars pulled a flute from his doublet and began to play. Another took a lute from a bag and struck a few chords; the rest began to sing, beating time on the heavy wooden tables, rattling the jars and wooden plates. Peslep, leaning back, watched them through heavy-lidded eyes. He was pleased with the way life was going: the threatening clouds had receded; all would be well.

Peslep intended to buy a new house, perhaps north of Clerkenwell. He opened his eyes as a young man entered the tavern, cowl pulled over his head, the spurs on his boots jingling; a war belt, carrying a sword and dagger, was slung over his shoulder. He snapped his fingers and whispered at Meg who hurried off to bring him a black-jack of ale.

The young man sat down. Peslep sniffed contemptu-ously and glanced away. A court popinjay! One of those foppish young men whom Peslep and his companions openly envied, yet secretly admired, with their wealth and lazy good manners. Alcest even aped them. One day Peslep would be like that. His stomach began to churn. He drained his tankard.

'Master taverner!' He rose, snapping his fingers.

The fellow came hurrying out of the buttery with fresh rags which he placed in Peslep's hand. The routine was always the same. Peslep came to break his fast, he would then go out into the privies and return for one final pottle of ale before going on to work. Peslep walked out into the yard, pinching his nose as he passed the midden. The privies at the far end, behind the scrawny hedgerow, were a series of cubicles set over a ditch. Peslep went inside, pulled down his hose and made himself comfortable.

Clutching the rags, he closed his eyes and sat thinking about the money he had salted away. Suddenly the door opened; Peslep, startled, tried to rise. He glimpsed the young man he had seen in the tavern and the sword aiming straight for his stomach. Peslep could do nothing; the sword was thrust in, turned, out again. Peslep writhed at the sheet of pain even as the swordsman struck once more, driving his pointed weapon deep into Peslep's neck.

—

Sir John Cranston and Athelstan had returned to study Master Drayton's counting house when there was a furious knocking on the front door. They both went up the stairs. Athelstan glimpsed a tall, elegant figure framed against the sunlight. The fellow came forward, jewelled bonnet in his hand; spurs on the heels of his boots jingled musically on the floorboards. He had no sword but one hand rested on the jewelled dagger pressed into his leather sword belt; his cloak of dark saffron was tossed elegantly over one shoulder. Cranston studied the handsome, swarthy face and mocking green eyes; he noticed how the young man's moustache and beard were clipped in the neat French fashion. A memory stirred.

'Do I know you, sir?'

'You are Sir John Cranston, coroner of the city?'

'I sincerely hope so. I asked you a question, sir.'

'I am Sir Lionel Havant, a member of His Grace the Duke of Lancaster's household.'

'Ah, one of John of Gaunt's boys, aren't you? One of the Regent's henchmen?' Cranston stood, feet apart, studying the man from head to toe. Then he walked forward, hand extended. 'Oh, don't take offence, man. I knew your father, Sir Reginald Havant of Crosby in Northampton.'

The young man smiled, then straightened up as if remembering his task. 'Sir John, it's good to see you but I come direct from the Regent. He would like his five thousand pounds in silver.'

'He'll have to wait!' Cranston snarled. 'I am a coroner, not a damn miracle worker!'

Havant looked at Brother Athelstan, who raised his eyes heavenwards.

'Sir Lionel,' Athelstan intervened, before Cranston got into full stride, 'we've scarce been here long; progress will be made.'

The young knight nodded.

'And you have a message for us?' Athelstan asked.

'Yes, how did you…?'

Athelstan pointed to the small scroll tucked into the man's war belt.

'Ah yes.' Havant took it out. 'Sir John.' He undid the piece of parchment. 'His Grace the Regent is also concerned about one of his clerks, Edwin Chapler of the Chancery of the Green Wax. His corpse was fished from the Thames last night. It now lies in the hands of the Fisher of Men. Chapler's been missing for about two days. His Grace wants you to claim the corpse, pay the fine and investigate the cause of death.'

'I am too busy for drunken clerks!' Cranston snapped.

'He wasn't drunk, Sir John,' Havant retorted. 'Chapler was murdered.'

A few minutes later Cranston, with Athelstan trotting beside him, strode across Cheapside and down Bread

Street. The coroner wanted to visit the 'Barque of St Peter', the rather eccentric name the Fisher of Men gave to his 'chapel' or death house. Cranston pushed himself through the crowds, making his way along the thronged streets. Above and around them the two- or three-storey houses, pinched and narrow, blocked out the sunlight and forced people to knock and push each other in the busy lanes below. The stalls and shops were open. The air dinned with the cries of apprentices, particularly the clothiers, their huge barrows or tables covered with a rich variety of materials: brightly embroidered with brilliantly coloured Brussels linen; English broadcloths; textiles from Louvain and Arras. Further down, along the streets of Trinity, the stalls were stacked high with merchandise from Lebanon to Venice: chests of cinnamon, bags of saffron and gingers; casks full of figs; bitter oranges and exotically scented candied lemon peel. There were crates full of locust pots, almonds and mace; sacks of sugar and pepper; casks of wine; writing tablets and boxes of chalk; leather goods in every shade of brown. Herrings were displayed in open crates beside stacked mounds of fruits and vegetables.

Athelstan would have loved to question Sir John but the noise was absolutely deafening. The coroner was busy shaking his fists at the cheeky apprentices who tried to jump up to catch his arm. Cranston would roar and shake himself as a bear would rage at baiting dogs. Athelstan trailed desolately behind, trying not to pay any attention to the shouts, the haggling and bartering. He was bumped and knocked by peasants, craftsmen and townsfolk. Now and again he would stumble and have to profusely apologise to some lady trying to walk arm in arm with her gentleman. As they went down La Réole, towards Vintry and the less salubrious parts of the city, Athelstan kept his hand on his purse. Here the quacks and fortune tellers had set up their temporary booths and attracted the pickpockets and cutpurses. These always gathered in such places, as quickly as bees round honey or, as Sir John would more caustically put it, 'flies round a turd'.

At last Athelstan glimpsed the rigging of ships and, on the morning breeze, smelt the fresh, tangy air of the river. Cranston, now in a black mood and taking copious swigs from his miraculous wineskin, turned down an alleyway leading to the Barque of St Peter. A relic-seller came whining up, carrying in his hands a box allegedly containing the toenails of the Pharaoh who had persecuted Moses. Cranston pulled back his cowl.

'Oh, Lord save us!' the man yelled and fled like a whippet back into the shadows.

The Fisher of Men was sitting on a bench outside his chapel. He was surrounded by his strange coven, beggars and lepers, their faces and hands covered with sore open wounds. Some were so disfigured they wore masks. Beside the Fisher of Men stood Icthus. The boy had no eyebrows or eyelids; he looked like a fish and could swim like one. Sir John stopped and bowed: he had great respect for the Fisher of Men.

'Good morning, Sir John.'

'And you, my lovelies.' Cranston smiled whilst Athelstan sketched a blessing in their direction.

The Fisher of Men rose, hands by his side, and bowed from the waist. 'Welcome to our humble church, Sir John.' His watery eyes shifted. 'And you, Brother Athelstan. Once again death brings us together.'

'The corpse of Edwin Chapler?' Cranston asked.

The Fisher of Men handed his pottle of ale to Icthus, opened the chapel door and beckoned Cranston and Athelstan forward. The inside was a long, narrow shed. Against the far wall a makeshift altar had been set up; on it stood two candlesticks either side of a huge crucifix. On the flanking wall were paintings, crudely drawn with charcoal then filled in with paint. One depicted Jonah being swallowed by the whale. The other showed Christ and his apostles, who looked suspiciously like the Fisher of Men and his coven, sailing in a laden barge across the Sea of Galilee. An eerie place, lit by rushlights and oil lamps. Down either side were tables; on each a corpse, plucked from the Thames, lay underneath a dirty piece of canvas. The air smelt stale and, despite the huge herb pots beneath each table, Athelstan detected the sickening odour of corruption. The Fisher of Men, however, seemed all at home, chattering to himself as he led them forward. He stopped at a table and pulled back the sheet. The corpse of a young man lay sprawled there, his hair, body and clothes soaked in river water, eyes half open, face a liverish white. Athelstan noticed faint crusts of dried blood on the corners of the mouth.

'It was no accident,' the Fisher of Men intoned. He turned the corpse over.

Athelstan, trying to control his nausea, studied the mass of loose flesh on the back of the young man's head.

'Any other wounds?' Cranston asked, helping himself to his wineskin.

This time Athelstan accepted the coroner's kind offer and took a deep mouthful himself.

'None that I could see.' The Fisher of Men held out his hand. 'Three shillings, Sir John! Three shillings for pulling a murder victim from the Thames!'

'The Guildhall will pay you,' Cranston retorted.

The Fisher of Men smiled; his hand remained outstretched. 'Come, come, Sir John, don't play cat and mouse with me. If you go to the Guildhall for three shillings, three shillings you'll get. If I go, I'll be beaten round the head and rolled down the steps.'

Cranston sighed and handed the money over.

'He was struck on the back of the head,' the Fisher of Men declared. 'We know he was Edwin Chapler, as his seals of office were found in his pouch. Being a royal clerk, we sent these to the Regent at his Palace of the Savoy.'

'Anything else?' Cranston asked.

'A few coins but...' The Fisher of Men shrugged.

Athelstan turned the corpse over and, kneeling down, began to whisper the words of absolution. The Fisher of Men waited patiently whilst Athelstan sketched the sign of the cross over the young man's face and whispered the Requiem.

'He was struck on the back of the head,' the Fisher of Men continued. 'And, knowing the run of the river, I believe he was thrown from London Bridge three evenings ago.'

'Wouldn't his body be bruised by the starlings and bridge supports?'

'No, Sir John, the river runs fast and furious between the arches of the bridge. He was certainly thrown down there: as his body swirled in the water, bits of seaweed became entangled in his clothing. If you climb down and look at the arches underneath the bridge, it's one of the few parts of the river where seaweed is caught and held.' The Fisher of Men laughed. 'But I'm showing off, Sir John. One of my lovely boys out there, he talks to old Harrowtooth, the witch, the wise woman, who lives in a hovel near the city end of the bridge. Three evenings ago, she went into the chapel of St Thomas à Becket, and met a young man who matches this man's description.'

'Of course,' Sir John breathed. 'And behind the chapel is a small, deserted area. It's well known as a place for suicides. What time did Harrowtooth see him?'

'Well after Vespers. The sun had disappeared. Very agitated he was, praying just within the porch, as if he didn't really want to be there.'

'I know old Harrowtooth,' Athelstan added. 'I'll have a talk with her.'

'And the corpse?' the Fisher of Men asked.

'Keep it for twenty-four hours,' Cranston replied. 'If no one claims it, send it to the priest at St Mary Le Bow for interment. There's a plot in the cemetery there...'

'I can't do that,' the Fisher of Men responded. 'They refused the last one and will continue to do so until the graveyard is cleared and a new charnel house is built.'

Athelstan stared down at the corpse, full of pity at this young life so brutally wiped out.

'Send it to St Erconwald's,' he declared. 'If no one wants him, St Erconwald's will take him.'

Athelstan abruptly turned as the door swung open. Havant, the Fisher of Men's coven protesting and fluttering like a group of starlings around him, swept into the corpse house.

'Oh, for the love of God!' Cranston breathed. 'Don't say I'm going to see you on the hour every hour, Sir Lionel?'

'A rash of deaths, Sir John. Another clerk has been murdered.'

'In the river?' the Fisher of Men asked hopefully.

Sir Lionel didn't even bother to acknowledge him. 'Luke Peslep was killed on the privy at the Ink and Pot tavern: stabbed through the belly and the gullet. The assassin has vanished like smoke.'

'Robbery?' Cranston asked.

'Nothing taken from him except his life, though this was left.'

Havant handed across a dirty piece of parchment; the ink was dark blue, the writing sprawling. Cranston passed it to Athelstan.

'My eyes are rather bad this morning.' Cranston's usual explanation when he'd drunk too much.

Athelstan read it in the light of an oil lamp.

'Two riddles,' he said slowly. 'The first reads: "A king once fought an army. He defeated them but, in the end, victor and vanquished lay in the same place."'

'What on earth does that mean?' Cranston asked.

'God only knows,' Athelstan replied. 'And here's the second: "My first is like a selfish brother." Did this belong to Peslep?' he asked.

'No,' Havant replied. 'The assassin must have left it on the corpse. You'd best come and see.'

Cranston and Athelstan thanked the Fisher of Men then followed Havant back out into the streets.

The bells of the city were pealing for midmorning prayers. The traders and their customers ignored this invitation, but had taken a rest for something to eat and drink so the crowds were thinner, the alleyways and lanes easier to manage. Nevertheless, Athelstan felt tired by the time they reached the Ink and Pot. Havant strode like a giant whilst Sir John, eager to accept the challenge, was intent, as always, on showing that he was a puissant knight able to compete with the youngest and the best. A crowd had assembled outside the Ink and Pot tavern, kept back by archers from the Tower wearing the personal escutcheon of John of Gaunt. Havant pushed his way through, spoke to the captain of the guard then led Cranston and Athelstan into the taproom and out across the dirty yard. An archer, gnawing at a chicken bone whilst flirting with Meg the scullion, indicated with his thumb.

'He's in there,' he shouted. 'The captain pulled up his hose and made him decent. He said no man should be found like that.'

Athelstan opened the door. Peslep was sitting slumped on the privy bench, his jerkin caked in blood from the wound in his neck and the deep sword thrust to his belly.

'Bring him out,' he whispered.

Cranston snapped out an order. The archer, assisted by Athelstan, removed the corpse and laid it down upon the cobbles. Athelstan gave absolution and examined the two wounds. He took out the dead man's purse and emptied the contents out on his hand: there was nothing except a few coins, a pumice stone and a small St Christopher medal.

Athelstan recited the short Office for the Dead, blessed the corpse and got to his feet. The landlord, his face creased in mock sorrow, came out rubbing his hands, eyes rolling heavenwards.

'Lord have mercy!' he wailed. 'Lord have mercy on us all! We'll all be slain in our beds!'

'Oh, shut up!' Cranston growled. 'Don't worry, master taverner, the corpse will be removed. You'll be back to coining your silver within the hour. Now, what has happened?'

'I sent a runner to the Tower,' the taverner gabbled. 'Because he's Luke Peslep, clerk in the Chancery of the Green Wax.'

'You didn't send the boy to the Tower,' Meg scoffed.

'For God's sake, gather your wits,' Havant snapped. 'You sent the boy to the Chancery Office off Fleet Street. I was there when he arrived.'

The landlord fluttered his fingers; he took a dirty rag from his greasy apron and mopped his face. 'Oh Lord, have mercy, Lord, have mercy! You are right, you are right! I kept thinking we should go to the Tower, maybe the French had landed.'

Cranston grasped the man's shoulder and squeezed it. 'Good friend,' he said. 'A royal clerk has been murdered and you are bleating like a lamb.'

'I didn't see anything,' the landlord whined.

'Too busy watching the customers,' Meg hinted.

Athelstan beckoned her over and slipped a penny into her callused hand. 'What did you see, girl?'

She sniffed and wiped her nose on the back of her hand. 'As normal, Peslep came in here to break his fast. As normal, he squeezed my tits and sat like a prince stuffing his face and then, as normal, he went out into the jakes to relieve himself.'

'And?'

'I don't know. I didn't see anyone leave after him. Simon, the ironmaster, went out, bladder full of ale he had. We hears him screaming. The rest you know.'

'Did you see anyone in the tavern this morning? A stranger?'

The girl closed her eyes and screwed up her face. 'We had some beggars,' she replied. 'Oh yes, and a young man.' She opened one eye and pointed at Havant. 'He was dressed like you. In good clothes. He carried a war belt, long leather riding boots with spurs on.'

Havant smiled bleakly. 'But it wasn't me?'

'Oh no, sir,' she replied coyly. 'You are much more handsome than he.'

'So you saw his face?' Athelstan asked.

'He was clean-shaven,' Meg responded. 'But no, Father, I really didn't have a good look. I was too busy.'

Cranston, who had been swaying on his feet, eyes half closed, smacked his lips noisily. 'I'll tell you what,' he declared. 'Master taverner,' he took the coins Athelstan had handed over from Peslep's purse, 'have the body removed.'

'Where to?'

'Your parish church,' Cranston retorted, grasping the man's wrist and squeezing it. 'Tell the priest there that Sir John Cranston sent it for burial.'

The landlord, followed by Meg, strode away.

'Why were you at the Chancery Office?' Cranston asked.

Havant shrugged. 'The Regent's orders, Sir John. I was to tell them about Chapler's corpse being discovered.'

'And?'

'They were upset, sad, then the boy arrived from the tavern.' Havant looked up at the blue sky. 'Sir John, I must be going.' He smiled at Athelstan, spun on his heel and walked back into the taproom.

Cranston sat down on a wooden bench and stared glumly at the corpse whilst Athelstan inspected the yard.

'You won't find anything,' the coroner moaned. 'This one came like a thief in the night.'

Athelstan went to the back of the privies and opened a small wicket gate which led into a mean alleyway. He looked up and down: at the far end a group of children played with a pet toad watched by a mangy cat; at the other, an empty gap between huddled houses led out into a street. Athelstan closed the wicket gate, returned and sat down beside Sir John.

'Too many killings,' the coroner murmured. He rubbed his face. 'Brother Athelstan, I need refreshments.' He nudged his companion, who was lost in thought. 'What are you thinking about, monk?'

'This friar, Sir John, is mystified, not just by Drayton's death: we have Chapler knocked on the head and thrown over the bridge, and now Peslep is stabbed to death in a privy.'

'Which means?' Cranston asked.

'These clerks were killed by someone who knew all their habits and customs.' Athelstan sighed. 'I wager Chapler was accustomed to praying in the chapel of St Thomas à Becket and, as Meg has just told us, Peslep was in the habit of coming here every morning.'

'And the killer?'

'That young man,' Athelstan replied. 'He came in here with his war belt. He waited till Peslep went out and followed. It would have been easy: Peslep sitting on the jakes, his hose around his ankles. The door is flung open, a thrust to his stomach followed by one to the neck, then

the assassin flees down the alleyway. Come on, Sir John.'
Athelstan rose to his feet. 'We'll have refreshment soon
enough. Let's go down to the Chancery Office.'

'I don't think so,' Cranston replied.

'Sir John?'

'The deaths of the clerks are important, Brother, but
the Regent is breathing down my neck. I want to go back
to Drayton's house. I want to search that counting house
from top to bottom.'

'Sir John,' Athelstan insisted, 'we are in the city now.
Chancery Lane is not far away. Drayton's murder is due
to a subtle mind rather than some secret passageway.
Moreover,' he pulled the scrap of parchment out of his
purse, 'why should these riddles be left? What message
did the assassin intend to leave? I believe, Sir John, that
Peslep and Chapler were killed by one of their number,
another clerk. So arise, Sir John, it's not yet noon.'

Cranston grudgingly conceded, hiding his bitter disap-
pointment at not being able to buy a juicy meat pie in the
Holy Lamb of God. They left the Ink and Pot, Cranston
barking orders at the landlord about Peslep's corpse, and
made their way up Cheapside, past the Shambles, the
noisy meat market outside Newgate prison, then into
Holborn Street. For a while they had to pause: a travelling troupe of players had attracted the crowds, those
who loafed about the streets or sprawled on church steps.
Anyone who had a measure of free time had flocked
on to a piece of nearby wasteland to watch the somer-
saulting, fire-sprouting, rope-dancing guild of entertainers

and jugglers. Garishly dressed whores had also clustered around and, as Sir John Cranston was recognised, the occasional catcall was heard, but the braggart boys, card-sharpers and pickpockets stayed well away from him.

At last Sir John, shouting and waving his ham-like fists, forced a way through. They passed the Bishop of Ely's inn and entered the lawyers' quarter, thronged with soberly dressed men in fur-edged robes, clerks and scriveners in dull browns and greens. They turned into Chancery Lane and Cranston stopped before a large, mouldering four-storey house. The windows were dusty, the plaster and woodwork fading and crumbling.

'It's been like this,' Cranston remarked, bringing down the iron knocker in the shape of a quill, 'since I was a boy.' He wagged a finger at Athelstan. 'A veritable house of secrets.'

He was about to continue when the door swung open. The man who greeted them was dressed, despite the heat, in a fur-edged robe stretching from neck to slippered feet. In one hand he held an eyeglass, in the other a quill; ink stains covered his fingers. He was balding, with a grey seamed face; his eyes were bright, his nose sharp and pointed like a quill. Bloodless lips puckered in irritation at being disturbed.

'What business, sirs?' He scratched his scrawny neck.

'King's business,' Cranston replied, pushing him aside.

'Well I never, I beg your pardon, sir.' The man grasped Cranston's arm.

'Who are you?' the coroner barked.

'Tibault Lesures, Master of the Rolls. How dare you...?'

Cranston gripped his hand. 'Sir John Cranston, coroner of the city here on the express orders of the Regent. This monk is Brother Athelstan, parish priest of St Erconwald's and my secretarius.'

'Then why didn't you say that in the first place?' Lesures' head came forward like that of an angry chicken. He plucked at the cambric belt round his waist and smiled at Athelstan. 'You are here about the murders?' He clucked his tongue. 'Two young men killed in their prime. Violent times, Father! Satan is always an assassin and there are more sons of Cain than there are of Abel. Ah well, come on.'

He led them along a gloomy passageway, past chambers where scribes and scriveners scratched away, copying or preparing rough drafts of documents.

'The Chancery of the Green Wax,' Lesures turned at the foot of the stairs, 'is on the first gallery. On the second gallery is the Chancery of the Red Wax and on the...'

'Thank you,' Cranston replied. 'I once worked in the Chancery myself, Master Tibault.'

'Did you really?' Lesures became all friendly.

'Please!' Cranston insisted.

Lesures took them up the stairs, along the gallery and into a large furnished room. This was more comfortable than the others they'd passed. Damask cloths and coloured tapestries hung above the wooden wainscoting next to shields bearing the arms of England, France, Scotland

49

and Castile. The floor was of polished wood; high desks and stools were placed neatly around but these were now empty. Four clerks were gathered at the far end of a long table which ran down the centre of the room. They were grouped round a fair-haired young woman who sat in a chair, her face in her hands.

The young men looked up as Cranston approached. They were all in their early thirties, dressed in jerkin and hose, white shirts with clean, crisp collars coming up under the neck. They were neat, tidy and all wore the Chancery ring on their left hands. Athelstan recalled how the Chancery always recruited the best from the Halls of Oxford and Cambridge: young men of good families. Some of them would enter the Church whilst others, if they won royal favour, would rise to be sheriffs, court bailiffs or royal commissioners.

Lesures introduced them: William Ollerton, small and thickset, his clean-shaven face marred by a scar which ran from his nose down to his mouth. His dark hair was carefully oiled and he wore an earring in one lobe. Quite the dandy, Athelstan thought. Robert Elflain was tall and thin as a spear shaft: arrogant, his face puckered in a permanent expression of disdain, his eyes watchful. Thomas Napham was tall, broad and chubby-faced, his hair not so neatly coifed as the rest, rather nervous, eager to please. Finally, Andrew Alcest, apparently the leader of the group: loose-limbed, rather girlish with his smooth-skinned face and large round eyes. Yet Athelstan sensed mischief, a man who, despite his innocent looks, was attracted to plotting as a cat to mice.

Lesures finished the introductions. The clerks shook Sir John's hand and that of Athelstan, then stood aside. The young woman, round whom they had been grouped, still sat in the chair, her chin resting on the heel of her hand. She smiled tearfully at Cranston who towered over her. Athelstan was struck by how pleasing her face was, not beautiful but pretty: large grey eyes, sweet mouth, her oval-shaped face still comely despite the tears streaming down her cheeks. She looked tired. Wisps of auburn hair peeped from under the serge-cloth wimple she wore. Athelstan noticed the mud stains on her grey cloak, slung over the arm of the chair, whilst her bodice and dress, clasped close at the neck, looked crumpled and travel worn. She wore a ring on one finger but otherwise, apart from a silver cross hanging on a chain round her neck, no other jewellery. The friar was fascinated by her fingers, long and very slender; he noticed the indentations around the nails and wondered if she was a woman who had spent her life as an embroiderer or seamstress. Cranston still gazed beatifically down at her until the young woman, rather disconcerted, blinked and turned to Athelstan for help.

'Sir John Cranston, mistress,' Athelstan explained. 'Coroner of the city. We are here to investigate the murders of Luke Peslep and Edwin Chapler.'

'Good!' the woman exclaimed, her face becoming hard. She rose, grasped Cranston's hand and, before he could stop her, kissed it. 'I am Edwin's sister, Alison Chapler. I have just heard the news, Sir John. I demand vengeance and justice for my brother's murder.'

Chapter 3

Sir John released the young woman's hand.

'Sit down, mistress,' he said softly, walking backwards.

Athelstan closed his eyes at the muffled giggles from the clerks. Cranston, the rich claret now making its full effect felt, gazed round benevolently.

'All of you, sirs, sit down at the table here.' He placed himself at the top, snapping his fingers for Athelstan to take the stool beside him. 'Now,' Cranston began, once the clerks were sat on either side of him. 'Now, now, a pretty mess, two royal clerks horribly murdered.' He wagged a stubby finger. 'And you know what they're going to say, don't you?'

'Are you a prophet as well as a coroner?' Elflain blurted out, grinning at his companions for support.

'No, sir, I am the King's officer,' Cranston snapped, all weariness disappearing from his face and voice. 'The murder of a royal clerk is treason. The punishment for that is to be half-hanged, disembowelled, cut down and the body sliced into quarters.'

The clerks became more attentive.

'Good,' Cranston purred. 'Now we have your attention, let us begin. Mistress Alison, you live in London?'

'No, Sir John, I do not. I came this morning from Epping, a village on the old Roman road through Essex.'

'Aye, I know it,' Cranston replied. 'Mistress Alison, I must apologise, but I have ordered your brother's corpse to be taken to St Erconwald's. Brother Athelstan kindly agreed to have it interred there.'

Alison smiled so dazzlingly at Athelstan that his heart gave a slight skip. It had been a long time since a comely young woman smiled at him like that. He blushed and lowered his head.

'Do you wish to take it back, mistress?' Cranston continued, glancing sideways at Athelstan, enjoying his secretarius's discomfort.

'No, Sir John, I do not. Brother Athelstan, it was most kind of you. St Erconwald's is in Southwark, is it not?'

'Yes, mistress.' Athelstan didn't even lift his head.

'I thank you, Brother.'

'What are you doing in London now?' Cranston asked.

'I came to see my brother,' Alison replied. 'Ten days ago a journeyman brought me a letter, a short note: Edwin said he felt unwell. I could see he was worried about something. I have it here.'

She picked up the battered leather saddlebag lying next to her chair, undid the clasp and rummaged amongst the contents. The letter was passed along. Athelstan took it and undid the crisp, square piece of parchment. The writing inside it was beautifully formed: *From Edwin Chapler to his sweet and beloved sister Alison*. The letter went on to describe that he felt unwell, burdened by certain troubles; that if he was free, he would go to visit her but could she not come and see him?

Athelstan noted it was written ten days earlier; he smiled his thanks and passed it back.

'I arrived this morning,' Alison continued. 'My brother had lodgings in St Martin's Lane near Aldersgate: a mere garret overlooking the city ditch. A rather foulsome place, especially in summer.'

'Quite, quite.' Cranston nodded understandingly. 'And so you came here, mistress, and found your brother had been killed?'

'Yes she did.' Alcest spoke up. 'We told her, sir, what Havant had told us, that her brother's corpse had been plucked from the Thames.'

'And now poor Peslep is also slain,' Napham added.

'Two deaths,' Cranston trumpeted, eyes rolling. 'Two royal clerks killed in a matter of days.' He drummed his fingers on the table. 'It's not accident, sirs. We are given to understand that Chapler was killed whilst praying in the chapel of St Thomas à Becket on London Bridge and his body thrown over into the Thames. Peslep was stabbed in the Ink and Pot tavern. To cut a long story short, sirs, the assassin knew where to strike. We have a story of a young man, a stranger, at the Ink and Pot dressed in a cloak, war belt and boots armed with spurs. How many of you here could fit that description?'

The clerks looked at each other in surprise.

'The Lord Coroner,' Athelstan broke in, 'asked you a question. How many of you might fit this description? Perhaps if you could indicate?'

Slowly, led by Alcest, each of the clerks held up a hand.

'But,' Elflain protested, 'there are countless young men in London who would fit that description.'

'And how many of those young men,' Athelstan asked, 'knew that Chapler prayed at St Thomas à Becket or that Peslep frequented the Ink and Pot?'

'You are saying that the killer is one of us?' Alcest demanded.

'Yes, sir, I am,' Athelstan replied. 'And please don't take offence or stand up to protest your innocence. We are here on the orders of His Grace the Regent, John Duke of Lancaster.' He was pleased to see their smugness and arrogance fade. 'Of course,' Athelstan continued, 'I could temper my words. At this moment, suspicion falls on all of you but, there again, if honesty is your guide and truth your response to our questions, suspicion might fall elsewhere.'

'What questions?' Ollerton asked.

Athelstan glanced at Lesures, who was sitting open-mouthed. The friar had already concluded that the Master of the Rolls, despite his title, exercised very little control over these young fighting cocks. These clerks earned good silver and were patronised by the great and mighty at court who always needed the services of a good scribe.

'Questions!' Cranston barked. 'Questions, sir! Yes, sirs, I will ask you questions, all of you. First, where were you this morning, when Peslep was killed?'

'Oh, for the love of God, Sir John,' Alcest replied, his handsome face twisted in disdain. 'All of us here live in different parts of the city. We arrived here just after Matins. Some of us go to Mass, others stroll the fields of Clerkenwell. Peslep liked to eat, drink and feel the tits of a young tavern wench.'

'And what did Chapler do?' Athelstan asked.

'A dutiful clerk.' Lesures now spoke up, as if eager to extol the dead man's virtues. 'He always went to Mass at St Mary Le Bow and said the Angelus at noon. He was known for his generosity to beggars along Cheapside.'

'Quite, quite,' Athelstan said, imitating Cranston. 'But none of you can account for where you were and what you were doing this morning when Peslep was killed?'

The clerks stared at him and shook their heads.

'You have no witnesses,' Athelstan continued, 'saying that such and such a person was there at such and such a time?'

'Does any man in London?' Napham scratched his head. 'Brother Athelstan, we get up, we wash, we get dressed and we go about our daily duties. We do not keep a faithful check of every minute and every second we spend.'

'Then let us discuss what you were doing three nights ago...'

Athelstan heard a snore and looked round. Cranston had leaned back in his chair, eyes closed, smacking his lips. The coroner burped gently. The friar stared round the table. The young woman was gazing, fascinated, at Sir John. In ordinary circumstances the rest of the group would have been sniggering, laughing behind their hands,

57

but now the clerks were watchful. They might dismiss Cranston as a drunken buffoon but they watched this little friar with his innocent face and short, barbed questions. It's all a sham, Athelstan thought. Sitting here in this chamber he had a feeling of sin, heavy and oppressive, of arrogance and secrecy. These men had something to hide; Athelstan was sure the killer was sitting with him.

'Does Sir John sleep a great deal?' Alcest cocked his head to one side, eyes rounded like that of a child.

Athelstan caught the sneer in the words. 'I once saw a lion in the Tower,' he replied. 'He used to sprawl in the sand but only a fool would dare wake him. You are not a fool, are you, Master Alcest?'

The clerk pulled a face and looked away.

'Then let's return to three nights ago when Chapler was killed,' Athelstan suggested. He caught Alcest's glance: the clerk had been waiting for that question to be repeated.

'Three nights ago,' Alcest replied. 'At what hour, Brother?'

'What time do you finish here?'

'As soon as the light fades in summertime, but three evenings ago was different. It was the feast of St Edmund, our patron: we left here just before Vespers.'

'And did Chapler go with you?'

'No, no, as usual he went about his own duties.'

'And you?'

'Go ask mine host of the Dancing Pig. We were there well before sunset. We hired a special chamber for a feast. Certain ladies of the town graced us with their presence.'

'And none of you left?'

'No!' Ollerton intervened, scratching at the scar on his face. 'Not one of us left and we can each stand surety for the other. Moreover, mine host at the Dancing Pig will tell you we had no reason to leave.'

'You were there all night?'

'From before dusk until just before dawn.'

'Ah, the poppets! Lovely lads!' Cranston murmured. 'Lovely boys, and a cup of claret for myself.'

Athelstan went red with embarrassment at the sniggers. 'A king once fought an army,' he declared hurriedly. 'And vanquished them but, when the battle was over, victors and vanquished lay together in the same place.'

The sniggers faded away.

'What on earth?' Alcest asked.

'My first,' Athelstan added, remembering the second riddle, 'is like a selfish brother.'

'Father, you are speaking in riddles!'

'Brother Athelstan,' Cranston opened his eyes and leaned forward, rubbing his face, 'Brother Athelstan is quoting from what we found this morning on the corpse of your dead friend Peslep. Two riddles, sir, eh, what do they mean? Come, sir, tell me.'

Cranston stretched, flexing muscles and wetting his lips. He would have sipped from the miraculous wineskin but Athelstan kicked his shin under the table.

'Riddles!' Lesures exclaimed. He glanced round the table, eager to join in this mysterious conversation. 'Why, sirs,' Lesures addressed the clerks, 'you are constantly posing riddles for the others to solve.'

'Is that true?' Athelstan asked.

'Yes, it's true,' Alcest replied. 'Sir John, you once served as a clerk. Brother Athelstan, you were engaged in your studies, yes?' Alcest spread his hands. 'Life can be tedious, even as a clerk in the Chancery of the Green Wax. So, yes, we have perfected the art of the riddle. We pose each other riddles and, at the end of the week, the one who has solved the most dines free.'

'Give me an example,' Athelstan asked.

Alcest scratched his chin. 'Tell me, Brother, where in the world is the sky no more than three yards wide?'

Athelstan looked at Sir John, who pulled a face.

'Think, Brother,' Alcest added teasingly. 'Where, in any part of the world, is the sky no more than three yards wide?'

Athelstan closed his eyes. He recalled the previous night, standing on St Erconwald's tower, staring up at the sky. Sometimes he gazed so steadfastly he thought the sky would come down and envelope him whilst the stars, dancing round him, waited to be plucked. Then he thought of the stairs leading up to the tower, winding and narrow; sometimes he'd leave the trap door open... Athelstan opened his eyes.

'Where in the world is the sky no more than three yards wide?' he asked.

Alcest nodded.

'Why, at the bottom of a well,' Athelstan replied.

Alcest clapped his hands. 'Well done, Brother.'

'I have answered the riddle,' Athelstan pointed out.

'Repeat yours,' Elflain asked.

Athelstan did so; the clerks murmured and whispered amongst each other, oblivious to the young woman sitting at the end of the table.

'They are new,' Napham declared. 'Brother Athelstan, you must give us more time.'

'And we will,' Cranston interrupted. 'But tell me, sirs, do you know of someone who, for any reason, wanted the deaths of Chapler and Peslep?'

A chorus of denials greeted his words.

'You are sure of that?' Cranston insisted.

'Sir John, we are clerks,' Elflain replied. 'We come from different parts of the country. We have no family here.' Elflain waved around. 'So our companions here, these are our kinsfolk. We would know of any danger which threatened any of us.'

Cranston whistled through his teeth. 'In which case,' he lumbered to his feet, 'none of you, sirs, will be leaving London!'

'We are busy enough,' Lesures declared primly. 'No one can leave.'

Athelstan stared round the Chancery. Each desk had manuscripts covering it. In the far corner were seven cups, red glazed earthenware with a letter inscribed on each. Alcest followed his glance.

'Our drinking cups, Brother.' His face became sad. 'Seven, if you include Master Tibault's. Now Peslep and Chapler are dead, we'll toast them ceremoniously tonight.'

'It's our custom,' Lesures intervened. 'After working hard at charters and writs, we always finish the day with a cup of malmsey. Tonight we'll toast our deceased friends.'

'What do you do here?' Athelstan asked, getting to his feet, his writing bag clasped in his hands.

'This is the Chancery of the Green Wax,' Lesures said in hushed, reverential tones.

'Yes, I know that.'

'If I want,' Cranston explained, 'to renew a charter, obtain a licence to go overseas, to beg or have the right to enter my father's property, secure a writ against an enemy, I petition the Chancellor. The Chancellor and his clerks will either approve or reject; if they approve, the writ, charter, or whatever document is needed, will be drawn up and sealed.'

'And that is done here?' Athelstan asked.

'Yes,' Napham replied. 'And, Brother,' he pointed to the hour candle fixed on a large iron spigot near the door, 'we have further work to do.'

'Where did Peslep live?' Athelstan asked, ignoring the hint to leave.

'In Little Britain, near St Bartholomew's Priory,' Alcest replied.

'And Edwin Chapler?'

'He had lodgings near the city ditch.'

'I think we should visit both,' Athelstan said. He glanced round quickly and caught it, a slight grimace of annoyance on Ollerton's face, an anxious licking of the lips by Elflain.

'Is that proper?' Alcest asked.

'I am the King's coroner,' Cranston retorted, swaying slightly on his feet. 'And I know what I can do, sir, and I know what I cannot. I will visit their dwellings.' He drummed his fingers on the table. 'Let us not forget, sirs: you are clerks of the Green Wax, an important office of state. God knows why your companions were killed but His Grace the Regent has a deep interest in the matter.' He waved a stubby finger around. 'Every preacher leaves with a good text, so will I. Two of your comrades are dead. Now that may be the end of the matter but, for all I know, the assassin may wish more, or even all of you, dead. So I beg you to be careful.' He glanced round, pleased to see these arrogant young men had lost some of their hauteur. 'I also ask you to think, to reflect. Have you made any enemies? Have the clerks of this office offended someone? Who may nurture a grievance against you? Brother Athelstan, the day draws on.'

'Can I come with you?' Alison picked up her cloak and swung it round her shoulders. 'I have lodgings at the Silver Lute,' she added hastily, 'on the corner of Milk Street.'

'Of course,' Athelstan replied. 'You are more than welcome, mistress! Your belongings?' he asked.

'They are already there,' she replied.

The young woman picked up her leather bag and made to swing it over her shoulder. Cranston gallantly took it from her. They made their farewells and left the Chancery. Outside, in the street, Athelstan paused.

'Daydreaming, monk?'

'No, Sir John.' Athelstan smiled at Alison. 'This friar is just thinking. There was something wrong with those young men.' He rubbed his hands together. 'Nothing of substance, just a look, a glance.'

'What makes you say that, Brother?' Alison asked.

Cranston brought his hand down on Athelstan's shoulder. 'Because, mistress, he has the mind of a veritable ferret, always scurrying about for the truth, and, if he's not doing that, he's listening to those woebegone parishioners of his or sitting on his tower staring up at the stars.'

'You study the heavens, Father?'

Athelstan smiled at the young woman's sweet face. 'Why yes, and as I walk, I'll tell you about a book I'm reading by a monk called Richard of Wallingford. He was abbot of St Albans...'

Athelstan, pleased to find someone so avidly interested in the works of astrology and astronomy, briskly chattered on. Cranston, rather sulkily, hung back, now and again muttering to himself about bloody monks and stars or taking an occasional swig from his miraculous wineskin.

They made their way along Holborn. The crowds had thinned; only the solitary cart, a late arrival at the markets, or the usual travellers, journeymen and chapmen were travelling into the city. Athelstan found Alison a ready listener with a keen interest in the working of astrology and astronomy, particularly in the effect of Saturn on men's affairs. Only once, as they passed Cock Lane, the usual haunt of prostitutes, did Athelstan stop. Usually the mouth of the alleyway was thronged with whores in garish wigs and even more colourful garb touting for custom. If they ever glimpsed Sir John, the air would ring with their catcalls and lurid descriptions of what they would do to him. However, this morning the entire area was quiet, not a whore in sight. Instead the alleyway was sealed off by two great timbers placed across the entrance and guarded by a line of archers. These were all dressed in black, a hood of the same colour covering their faces. They were armed with sword and dagger, quivers on their backs; in their hands the longbows were already strung, an arrow notched to the string. Over the wooden barrier someone had draped a piece of white cloth bearing a large red cross with the words 'Jesu Miserere' scrawled beneath.

'Lord have mercy on us!' Cranston whispered. 'The plague is here!'

Athelstan felt the hairs prickle at the back of his neck; one of the great nightmares of London had returned. Every so often the pestilential miasma would seep into the city. Sometimes it would infect every place; at others, like now, just one alleyway, street or quarter would be blighted. When this happened all the inhabitants were locked and barred in their houses, dying in bed together. Children would cry beside the corpses of their parents; priests would refuse to administer the sacraments, doctors decline to visit; even the gravediggers would not touch the dead.

'The Plague Virgin!' Alison whispered.

'The what?' Cranston asked, staring across at the barricades.

'A Norfolk legend,' the woman replied. 'The Plague Virgin's a spectre who flies through the air like a bluish flame and stops at the place of her choice. She then takes human form and goes from house to house anointing doors and windows with her feverish poison. Sometimes you can even glimpse her blood-red scarf fluttering in the wind. If you see or touch it, you die within the day.'

'What does your Richard of Wallingford say about that?' Cranston asked sardonically.

'Something similar,' Athelstan replied.

He made to walk towards the barricades. One of the archers lifted his bow. Athelstan held his hand up in a gesture of peace and stepped back. The friar sighed and made to go on.

'Richard of Wallingford says something similar,' he repeated. 'He talks of black dogs roaming about at night with burning eyes and mangy coats. Every age,' Athelstan continued, 'has its own signs and wonders about the plague.'

'I know,' Cranston replied, eager to walk beside the pretty young Alison. 'When I was a lad, knee-high to a cricket, my grandfather said the plague rode a black horse over London Bridge or floated down the Thames in a sombre barge.'

'In Epping,' Alison interrupted, 'the peasants see the plague as a reaper who digs the earth with his scythe and lets out serpents, black blood and repulsive vermin. Last year, when the pestilence visited the town, a dismal wailing was heard from the cemetery. Some people saw ghosts dancing in the meadows. A taverner claimed he had seen thirty coffins in a neat line covered with black palls. On each stood a dark figure, a gleaming white cross in its hand.'

Athelstan stopped and turned to face the young woman. 'You are very knowledgeable, mistress. You know of Richard of Wallingford, astronomy, astrology, the Plague Virgin.'

'My father schooled both myself and Edwin,' she replied, a slight blush to her cheeks.

Athelstan grasped her fingers. 'But you don't study your horn book now?'

She smiled coquettishly and glanced at the friar from under lowering eyelashes.

'No, Brother, I am a seamstress and a very good one.' She came closer and kissed Athelstan gently on each cheek. 'I thank you for your generosity and kindness, Brother. When Edwin is buried, and this is all finished, I shall fashion new altar cloths for your church.'

Athelstan saw Cranston grinning eagerly behind him, thoroughly enjoying his discomfiture. 'Thank you,' he murmured and coughed in embarrassment. 'But we really should move on, Sir John. Mistress Alison, there's really no need for you to accompany us.'

'Oh, I couldn't care less about Peslep,' she replied. 'But I want to be there when you visit Edwin's lodgings.'

They continued across the great open expanse of Smithfield. A water-tippler, who had drunk too deeply, staggered about, the buckets slung over his shoulder slopping out, much to the merriment of a group of ragged-arsed urchins.

Athelstan made for the looming mass of St Bartholomew's Hospital. At first he thought the crowd assembled there was waiting to make their devotions at the tomb of the Blessed Rahere in the nearby priory or, perhaps, seeking sustenance from the hospital until a shriek of pain curdled his stomach.

'Oh lord, no!' Cranston whispered. 'It's branding day!'

Athelstan walked more quickly. 'Don't look,' he whispered to Alison. 'When you pass the door of the hospital, turn away.'

He pulled his cowl over his head, half closed his eyes and recited a prayer. Cranston, walking more leisurely behind, stared over the heads of the crowd to a small platform set up beside the hospital door. Beside it a line of felons from the Fleet and Newgate prisons waited to be branded: an 'F' for forger, a 'B' for the blasphemer, a 'T' for the twice-convicted thief. Pickpockets would have their ears clipped; whores, caught plying their trade within the city limits for the fourth time, had their noses slit. Some bore it stalwartly, others shrieked and protested, crashing their chains about as they were held down by burly city bailiffs.

'Come, Sir John!' Athelstan called over his shoulder. 'This is no place for a lady.'

'It's no place for anyone,' Cranston grunted. 'Now, in my treatise on the governance of this city...' He stopped, closing his eyes. 'Yes, in *Caput Decimus*, in chapter ten,

"On the inflicting of petty punishments", I argue that these brandings should be carried out in the prison yard.'

He opened his eyes but Athelstan and the young woman were now twenty paces ahead, going down Little Britain. Cranston hurried to catch them up. Athelstan paused to ask directions from a stallholder, then they continued on until he stopped before a four-storey, well-furnished mansion, which stood in its own small plot of land with an alleyway at either side. He brought the iron knocker down on the door. A young maid opened it, her face thin and white under a small mobcap. Her eyes rounded in fear as she looked at Brother Athelstan and then at the huge bulk of Sir John.

'Did Luke Peslep live here?' the coroner boomed.

'Oh yes, your grace.' The young maid bobbed and curtsied. 'He has two chambers on the second floor.'

'Two?' Cranston murmured. 'A wealthy man our clerk. Do you have a key?'

'The master's out,' the maid replied. 'But,' she added hastily as Sir John drew his brows together, 'I have a key here.'

She led them into a sweet-smelling passage, up the brightly polished oaken stairs and into a small recess. She inserted the key and flung open the door. Sir John, followed by Alison and Athelstan, entered.

The room was dark, so the maid opened some shutters. As she did so, Cranston whistled and Athelstan exclaimed in surprise. Peslep's lodgings were no paltry chamber but two rooms, a small parlour and a bedroom. As the maid lit candles and opened more windows, Athelstan could see that Peslep had lived a most luxurious life: damask hangings on the wall; a velvet cloth-of-gold bedspread; tables, chairs, stools and chests. On the far wall were two shelves, one with silver and pewter pots, the other with three books and a collection of rolled manuscripts. On the wall facing the bed hung a small tapestry depicting a scene from the Old Testament showing Delilah seducing Samson. Delilah wore hardly any clothing and stood in the most delightful poses.

'Even the devil can quote scripture,' Cranston whispered in Athelstan's ear.

The young maid hurriedly left.

'Come back!' Athelstan called.

The young girl did so. Athelstan pointed to the key. 'You know Master Peslep's dead?'

She just stared blankly back.

'We found no key on his corpse,' Athelstan explained.

'Oh,' the young girl replied, 'he always left it with me, sir, so I could clean the chamber.'

'And he did so this morning?'

'Oh yes.'

'And no one came here after he had left?'

'No, sir, they didn't,' the maid replied. 'But I saw Master Peslep go down the street. I was brushing the front step and, as I did so, I noticed someone else, another young man cloaked and cowled, spurs on his boots. He followed Master Peslep as if he'd been waiting for him.'

Chapter 4

'Would you recognise him again?' Cranston asked.

'Oh no, sir, just a glimpse then he was gone, Master Peslep with him.'

The young maid left. They went back to their searches. Alison seemed bored. She sat on a quilted cushion, tapping her foot as if impatient to be gone. At last Athelstan found the dead clerk's writing box. It was locked, so Cranston prised the clasp loose with his dagger and emptied the contents on to the table. Prominent amongst them was a roll of parchment containing a list of riddles. Athelstan scrutinised this.

'These clerks really love puzzles,' he murmured.

'It's more than a game.' Alison spoke up. 'My brother was always talking about it, asking me to search for fresh ones.'

'And the assassin knew that,' Athelstan replied. He picked up a smaller scroll, undid it and whistled under his breath. 'Sir John, look at this.'

Cranston grasped it and studied the list of figures.

'It's from Orifab, the goldsmiths in Cheapside,' he muttered. He looked at the total at the bottom near the date, given some two weeks previously. 'Master Peslep was a very rich man,' he remarked. 'So rich I wonder why he worked as a Chancery clerk.'

'Many of them are from wealthy families,' Alison intervened. She came across and peered over Sir John's shoulder. 'The younger sons of nobles,' she continued. 'Their elder brothers either inherited the estates or entered the Church.'

Cranston tossed the roll back into the box. 'I'll tell my bailiffs to come and seal the room,' he declared. 'Is there anything else?'

Athelstan shook his head. 'Personal effects but nothing remarkable.'

They left the chamber, Cranston turning the lock and telling the maid he would keep the key himself, and went back down into the street. Alison grew silent, hanging back as Cranston and Athelstan made their way through the midmorning crowds towards the city ditch. At last they reached the house where Chapler had lodged, a shabby, two-storeyed tenement which looked as if it had been pushed between the alehouse on one side and a vintner's shop on the other. The timbers were crooked, the plaster sagging, the white paint flaking and falling like pieces of snow. A garrulous old woman was the door-keeper; she smiled rheumily at them, chewing on her gums.

Yes, she gabbled. Master Chapler lived here. And the door to his chamber was open. After all, Chapler's friend had also called.

'When?' Cranston asked.

'Very early this morning,' she replied. 'Just as the bells were tolling for Matins.'

The old woman gave the same description as the maid: a young man, cowled and hooded, spurs clinking on his riding boots. He had kept his face turned away but had given the old crone a coin and who was she to object?

They climbed the rickety stairs, Athelstan wrinkling his nose at the stale odours. Mice scampered before them and the friar wondered what his great tom cat Bonaventure would have made of all this. The door at the top was half open. Athelstan went in first, crossing the room to open the shutters. Despite the house's decay, this chamber was pleasant, the plaster freshly painted in a light, soothing green. The floor of both the parlour and the small scullery beyond was scrubbed, the furniture was roughly hewn but sturdy and clean. Alison looked around, put her face in her hands and sobbed quietly. Cranston lumbered across. He put one great arm round her.

'There, there, my girl! There, there! My sister lost her husband. He was killed fighting the Spanish in the Narrow Seas. These things pass. You never forget them. You just live with them.'

Athelstan, sitting on the four-poster bed, caught his breath at Sir John's words. He felt the same about his brother Francis when, what seemed like an eternity ago, they had both joined the King's armies in France. Francis had been killed and Athelstan had returned to his novitiate. For his crime of desertion and for having had a hand in his brother's death, he had paid a terrible price.

His parents had died broken-hearted and his order had never forgotten. Now, instead of being a scholar, he was parish priest of St Erconwald's in Southwark, but would he be for much longer?

'Brother?'

Athelstan shook himself free from his reverie and joined Cranston in his search. They found the usual riddles, letters, lists of provisions, but nothing remarkable. Certainly not the lavish wealth found at Peslep's. Athelstan came back to where Sir John hugged a quietly weeping Alison.

'There's nothing here, Sir John. Nothing at all.'

Cranston dropped his arm and stepped away, catching at Alison's hand. He cupped her chin gently, lifting her tearful face. 'I'll have this room sealed as well,' he promised. 'I'll send a bailiff, a man called Flaxwith, he's a trusty fellow. He'll pack all your brother's possessions away. Store them in chests in the Guildhall.'

The young woman thanked him. 'I'd best go. As I've said, I'm at the Silver Flute on Milk Street. My brother's possessions should be sent there.'

'Do you want us to accompany you?' Athelstan asked.

'Oh no. I'll find my own way.' She stepped forward and kissed Athelstan lightly on the cheek. 'If I may, Brother, I'll come to St Erconwald's later on to watch over my brother's corpse.'

'Of course,' Athelstan replied.

Alison left. They heard her steps fade away on the stairs.

Cranston rubbed his face. 'Brother, I need a beef pie: the crust gold and soft, the juices running fresh in my

74

mouth.' He grasped the friar by the arm. 'And, by the power given to me, I must ask you to accompany me to the Holy Lamb.'

'You have no power over Holy Mother Church,' Athelstan joked.

'Then come as a friend,' Cranston whispered.

They found Sir John's favourite tavern half-empty, the air thick with fragrant smells from the buttery beyond. Leif the one-legged beggar was sitting in Sir John's window seat overlooking the small garden. He leapt up as the coroner came in.

'Oh, devil's paps!' Cranston swore.

The beggar, his red greasy hair pushed back from his white emaciated face, hopped like a grasshopper towards them.

'Sir John! Sir John! A thousand blessings on you, Brother! Lady Maude has sent me! The table is set. Three cutlets of lamb cooked in rosemary! The twins have been fighting and Gog and Magog have stolen the beef you had hoped to eat this evening. Blaskett your manservant says he needs your key to clean your chamber. Master Flaxwith the bailiff has been looking for you. A young nobleman, Sir Lionel Havant, has called at your house. Two pickpockets have been caught in the market. Osbert your clerk...'

'Shut up!' Cranston roared, silencing even the clamour in the kitchen. 'Leif, for the love of God, would you shut up!'

'Very good, Your Grace.' Leif bobbed and bowed. 'I'll go straight to Lady Maude to tell her you are here but you'll be home shortly.'

Sir John's great arm shot out. He grasped Leif's shoulder. The beggar winced.

'On second thought, Sir John, perhaps if I was given a penny for some ale, I'd sit in the garden and...'

—

He took the penny Sir John thrust into his hand and fled from the taproom. He took his seat above the herb garden, his back half turned; now and again he'd turn the glower in the direction of the coroner. Cranston, however, was now enthroned, rubbing his hands whilst the taverner's wife fluttered round him like a solicitous chicken.

'A blackjack of ale,' Cranston boomed. 'One of your meat pies, with the onions soft, blending with the meat. A cup of...?' He looked at Athelstan.

'Watered ale,' the friar replied.

'Some ale for my monkish friend and, if you come here, lady, I'll give you a kiss on those red fat cheeks of yours.'

The landlord's wife, fluttering and cooing, fled the taproom for the kitchen.

Athelstan leaned back against the wall. The plaster felt cool on the back of his head. He half listened to Sir John's chatter. Closing his eyes, he thought of all he had seen this morning. Those two young men: death had sprung like a trap upon them. Alison crying. Those smug clerks of the

Green Wax, the sneering faces of Stablegate and Flinstead, and Drayton's corpse in that lonely counting house. How had that moneylender been killed?

A servant brought Sir John's pie and ale. Athelstan sipped at his and let the coroner enjoy himself, exclaiming in pleasure at the fragrance of the beef and the sharp sweetness of the onions. Athelstan just prayed that Cranston would not return to the usual questioning: was Father Prior going to send him away from Southwark? Was it true Athelstan was bound for the Halls of Oxford? So, as the coroner wiped his hands on a napkin, Athelstan took the initiative.

'I really should be going, Sir John. We have a bubbling pot of mystery here. I am sure Stablegate and Flinstead are as guilty as Judas, but how they killed poor Drayton is a mystery.' He sighed. 'As for the murder of those two clerks of the Green Wax, their deaths are as puzzling as their lives.'

'What do you mean?' Cranston ignored the pun.

'Well.' Athelstan cradled the blackjack in his hands. 'Here we have one clerk knocked on the head and thrown in the Thames; the other is stabbed to death whilst sitting on a privy. Riddles are left with the second corpse. Chapler was poor but Peslep rich. And who is this strange young man who apparently knew both of them?'

'So, what do we do now?' the coroner asked.

'Get Flaxwith,' Athelstan drained his tankard, 'to check that Stablegate and Flinstead were where they claimed to be. And the same with those clerks of the Green Wax. Did they spend the night at the Dancing Pig? And where was Master Lesures, the Master of the Rolls?'

'Anything else?'

'Yes. Use your authority, Sir John, to question Orifab. Discover the source of Peslep's wealth.'

Cranston looked at him mournfully. 'You'll stay for another blackjack of ale?'

'No, Sir John, and neither should you. Lady Maude and the poppets are waiting.'

Athelstan rose, sketched a blessing in the air and left the tavern. He pulled the cowl over his head and, wrapping his hands in the sleeves of his gown, made his way through the crowds. He kept his eyes to the ground. As he turned up the Poultry to Walbrooke, he felt hot and sticky and wondered if he should go down to the riverside. Moleskin the boatman might take him across to Southwark. The river breeze would be cool, fresh, and Athelstan liked its salty tang. Moreover, he was forever curious about what ships came into port. Sometimes, if there was a Venetian caravel, Athelstan would love to seek out the navigator, for there had been whispers in his order that the Venetians owned secret maps and were sailing seas where no English cog would dare to go. Legendary stories about slipping out through the Pillars of Hercules and, instead of turning north into the Bay of Biscay, sailing south down the west coast of Africa.

Athelstan paused before a small statue of Our Lady placed near the London stone in Candlewick Street. He closed his eyes and said the Ave Maria but he was still distracted. He would love to talk to these navigators. If the earth was flat, why didn't they ever reach the edge? And were the stars in heaven different the further south they sailed?

A child ran up, smutty-faced. 'Give me your blessing, Father!' he piped, jumping from foot to foot.

'Of course.' Athelstan pulled back his cowl.

'A real blessing, Father.' The young boy's eyes were bright.

'Why?' Athelstan asked curiously.

'Because I've just nipped my sister,' the urchin replied. 'And my mother will beat me, but if you've given me a blessing...'

Athelstan put his hand on the boy's hot brow. 'May the Lord bless you and protect you,' he prayed. 'May He show you His face and have mercy on you.' He raised his right hand for the benediction. 'May He smile on you and give you peace. May the Lord bless you and keep you all the days of your life.' He still grasped the boy as he dug into his purse and took out a penny. 'Now, buy your sister some sweet-meats. Give some to her and to your mother. Always be kind and the Lord will be kind to you.'

The young boy grabbed the coin and scampered off. Athelstan felt better. I won't go to the river, he thought, I'll go along to see old Harrowtooth.

He continued along Candlewick into Bridge Street. Near the gatehouse he met Master Robert Burdon, the diminutive constable of the bridge and the proud father of nine children. The little fellow was strutting up and down, gazing at long poles which stretched out over the river bearing the heads of executed traitors.

'Goodmorrow, Master Burdon, do I have permission to cross your bridge?'

'You carry the warrant of Holy Mother Church,' Burdon teased back. 'Not to mention the Lord Coroner's. May the Lord bless his breeches and all that's within them. What do you really want, Father?'

Athelstan took a deep breath but gagged at the stench from the corrupting pile of rotting fish piled high against the rails of the bridge. Burdon followed his gaze.

'I know, Father. I'll throw that lot over as well as the insolent bastard who put it there.'

'Where does old Harrowtooth live?' Athelstan asked.

Burdon clicked his fingers. Athelstan followed him along the bridge. He felt that strange sensation he always did: the bridge was really a street with houses and shops on either side, yet he was aware of the rushing water below, caught like some soul between heaven and earth. Burdon stopped at the side door to a clothier and rapped noisily upon it. Harrowtooth, her iron-grey hair streaming about her, flung open the door.

'Go to hell!' she screamed when she saw Burdon.

'Only after you, you foulsome bitch!' Burdon yelled back.

'Now, now,' Athelstan intervened swiftly. 'Master Burdon, I thank you. Mistress Harrowtooth, a word?'

Burdon skipped away, turning to make an obscene gesture with his middle finger. Harrowtooth was about to reply but Athelstan grasped her hand.

'Mistress, please, just a few minutes of your time?'

The old woman turned, eyes screwed up against the sun. 'You are the Dominican from Southwark?'

'Can I come in?'

'No, you can't. I don't allow priests in here: thieving magpies they are.'

'I really won't steal anything.' Athelstan held his hands up.

'It's a fine day,' Harrowtooth replied. She pointed across the street. 'Let's go down the alleyway, it overlooks the river.'

Athelstan sighed. He had no choice. The alleyway was a sordid, stinking mess, rubbish piled on either side. He was pleased to stand against the rail of the bridge. The breeze was cool and from below he could hear the shouts of the watermen and wherry boys. Further down the river two huge cogs, royal men-of-war, were preparing to leave to patrol the Narrow Seas: bumboats and barges bobbed like little sticks around them.

'I love this place,' Harrowtooth said, coming up behind him. 'My father used to bring me here.'

'Father?' Athelstan asked.

'He was a priest.' Harrowtooth grinned. 'Mother died, so he made reparation by going on pilgrimage. The lazy bugger never came back.'

'Edwin Chapler?' Athelstan abruptly asked.

'Ah, the young clerk who was flung over the bridge.' Harrowtooth sniffed. 'I sees him, you know. I was probably the last person to see him before he met God.'

'Except for his murderer,' Athelstan corrected.

'Ah yes!'

'So, what did you see, Mother?'

'I am not your mother!' Harrowtooth snapped but then, leaning against the rails, she told Athelstan of how she had visited the chapel of St Thomas, how Chapler had been praying there, how he looked agitated when she left him.

'And you saw no one else?'

'No one, father.'

'Did Chapler often visit St Thomas à Becket?'

'Oh yes. Oh yes. Sometimes he'd be by himself. I sees him once.' She hurried on, eyes glinting at the penny in Athelstan's hand. 'I sees him, Father. Oh, and by the way, you can call me Mother any time you want. I sees him with a young man, well dressed. Here on the bridge.'

Athelstan pressed for a description but the old woman shook her head. 'I told you what I can, Father.'

Athelstan handed over the penny. He followed Harrowtooth back across the bridge. She waited for a break in the carts and sumpter ponies being led across and scurried away like a spider hiding from the sunlight. Athelstan made his way to Southwark side. Near the priory of St Mary Overy, Mugwort the bell clerk and Pernell the old Flemish woman, her hair now painted a hideous orange, were standing talking to Amisias the fuller. All three parishioners turned to greet Athelstan. The friar would have liked to stop and ask why they'd had their heads together, talking so animatedly, but he walked on.

He passed the house of Simon the carpenter, pleased to see that Tabitha, a widow, her husband recently hanged at Tyburn, seemed to be coping better. Athelstan wondered if the whispers were true, that the deceased carpenter had been too quick with his fists, and regularly beat upon his poor wife.

He made his way past the shabby stalls, the little hovels and cottages of his parishioners. The air was thick with the pungent smells from the tanning yards but the aroma from Merryleg's pie shop was as sweet and savoury as ever. The day seemed busy enough: dogs and children ran about, thin-necked chickens dug into the midden heaps. Lurching out of an alleyway, ears flapping, flanks quivering with fat, trotted Ursula the pig-woman's favourite sow. The beast stopped, snout up, and stared at Athelstan. The friar was sure that, if a pig could grin, this one did.

I'd love to have a stick, Athelstan thought, quietly mourning the succulent cabbages this great beast had plucked from his garden. Instead he sighed, sketched a blessing in the direction of the sow and continued up the alleyway. The church steps were deserted except for Bonaventure, the great one-eyed tom cat who lay sprawled there like some dissolute Roman emperor. He cocked his good eye open as Athelstan came and crouched beside him.

'Oh, most pious of cats,' Athelstan breathed, gently rubbing the cat's tattered ears between his fingers.

He opened the door of the church and went inside, relishing the cool, incense-filled air. The nave was empty.

Athelstan felt guilty because there should have been a school today. He checked the sanctuary lamp, a little red beacon in the darkness glowing under the silver pyx hanging from its chain above the high altar. About to go back down the steps, Athelstan sniffed. 'Fresh paint,' he murmured.

Then he remembered how Huddle the painter, together with Tab the tinker, had finished a new crucifix to hang in the small alcove behind the baptismal font. Athelstan went to inspect it. The wall behind the font had been covered with a vivid garish painting depicting souls, in the form of worms, being pushed into a fiery furnace by a devil which had the body of a monkey and the head of a wild goat.

'It's too savage,' Athelstan murmured, studying the flames Huddle had painted devouring the black imps and the grotesque beasts of the underworld. However, it was the new crucifix which caught his attention. Huge, at least three foot high and two foot across, the rood was black with the figure of Christ in alabaster-white. This twisted in agony, the head covered with thorns, the face drooping, whilst Huddle had vividly painted the blood pouring out of the wounds in the hands, feet and side. Beneath it, the work of Watkin the dung-collector, leader of the parish council, was a new candelabra made of wrought iron with little spikes for devotional lights to be placed on.

Athelstan studied the scene carefully. 'A little too vivid,' he commented but, there again, he admired Huddle's consummate skill and knew that every aspect of the cross would be carefully studied by each and every one of his parishioners at the parish council tonight. Athelstan genuflected towards the sanctuary, closed the door and, followed by an inquisitive Bonaventure, went across to the priest's house.

He first checked on Philomel, the old destrier he had bought. The horse seemed happy enough, leaning against the wall, eyes closed, munching the remains of what was left of his oats. Athelstan went into the house. The small kitchen and parlour were clean and swept, the rushes changed and sprinkled with spring flowers and herbs. The wooden table before the kitchen hearth had been scrubbed whilst fresh bread, cheese and a small jar of comfit were in the buttery. Athelstan closed his eyes and thanked God for Benedicta, the widow woman. He took the food and returned to the parlour, filling Bonaventure's bowl with milk. The great cat sat on the table, sipping at it, now and again raising his head to study his master. Athelstan's thoughts were elsewhere. He chewed his food carefully, eyes half closed, remembering the problems which had confronted him earlier in the day. He could make no sense of the moneylender's murder.

Think, Athelstan. For the love of God there must be a solution.

He put the piece of cheese down, closed his eyes and recalled Drayton's counting room. No entrances, a square of stone, walls, ceiling, floors all sealed in by that great oaken door with its metal studs, locked and barred. How had the assassin got in and out with the stolen silver? If he had knocked at the door, Drayton might have admitted him, but who would have locked and bolted the door behind him? And Athelstan recalled the house: how did the murderer leave, making sure every window and door was locked behind him? Athelstan opened his eyes and shook his head. When he looked down, the piece of cheese had gone. The friar wagged a finger at the cat.

'Thou shalt not covet thy neighbour's cheese, Bonaventura.'

The cat's little pink tongue came out. Athelstan then thought of the murders amongst the clerks of the Green Wax. Chapler's was brutal, a bang on the head and tossed over London Bridge. But why? Who would kill a clerk? For what reason? And who was this mysterious young man whom Chapler had met and who was probably responsible for Peslep's death? And the latter's wealth, was it ill-gotten? And his companions? Why had Athelstan caught that sense of...? He paused in his thoughts: yes, wickedness, that's what it was, a sense of evil. And the riddles? What did it mean: a king vanquishing his opponents but, in the end, victors and vanquished lying together in the same place? And the riddle that was left on Peslep's body?

My first is like a selfish brother.

Athelstan shook his head. 'Sufficient unto the day is the evil thereof,' he declared.

At least, thank God, Cranston had not questioned him. What the coroner did not know, nor did anyone here in Southwark, was that Father Prior seemed intent on moving Athelstan to the Halls of Oxford. Athelstan had protested and, in doing so, realised how much he loved this small poor parish on the south side of the Thames. Moreover, despite the bloody murders they investigated, Cranston was his friend.

Athelstan sighed: his brooding would do no good. He let Bonaventure finish what was left of the cheese and climbed up the steps to the little loft which also served as his bedroom. He sat down on the bed and picked up the book his brethren at Blackfriars had so kindly lent him: the writings of Abbot Richard of Wallingford, the eminent scholar and instrument maker who, a hundred years ago, had built a great clock at St Albans.

I must go and see it, Athelstan thought. He turned the pages of the folio and studied Wallingford's drawing of the Albion, an elaborate astrolabe, but he couldn't concentrate. His mind kept jumping like a flea. Drayton's corpse locked and sealed in a vaulted chamber; Peslep stabbed whilst sitting on a privy; Chapler's corpse; the riddles; something else he had seen or heard today which had escaped his tired brain. He put the book down and lay on the bed. He felt Bonaventure come and snuggle up behind him.

'According to the laws of my order,' he murmured, 'a Dominican is supposed to sleep alone, Bonaventure! Whatever would Father Prior think?'

Athelstan closed his eyes and drifted into a dream about constructing, with the help of Sir John Cranston, a marvellous clock at the top of St Erconwald's tower.

A few hours later, in the writing room of the Chancery of the Green Wax, the clerks were finishing the major tasks of the day. They had, Master Lesures reflected, been quiet, not the respectful silence due to the deaths of two of their colleagues, but something else, as if they were afraid. He walked into the centre of the room and rang his small handbell.

'The day's work is done,' he declared. 'So it's time we took a little refreshment, a break from our duties. Perhaps toast the memory of our dead comrades?'

The others agreed, climbing down off their high stools. They left their quills on their desks, or pushed them into the pouches on their belts. They stood in a small group talking softly amongst themselves, almost ignoring him. Lesures shrugged and walked across to the table where their cups were kept. He picked up the jug of malmsey, removing the linen cloth which covered it, and filled the cups. He then took the tray round the room. Each clerk picked up the cup which carried the letter of their surname; they sipped appreciatively, savouring the rich, honey-fused drink. This evening, however, Lesures felt like a stranger. They looked at him out of the corner of their eyes and he could see that they wished him else-where.

'Are we to attend the funerals?' he asked.

'Chapler was an acquaintance,' Alcest retorted. 'But he was not a friend. I don't like Southwark and I want to keep far away from Brother Athelstan and that drunken coroner.'

'And Peslep?' Lesures asked.

'I suppose he'll be buried in St Mary Le Bow,' Napham replied. 'We'll pray for a priest to sing a chantry Mass and watch his body being tossed into the grave.'

'You're rather hard,' Lesures stuttered.

'It's what Peslep would have wanted,' Elflain responded. 'I don't think he believed in God so why should we make a mockery in death of what he made a mockery in life?'

Lesures was about to object when Ollerton staggered back, the pewter cup dropping from his hand, his face contorted in pain. He clutched at his throat and stomach.

'Oh my God!' he whispered. 'Oh heaven and all the...!' He slumped to his knees.

His companions hurried to assist but Ollerton, the pain so intense, drove them off with his hand before crashing face down to the floor. He lay there convulsing in agony. Alcest managed to secure him, gripping him under the shoulders. All he could do, whilst the others shouted and exclaimed around him, was try to control the terrible spasms which racked his friend's body. Ollerton was already losing consciousness, eyes rolling back, mouth open, jaw tense, a long line of saliva drooling down his chin. He closed his eyes and coughed, his body shaking again. Suddenly he went rigid and then slack, head falling away, eyes and mouth half open. Alcest put him gently back on the floor. The others stared, horror-struck.

'Don't drink,' Elflain whispered, putting his own cup back on the table.

'Apoplexy?' Lesures asked.

'Apoplexy!' Alcest sneered. He turned Ollerton's face over; it was now a garish white, with dark rings under the staring eyes. 'This is no *coup de sang*. Ollerton has been poisoned.'

He edged across the floor and picked up the fallen cup, whose contents had now soaked into the floorboards. Alcest sniffed at the rim but realised the sweet honey taste could hide any potion. He went across to the jug.

'You poured the cup, Lesures?'

'I…' The Master of the Rolls lifted his hand in alarm. 'We should send for a physician,' he wailed.

'Unless,' Alcest sneered, 'you know one who can bring the dead back to life, Master Lesures, perhaps a priest would be better? One of the good brothers from St Bartholomew's. I'd be grateful.'

Lesures took the hint and fled. Once the door closed behind him, the rest grouped round the corpse.

'Three now!' Napham whispered. 'Three dead!'

Alcest was already going through the man's wallet and purse.

'Is that necessary?'

'Yes, it is,' Alcest snarled. 'And tonight, before the snooping coroner arrives, we visit his chambers.'

He paused at the sound of footsteps on the stairs. Lesures hurried in, clutching a piece of parchment. He thrust this at Alcest. The clerk read aloud the riddle scrawled there.

'"My second is the centre of woe and the principal mover of horror."' He glanced at his companions. 'We are being hunted,' he said. 'Ollerton's death will not be the last!'

Chapter 5

Athelstan was standing on the top of St Erconwald's tower looking through a huge telescope. Bonaventure was talking to him but Cranston was calling from below. Athelstan opened his eyes; roughly woken from his dream, he gasped and looked around. Bonaventure was gone. The sunlight in the small window above his bed was fading. He swung his legs off the bed and realised that what had woken him was the knocking on the door below.

'Father, Father, are you all right?'

Benedicta had now come into the kitchen.

'I'm up here, Benedicta,' Athelstan called, rubbing his face. 'I went with the cat for a nap.' He paused. 'That's witty,' he whispered. 'For a man just woken up.'

'Athelstan, are you all right?'

The friar rose and looked down the ladder at Benedicta. She was dressed in a summer smock made of light green cloth. She had a small silver chain round her neck. Someone, probably one of the children, had made a daisy chain; she still had this over her jet-black hair. She had such a look of concern in her beautiful dark eyes that Athelstan's heart skipped a beat. Deep in his soul he loved this widow, but never once would he dare tell her. I love you passionately, he thought, and ruefully recalled the advice of his novice master.

'It's not the body, Athelstan, that hungers, it's the soul. Physical desire is like a flame. Sometimes it leaps up, at other times it burns low. The love of the soul, however, is a raging fire that is never quenched.'

'Athelstan!' Benedicta stamped her foot. 'Have you lost your wits? You are staring at me!'

'I was thinking.' Athelstan smiled. 'I know what it's going to be like in heaven.'

Benedicta sighed in exasperation. 'Athelstan, the council will be meeting soon. You know what Watkin is like. If you're not there, he'll start saying Mass. We also have a visitor, a young woman, Alison Chapler. I didn't know there was a corpse in the death house!'

Athelstan's fingers flew to his lips and he groaned. 'Oh Lord save us!' he exclaimed. 'I'd forgotten about that, Benedicta. I've been with Cranston. You know what it's like.'

He hurried down the ladder, grasped Benedicta by the shoulder and gave her a kiss on each cheek.

'What's that for, Father?'

'One day I'll tell you. That poor woman.'

Athelstan quickly grabbed his stole and the phial of holy oils he kept in the cupboard in the far corner of the kitchen. He tightened the girdle round his robe and hurried out. The evening was a gorgeous one; the sun not so strong and bright whilst a refreshing breeze bent the grass and flowers in the cemetery. Crim the altar boy was having a pee in the corner just inside the gate.

'Hello, Father!' he called out over his shoulder.

'Pull up your hose!' Athelstan ordered. 'I've told you not to do that in God's acre.'

'Sorry, Father, but the water-tippler gave me a free drink, cool and sweet it was. Where are you going, Father? I did chase the sow from your garden! It's a good job you didn't come earlier.' Crim chattered on, running along-side Athelstan and looking over his shoulder at Benedicta. 'Cecily the courtesan has been here!'

'What?' Athelstan paused. 'And who was with her?'

'I don't know,' the boy mumbled, his face crestfallen.

Athelstan ruffled the boy's hair. 'Go and bring a lighted candle,' he said kindly.

'Oh, there's a woman in the death house,' Crim retorted. 'Is there a corpse there? Can I see it?'

'Get a candle.'

Athelstan continued down the narrow path which wound by the burial mounds, battered crosses and worn gravestones. The small corpse house stood under the shade of a yew tree in the far corner of the cemetery. The door was open. Inside, Alison knelt beside the corpse which lay in a wooden casket. She'd already lit a candle and put it on a niche in the wall. The air was sweet, not the usual stale, rather dank odour. Alison got up as Athelstan entered, her cheeks soaked in tears.

'I'm sorry,' Athelstan apologised. 'I came back and I forgot.'

'It's all right, Father,' Alison replied. 'I bought a coffin from a gravedigger who lives near Crutched Friars. He also brought it across for me.'

95

She went to lift the lid of the coffin. Athelstan helped her to take it off. Chapler's corpse did not look so ghastly now. Even the hair had been combed, whilst Alison had filled the coffin on either side of the body with crushed rosemary. She stood, hands joined, Benedicta behind her, as Athelstan began the service for the dead. He anointed the corpse, its forehead, eyes, nose, mouth, hands and chest. Crim stole in, a lighted candle in his hand. When Athelstan had finished, he recited the Office for the Dead and ended it with the Requiem.

'Eternal rest grant to him, O Lord.'

Benedicta and Alison took up the refrain: 'And let eternal light shine upon him.'

Once they had said the prayer, Athelstan ordered the lid to be replaced and screwed down. 'It can now be taken into church,' he declared.

'No, Father, leave it here for the night.' Alison's sweet face puckered into a smile. 'Edwin liked the grass, the loneliness, the flowers. It's pleasant out here.'

'You are sure you want him buried at St Erconwald's?' Athelstan asked.

'Oh yes, Father.'

'Then I'll say a Requiem Mass tomorrow morning, just after dawn.' He turned. 'This is Benedicta.'

Both women exchanged smiles.

'You can stay with her. I'll have Pike the ditcher prepare a grave.' Athelstan walked out and pointed across the graveyard. 'Perhaps there in the corner? In summer it catches the sun.'

Alison tearfully agreed. Athelstan took off his stole. He handed that and the oils to Crim, asking him to take them back to his house.

'So, Mistress Alison, will you accept my offer to stay?'

'Yes, Father, I will.'

Benedicta came over and linked her arm through that of the young woman. 'Do you have enough money?' she asked.

'Oh yes,' Alison replied. 'Edwin was a good brother. What he earned he sent to me.'

'We have a parish council meeting now,' Athelstan explained. 'You can wait here or, if you want to join us…?'

Alison squeezed Benedicta's hand. 'I'd like to come, Father.'

Athelstan made to lead them down the path.

'Brother Athelstan.' Alison was now standing straight.

The friar was slightly alarmed at the expression in her face and eyes; there was something about this young woman, a steel beneath the velvet.

'What is it, mistress?'

'My brother's assassins. You will apprehend them? They will hang for what they did?'

'Them?' Athelstan came back. 'Mistress Alison, what makes you think there are more than one?'

'Oh.' Alison pulled a face. 'Edwin was a vigorous young man. He would not have given up his life so easily.'

'Do you suspect anyone?' Athelstan asked.

'One of those clerks,' she replied. 'Especially the arrogant one, Alcest. Edwin often talked about him: he didn't like him and Alcest certainly didn't like Edwin.'

'But murder!' Athelstan exclaimed. 'Mistress Alison, sometimes I do not like some of my parishioners, yet that's no excuse for the most terrible crime of all!'

'Just a feeling,' Alison replied, running a finger along her lower lip. 'Something in the soul, Father.'

Athelstan knew the young woman was right. The clerks of the Green Wax had a great deal to answer for, but what? Murder? How, if they had spent the night Chapler had been killed carousing in some tavern chamber? Athelstan walked down the cemetery path; behind him Benedicta consoled Alison, listening to details about her brother's murder and reassuring her that Sir John Cranston, for all his love of claret, had a mind as sharp as a razor and a passion for justice.

They went round to the front of the church and Athelstan smiled at his parish council.

'We've been waiting, Father. You're late!' Hig the pig-man bellowed, his dark-set face made even more ugly by a scowl.

'I had to anoint a corpse,' Athelstan explained. He introduced Alison.

'Don't you go lecturing our priest.' Watkin the dung-collector came down the steps, almost knocking Hig the pig-man flying. Watkin's bulbous face was red, his eyes popping and, even from where he stood, Athelstan could smell his ale-drenched breath. 'I am leader of the parish council.' Watkin turned. 'I am the one who speaks to Father.'

'Not for long!' Pike the ditcher's wife called out from the back.

Athelstan clapped his hands. 'Come on! Come on!' The friar intervened before a fight broke out.

Ranulf the rat-catcher, dressed in his black tarred hood and jerkin despite the weather, opened the church door and ushered them in. Athelstan plucked the sleeve of Cecily the courtesan. She was climbing the steps slowly, clutching at her dress and swinging her bottom provocatively at Pike the ditcher.

'Cecily,' Athelstan whispered.

'Yes, Father?' The woman's cornflower-blue eyes and lovely girlish face, framed in a mass of golden curls, looked more angelic than ever.

'Cecily, when will you learn,' Athelstan whispered, 'that only those who are dead are supposed to lie down in the graveyard?'

'Why, Father.' Cecily's eyes rounded even further. 'I only went to pick some flowers.'

'Is that the truth?'

'No, Father, but that's all I'm going to tell you.' And the minx scampered off.

The parish council met near the baptistry, sitting on benches formed in the shape of a square. Watkin took the place of honour on Athelstan's right, Pike the ditcher on the left, followed by the usual fight for places amongst the rest. Benedicta and Alison found seats on the bench opposite Athelstan and he began the meeting with a prayer. There were the usual items of business: the grass in the cemetery needed cutting; the arrangements for tomorrow's funeral. Everyone looked sympathetically at

Alison. Pike offered to dig the grave, Hig and Watkin to carry the coffin. Athelstan asked who had been drinking raucously two nights previously just outside the church. No one answered, though Bladdersniff the bailiff, Pike and Watkin stared at the floor as if they had never seen it before.

'Now,' Athelstan continued. 'The preparations for Holy Rood Day. In about a month's time, on the fourteenth of September, we celebrate the feast of the Exaltation of the Holy Cross.'

That was the signal for everyone to get up and admire Huddle's new crucifix. The painter, his long, horsy face bright with pleasure, described how he had achieved his masterpiece. Everyone 'oohed' and 'aahed', followed by general agreement that, this time, Huddle had surpassed himself.

'Now,' Athelstan continued when they had resumed their seats. 'Rood Day is a holy day. We will have Mass followed by a solemn blessing of the crucifix.'

'I will carry it,' Watkin bellowed.

'You bloody won't!' Pike roared back. 'You do everything, Watkin!'

'I don't lie down in the cemetery,' the dung-collector hissed spitefully.

'What's that?' Pike's virago of a wife leaned forward.

'Hush now.' Tab the tinker, sitting next to her, grasped her hand. 'You know Pike has to dig the graves and look after them.'

Pike smiled across at the tinker and Athelstan sensed there were new shifting alliances on the parish council.

'After the blessing,' he continued, 'we will have church ales and some games, followed by the parish feast in the evening.'

'What about the ceremony?' Pernell the Fleming pulled her hair away from her face.

Athelstan quietly groaned: he'd hoped they had forgotten that.

'You know, Father,' Pernell continued, 'a cross is always taken round the cemetery. Who'll be Christ this year?'

After that came the descent into hell, as bitter words were exchanged about who would do what. Athelstan stared across at Alison. She, like Benedicta, was desperately trying not to laugh. At last peace reigned but only after Athelstan had got up, clapped his hands and glared around. Ranulf the rat-catcher would carry the cross, he decided; Watkin and Pike would be Roman soldiers; other roles were shared out. In the end, only one person didn't have a part, Pike the ditcher's wife. She boiled with fury as she paid the price for her spiteful tongue and malicious comments. Time and again Athelstan tried to reallocate or introduce a new role but the woman refused to be mollified. More dangerously, the virago was glaring malevolently at Cecily the courtesan who, of course, smiled sweetly back.

'Father.' Alison Chapler got to her feet. 'Father, I have a suggestion. My family originally came from Norfolk. We always celebrated Holy Rood Day. I notice you have one thing missing, the Kitsch Witch.'

'Who?' Athelstan asked.

'According to legend,' Alison continued, clearly enjoying herself, 'the witch was a woman who lived in the Valley of Death near Jerusalem: she was despised by all.'

Athelstan just prayed that no one would make a comment.

'Anyway,' Alison continued, 'when Christ was crucified, she stood far off and, because of her faith, she was transformed and became a saint.'

Everyone clapped and peace was restored.

-

In a small chamber on the ground floor of the Chancery of the Green Wax, Sir John Cranston surveyed the ruined corpse of William Ollerton, former clerk.

'The poison must have been deadly.' Cranston tapped the dead man's boot with the toe of his own. 'Pernicious and venomous, eh?'

The coroner drummed his fingers on his stomach. He had been sitting in his garden, watching the poppets play with Gog and Magog and reflecting on his learned treatise, 'On the Governance of London', when Bailiff Flaxwith had arrived with the news. Cranston had cursed but left: the report of Ollerton's death would soon reach the Savoy Palace and the Regent would begin asking questions. Now Cranston had a few of his own. Beside him Master Tibault Lesures seemed to be on the point of fainting, his face pallid and sweat-soaked, eyes blinking. The Master of the Rolls licked his lips, making small, nervous gestures with his fingers. The three clerks Elflain, Napham and Alcest were more composed.

'Let us begin again,' Cranston said. 'You have a cup...?'

'Yes, Sir John,' Lesures agreed. 'Each of us has a cup with the first letter of our surname on it. Late in the afternoon, just before we finish, it is customary for us to have a goblet of malmsey. It washes away the dust and sweetens the mouth.'

'And these cups were on a tray?'

Cranston left the corpse and walked over to a small table where all the cups, some still half full, stood on a pewter dish. He picked up Ollerton's and sniffed at it. He caught the sweet smell of honey and a more acrid odour. Sir John recalled Athelstan's words about arsenic and deadly nightshade.

'They are both deadly in their effect,' the friar had declared, 'yet easy to disguise.'

Cranston picked up all the cups and sniffed carefully. He tried to stop the juices in his own mouth gathering by remembering the corpse now lying stretched out on the floor.

'And who washed these cups every morning?'

'We took it in turns, Sir John.'

'And this morning?'

Napham lifted a hand. 'But, Sir John, they were all clean.'

'Fine, fine.' Sir John leaned against the wall; he wished Athelstan was here.

'And who entered the Chancery of the Green Wax today? Give me a list.'

'Well, well.' Lesures came forward, ticking the names off on his fingers. 'Myself and the clerks, Sir Lionel Havant, yourself, Sir John, Brother Athelstan and Mistress Chapler.'

'And anyone else?'

'Oh, the occasional servant. They would come in with messages or bring fresh parchment and quills.'

'But it's interesting, isn't it,' the coroner continued, 'that the poison was put in at the same time as this cryptic message arrives, about the second being the centre of woe and the principal mover of horror.' Cranston glanced at the clerks. 'I thought you liked puzzles and riddles. Do any of you know what it means?'

They shook their heads.

'Let me continue,' Cranston said. 'Whoever put the poison in knew what time you drank the mead. He also arranged for the message to be delivered at the same time: that reduces the number somewhat, doesn't it?' He leaned forward.

'What are you saying?' Alcest snapped.

'What I am saying, young man, is this. When Ollerton died, I was in my garden, Athelstan and Mistress Chapler were in Southwark. Havant was probably at the Savoy Palace – that takes care of the principal visitors here. In my view, Ollerton's assassin works in the Chancery of the Green Wax and could very well be in this room.'

A chorus of hoarse denials greeted his words. Cranston clapped his hands for silence.

'I am a man of law. I show where the evidence lies. Now I could ask for you to be searched: not everyone carries a small bag of poison around with them.'

'Pshaw!' Napham made a contemptuous gesture with his hand and walked to the door as if to leave.

'Do so,' Cranston shouted, 'and I'll have you arrested, sir! My bailiff's in the street outside.'

Napham returned.

'Anyone could have come in here!' Alcest cried.

'Anyone?' Cranston asked. 'You were here when Ollerton died and any one of you could have visited that tavern and killed Peslep.'

'But what about Chapler?' Alcest declared defiantly. 'Sir John, we can prove that we were carousing in a chamber at the Dancing Pig when our companion died.'

'Did you like him?' Cranston asked abruptly.

'Who?'

'Chapler. Did you like him? You called him your companion.'

'He wasn't one of us,' Alcest retorted. 'Ask Master Tibault here. Chapler kept to himself. When the office closed on Saturday morning before the Angelus, he would leave for his beloved sister in Epping.'

'Was Peslep a rich man?' Cranston asked.

'He came of good family.'

Cranston closed his eyes; he felt so tired. He would have loved to question these young men but there was nothing more he could say. No real evidence to work on. The coroner walked to the door.

'Have the body sheeted,' he ordered. He thought of the Holy Lamb and then recalled Alcest's words about the Dancing Pig. He turned, hand on the latch. 'Master Alcest, the night Chapler died. You left the Chancery of the Green Wax and went straight to the Dancing Pig?'

'Yes, we did.'

'And you were in a chamber all by yourselves?'

'Well, with the rest.'

'And some young ladies? Where were they from?'

Alcest rubbed his mouth.

'Come on!' Sir John barked. 'You hired a group of whores, didn't you? Young courtesans. Who was the mistress of this troupe?'

'Nell Broadsheet.'

Cranston grinned. 'By, sir, you pay well. Broadsheet's girls are the comeliest and most expensive in London. They keep a house, do they not, near Greyfriars, just past Newgate?'

The young man nodded.

'Good, then I think I'll pay her a visit.'

Cranston walked out into the street where Flaxwith leaned against a wall, his ugly dog beside him.

'Keep that bloody thing away from me!' Cranston growled. 'Now, Henry, I'm going to give you a treat. We are going to visit Mistress Broadsheet's establishment. You know it well?'

The bailiff's face coloured and he shuffled his feet; even Samson seemed to hang his head a little lower.

'Henry, Henry!' Cranston chucked the bailiff under his chin with his finger. 'Don't say you've been dipping your quill in Dame Broadsheet's inkhorn?'

'A man gets lonely, Sir John,' Flaxwith murmured.

'You have a wife,' Cranston replied. 'The beloved Ursula.'

Sheer terror now replaced the confusion in Flaxwith's face. Cranston recalled Mistress Ursula, a woman built like a donjon, with eyes of steel and a tongue like a lash.

'Oh, Sir John, it's our secret, isn't it? The Lady Ursula...' Flaxwith leaned down and patted Samson, who was cowering even more on hearing Mistress Flaxwith's name.

'Yes?' Cranston asked sweetly.

'The Lady Ursula,' Flaxwith swallowed hard, 'does not like the pleasures of the flesh.'

Cranston recalled his own merry trysts with his lady wife; he patted the man sympathetically on the shoulder.

'Well, let's visit Dame Broadsheet. Let's see what she has to say about our young clerks.'

'I was supposed to do that,' Flaxwith grumbled as they walked along.

'Well, Henry,' Cranston nudged him playfully, 'I am going to make sure you leave with me. Oh, by the way, I still want you to find out about Master Drayton's two clerks, Stablegate and Flinstead. Just where did they spend the night their master was murdered? You'll enjoy visiting taverns,' the coroner continued, 'and so will Samson.'

The mastiff turned its head, lips curled in a soft growl. Cranston smiled tactfully and they continued up Holborn past Cock Lane, still sealed off by royal archers, through the old city wall into Newgate. All the butchers' stalls had been cleared away but the smell of blood and offal made Samson excited. He pranced around, straining at this morsel or that. Cranston caught a cutpurse who was following two old ladies down to St Mary Le Bow where the bells were clanging for Compline, the beacon light already lit in the belfry. Cranston grabbed the weasel-faced knave by the collar, gave him a whack on the ear and sent him about his business.

'Do you know, Henry.' Cranston stopped before the dark, forbidding mass of Newgate prison where people thronged, waiting to pay a visit to their friends inside. 'If my treatise on the governance of this city was accepted by the Regent, I'd have torches lit along every highway.'

He pointed to the scaffold where the corpses of four felons, hanged earlier in the day, were now being given a coat of tar and pitch. They would then be placed in iron gibbets before being taken out and hanged as a warning at the crossroads leading into London. The two execu-tioners were whistling, happy in their work. Now and again flicking spots of tar at the orange-haired whores who clustered there, the hangmen were impervious to the misery of the dead men's friends and relatives who patiently waited to see where their beloved ones would be gibbeted.

'You were going to say, Sir John?' Flaxwith asked.

'I'd have all that removed,' Cranston growled. 'Come on!'

Dame Broadsheet's establishment stood in a small, quiet alleyway: a three-storeyed mansion in its own grounds, the bottom floor was an alehouse with a bush strung up over the door. The upper storeys were what Dame Broadsheet called her 'chapel of repose', where clients could meet the sweetest professional doxies in London. Flaxwith tied Samson up outside and told him to be a good boy. The dog, his jaws full of offal he had picked up, whimpered back.

The taproom was quiet and very pleasant, the ceiling high, the rushes on the floor clean and supple. The tables were ringed with proper stools, not overturned kegs. Vats and beer barrels stood neatly at one end; hams and bags of onions hung from the rafters and baskets of flowers were placed on window ledges. By the sweet tang from the buttery, Cranston knew Dame Broadsheet's French cook was busy. He smacked his lips, patted his stomach but kept within the shadows of the doorway, revelling in the sights and sounds. Flaxwith, behind him, kept his hand on his dagger. Dame Broadsheet's establishment was well known as a retreat for the highwaymen and footpads of the city: Sir John would not be a welcome guest.

Cranston wondered whether to make a grand entrance or rush across and up the stairs at the far end. He decided on the latter. He stared around the taproom. He recognised many of the faces: scrimpers, foists, counterfeit men, cunning women, professional beggars, hardened bully-boys as well as some young men out for an evening, intent on carousing until cockcrow. All around them were the ladies of the town, not the common whores or strumpets, but, as Dame Broadsheet proclaimed, 'ladies of refinement who knew how to please a gentleman'. The coroner had decided to make a dash for the stairs when a voice abruptly sang out.

'Oh hell's jakes, it's Cranston!'

The young boys playing the rebec, flute and tambour abruptly stopped their soft music. The chatter died. Cranston swaggered into the centre of the room. He pulled off his beaver hat and gave the most mocking bow.

'Lovely lads and lasses. Good evening. Jack Cranston presents his compliments.'

'Oh piss off!' A voice shouted.

Cranston didn't even bother to look round. 'It's Ned, isn't it? Ned the Limner? I'd keep a tidy tongue in your head, otherwise tomorrow, Ned my lad, I'll be issuing warrants for your arrest. Charges of contumacy against a King's officer. Now, now, now!' Cranston spread his legs and tucked his thumbs into his broad sword belt. 'Don't be cruel to old Jack. I've got Henry Flaxwith here and a dozen more of his burly boys outside. Not to mention Samson the dog. You know Samson, don't you? He likes nothing more than to gnaw on a nice juicy ankle.'

'There's no need for talk like that, Sir John.'

A lady came down the stairs, her blonde hair coifed under a silver-edged linen veil. Her gown was of dark burgundy, a gold chain round her slender waist. She moved slowly, languorously, head held high like a young noble-woman rather than mistress of a house of ill repute.

The skin of her face was smooth, almost golden, the eyes big and smiling. It was the mouth that gave her away: sharp, thin lips, slightly sneering.

Cranston bowed again. 'Mistress Broadsheet, how pleasant it is to see you.'

'I'd love to return the compliment, Sir John.'

Cranston noticed her voice suddenly rose. She seemed reluctant to come any further down the stairs but stood holding on to the rail.

Sir John stiffened. 'So, I'm welcome here?' he asked curiously.

'Of course you are, Sir John Cranston. You are coroner of the city. My house is your house...'

That was enough for Cranston. He reached the foot of the stairs in two bounds, brushed by her and reached the top. He heard the sounds of muffled footsteps above him. Despite his weight and tiredness, Sir John went up the next flight as nimble as a monkey, so quick he almost crashed into the man standing there; he held a small arbalest, the winch pulled back, the barbed bolt pointed directly at Sir John's chest. Cranston paused and stared at the smiling face of the young man. He reminded the coroner of Athelstan: gentle eyes and olive skin under a mop of dark, glossy hair.

'Well I never, the Vicar of Hell!' Cranston studied the young man from head to toe, dressed as usual in black leather. Behind him, a young woman, a sheet wrapped round her, peered anxiously at the coroner. 'Go back to your room, sweet one!' Cranston called, feeling for his dagger.

'Now, now, Sir John.' The young man edged a bit closer. 'You are not to do anything stupid.'

'I want you,' Cranston growled.

'Wanting and having are two different things, Sir John.'

The Vicar of Hell lifted his arbalest. Sir John flinched but, instead of loosing the quarrel, the Vicar of Hell abruptly pushed Cranston, sending him tumbling back down the stairs.

Chapter 6

Sir John Cranston, coroner of the city, was in a terrible rage. He had been sent crashing down the stairs but his pride was hurt more than his bones. The Vicar of Hell, of course, nimble as a squirrel, had scampered off down the gallery and through a window. Sir John knew any pursuit would be futile.

He now stood raging in the taproom; all the customers had fled, frightened by the coroner's roaring, a fearsome sight with his red face, bristling whiskers and naked dagger. Flaxwith had come rushing in, followed by Samson snarling and biting any available ankle.

Sir John glared at Dame Broadsheet who, despite all her hauteur and poise, now trembled on a stool beneath the coroner's fearsome gaze.

'Do you understand what I'm saying?' Cranston roared, hands on hips.

Dame Broadsheet blinked.

'I'll tell you what I'm saying,' Cranston continued. 'You, madam, will stand in the stews for two days. Your ladies alongside you. This house will be closed down, sealed and all its goods and appurtenances transported to a cellar in the Guildhall!'

Dame Broadsheet stared into the icy blue eyes of Cranston. She knew there would be no bribery for this man of integrity either in cash or kind. However, she knew his weakness: her lower lip quivered and two large tears ran down her cheeks. Cranston swallowed hard, the sign for Dame Broadsheet to put her face in her hands and sob uncontrollably. Like a chorus in a play her young ladies, in different stages of undress, also began to weep, followed by the bully-boys and cross-biters, the cooks, the scullions and the tapsters. Some of the women even fell to their knees, hands clenched beseechingly. Cranston gazed around. Even Samson put his head back and howled mournfully.

'Oh woe is us, Sir John!' Dame Broadsheet let her hands fall away from her face. 'Woe is the day I was born! Oh, Sir John, we are sorry!'

Cranston stared at the beautiful, tear-filled eyes and his rage began to ebb. The wailing grew even louder and Samson, head back and throat stretched, joined in with relish. Flaxwith looked pitiful. Cranston sat down on a stool.

'Shut up!' he bellowed. 'For all that is holy, shut up!'

The wailing stopped. Dame Broadsheet looked tearfully at Sir John from under fluttering eyelids.

'You are a minx,' Cranston said.

'Sir John, you looked so brave,' she cooed. 'Dashing upstairs ready for a battle, lance couched.' She caught the warning look in Cranston's eyes. 'A true knight.' She added hastily, 'The Lady Maude must be a very fortunate woman.' She lifted her hand and clicked her fingers.

'Some refreshment for Sir John: a small meat pie, my Lord Coroner?'

Cranston's anger disappeared. He moved across to the window seat, Dame Broadsheet with him. She leaned across the table. Somehow the buttons at the top of her dress had come unloosed so, if he had wanted to, Cranston could catch a glimpse of her soft, luxuriant breasts. He coughed, waved his fingers, and Dame Broadsheet, as prudish as a nun, quickly did up the offending buttons. She watched as Cranston bit into the pie and sipped at the wine.

'I didn't know he was there,' she began as Sir John pushed the platter away.

'Yes you did,' Cranston retorted. 'You know who the Vicar of Hell is, Dame Broadsheet: a defrocked priest, a rapscallion, responsible for more cunning and devilment than a village full of rogues. He steals, he foists, he receives and smuggles!'

'But he has a heart of gold.' Dame Broadsheet blinked her eyes. 'He has a heart of gold, Sir John. He could have hit you with that crossbow bolt.'

'Well, the Vicar of Hell will have to wait, won't he?' Cranston picked up his wine cup and sat back against the wall. 'But it's good to hear he's back in the city. If he's in London he can be trapped. Last time I heard of him he was organising pilgrimages to St Eadric's well which, supposedly, lies in the heart of Ashdown Forest. There's no St Eadric and certainly no well.'

Dame Broadsheet lowered her face to hide her smile.

'But I'm not here about the Vicar of Hell,' Cranston continued. 'And my threats still stand. Your cooperation, madam, or I'll be back in the morning with the bailiffs.'

'Cooperation over what?' she asked archly.

'Three nights ago,' Cranston replied, 'you and some of your ladies were not in residence here but at the Dancing Pig, entertaining clerks from the Chancery of the Green Wax.'

'Yes, we were there from sunset till dawn,' she replied. 'There's no crime in that. We were guests at a private party.'

'You are harlots,' Cranston replied. 'You say you were there from dawn till dusk?'

She nodded.

'Well, go on!' Cranston barked.

'We arrived before sunset,' Dame Broadsheet replied. 'There was myself and four other girls. Roesia, Melgotta, Hilda and Clarice.'

'I see.'

'The clerks had hired a private chamber, a large spacious room. A table was laid out and we supped and dined. Afterwards,' she hurried on, 'two young boys came up with rebec and tambour. They played tunes and we all danced. This was early on in the evening, it was not yet dark.'

'And then?'

'We each went off with our partners. I was with a young man called,' she closed her eyes, 'Ollerton.'

'Ollerton's dead,' Cranston declared.

Dame Broadsheet's eyes flew open in alarm. 'Dead?'

'Yes, poisoned by person or persons unknown. And,' Cranston added flatly, 'another one, Peslep, was stabbed whilst sitting on the jakes this morning.'

'Oh Lord save us, Sir John!'

Dame Broadsheet's fingers flew to her lips. Nevertheless, Cranston caught a sly look in her eyes. He grasped her hands and squeezed them tightly.

'You know, don't you?' he remarked. 'Don't act innocent.'

'Sir John!'

'Yes, you bloody well do!' Cranston squeezed tighter. 'Now why should Dame Broadsheet know about the deaths of two clerks, one of whom was killed only a short while ago?'

'The Vicar of Hell told me.'

'The Vicar of Hell? And what would he have to do with important clerks in the Chancery of the Green Wax?'

Dame Broadsheet withdrew her hands, her eyes rounded in what she hoped was an innocent look. 'I'll tell you the truth, Sir John. I know nothing of it. He came here; we shared a cup of wine before he retired with young Clarice. He asked me if I knew about the deaths at the Chancery, I replied I didn't.' She shrugged. 'We left it at that.'

Cranston sipped from his wine cup. 'And the night of the festivities?' he asked.

'As I said, Sir John, we feasted and drank and then each of us went to a small garret or chamber with our partner.

From what I can gather the clerks were as lusty as cocks in a barnyard. A merry coupling, Sir John!'

'And in the morning?'

'I woke up, it must have been before dawn. Ollerton was fast asleep in the sheets beside me. I dressed, collected the rest of the girls and we came back here to rest. After,' she added quickly, 'our night's labours.'

'Bring the girls here,' Cranston ordered.

Dame Broadsheet did. All of them were now dressed in long gowns, their hair tidied up under pure white wimples. If it hadn't been for their laughing eyes and saucy looks, they could have been taken for a group of dutiful novices in a nunnery. They stood trouped round the table, hands clasped before them, eyes lowered.

'Lovely girls,' Sir John breathed. 'Who was the leader?' he asked Dame Broadsheet.

'The leader, Sir John?'

'Amongst the clerks? Who organised the night's festivities?'

'Why, Alcest.'

'And who was with him?'

'I was,' a young, blonde-haired girl whispered.

Cranston leaned over. 'Raise your head, girl. You are...?'

'Clarice, Sir John. Clarice Clutterbuckle.'

Sir John chose to ignore the sniggers: he realised this was no more the young lady's name than it was his.

'Clarice, you were with Alcest all night?'

'Oh yes,' she purred, rolling her shoulders, reminding Cranston of a cat. 'We retired to an inner chamber, my

Lord Coroner, no bigger than a cupboard but it had a bed.'

'And?'

'We frolicked, we drank some wine.' She smiled. 'I fell asleep and the next minute it was morning and Dame Broadsheet was rousing me from bed.'

'And Alcest was still with you?'

'Oh yes, Sir John, snoring fit to burst.'

'And he never left you during the night?'

'No one ever leaves me, Sir John.'

'Less of your sauce!' Cranston barked.

'Sir John, I was asleep but I would have heard him leave. His clothes were where I,' she smiled quickly, 'put them the night before.'

'And is this true of all of you?'

The other three girls nodded in unison.

'You saw nothing suspicious?' Cranston asked.

'Oh no, Sir John.'

Cranston dismissed them; he turned back to Dame Broadsheet. 'This must have cost a pretty penny.'

'I mentioned that,' she continued hurriedly, 'to Alcest: how costly the evening was. He said he'd been to Master Drayton.'

'Who?' Cranston leaned across the table.

'Master Drayton the moneylender. Alcest had taken a loan out.' She added in a rush, 'I mean, clerks of the Green Wax are well paid, but the evening was costly.'

Cranston sat back, mouth half open. Alcest, he thought, going to a moneylender, offering surety to raise

119

monies for an evening of revelry? And why should he do that? Peslep was a wealthy man. All five clerks would have contributed to the evening. So why a loan? And why Drayton? Why not the Italian bankers down near the Thames?

'Sir John?'

Cranston stared at Dame Broadsheet. 'Yes, mistress.'

'Are you well? Would you like to lie down?' she asked mischievously.

'No, madam, I would not.' Cranston lumbered to his feet. 'I am finished with you for the time being.'

'So there'll be no bailiffs?'

'No, madam, there'll be no bailiffs.'

Cranston walked across the room, beckoning at Flaxwith who was sitting just within the doorway nursing a tankard of ale.

'What now, Sir John?' he asked.

'Go to the Dancing Pig. Ask the landlord there if any of the clerks left during the revelry.'

'Anything else, Sir John?'

'Yes, don't forget Stablegate and Flinstead.'

'And there's something else, isn't there?'

'Yes, Henry, there is.' Cranston put an arm round Flaxwith's shoulder and pulled him closer in order to whisper in his ear. 'Get your best men. Have this house watched. I wager a jug of wine to a jug of wine that the Vicar of Hell will return!'

Cranston stepped back as the door of the tavern was flung open. Sir Lionel Havant strode in, hand on his sword. He bowed mockingly.

'Sir John Cranston, I bring a personal invitation from His Grace the Regent. You are to join him in his private chambers at the Savoy Palace.'

Cranston groaned. 'Sir Lionel, I am tired, my feet ache, I have been tramping the streets, not to mention falling downstairs.'

Sir Lionel smiled. 'Sir John, it's one of those invitations I would beg you not to refuse. We are to escort you to the Savoy.' Havant sucked at his lips. 'Whether you like it or not.'

Cranston sighed and turned to Flaxwith. 'Carry out the tasks I have assigned to you. Tell the Lady Maude that I am His Grace's most honoured guest, so God knows when I'll crawl into my own bed tonight.'

Cranston went through the doorway. He heard a bark behind him and the coroner grinned slyly. He really should tell Sir Lionel Havant to keep his ankles well out of the nip of Samson's jaws. I only wish, the coroner thought, I could take that bloody dog to the Savoy where he could piss and nip ankles to his heart's content.

–

The funeral of Edwin Chapler at St Erconwald's the following morning was a solemn and dignified affair. The coffin had been carried in and laid at the entrance to the rood screen; purple candles ringed it whilst Athelstan celebrated a solemn Requiem Mass. Mistress Alison, supported by Benedicta, had maintained a dignified silence even as the coffin on which she placed a single white rose was lifted out of the church and taken to the fresh plot dug by Pike the ditcher just before dawn. The coffin had been lowered into it. Athelstan had sprinkled holy water with the asperges rod then incensed it with the thurible, the fragrance spreading throughout the graveyard. The earth had been piled in and a suitable wooden cross laid over the fresh mound of earth until Tab the tinker made a proper one. Athelstan and Alison were discussing this when a parishioner, Simplicatas, came running out of the church screaming that a miracle had occurred.

'The new crucifix!' she cried. 'Huddle's crucifix near the baptistry! It's bleeding!'

Athelstan, followed by the rest, rushed up the steps of the church. A crowd had gathered round the small recess where the crucifix hung. At first Athelstan could not believe his eyes. The wounds on the hands, side, feet and head of the crucified Christ were glistening red. Indeed, one small drop of blood, like a small ruby, was ready to drip down. Huddle was kneeling there, hands joined; on either side of him were Watkin and Pike the ditcher, reminding Athelstan of the Three Wise Men before the crib.

'Huddle!' Athelstan bellowed. 'Is this some trick of yours?' He nearly added that miracles couldn't occur in a place like St Erconwald's but bit back the words.

The painter just stared at him and swallowed hard. 'Father, how can you say that?'

Alison went forward and touched the glistening drop. She brought it back on the edge of her finger. She held it to her lips and licked it.

'It's blood,' she declared, her face white as snow. 'Father, it's not fake blood.' She paused. 'The type mummers use.'

Athelstan went and also took a drop. He raised it to his lips. He had the same sensation as when he had cut his lip the previous week: a salty, tangy taste. He stepped back, trying to hide the tremors in his own body. The news had spread; more parishioners were already crowding into the church.

'Go away!' Athelstan ordered, hands raised. 'Go back to your homes! For the love of God!' His mind raced. This was not the first time a miracle had occurred at St Erconwald's. He gazed suspiciously at Watkin and Pike but they were engrossed in their devotions.

Athelstan quickly took off his chasuble and surplice. He almost threw them at Crim and, grasping the lavabo cloth, the piece of linen he used to dry his hands after touching the sacred species, he thrust his way through to the cross. He dabbed at the red marks and gazed down at the cloth – they did look like bloodstains.

'What are you doing, Father?' Benedicta whispered, coming up behind him.

'Maybe it's some trick,' Athelstan replied. 'The crucifix is new, it might be some pigment...'

'I only used ordinary paint,' Huddle sang out.

Athelstan stood staring at the cross. He'd wiped the red glistening liquid away. His heart lurched: more was beginning to form.

'Have the crucifix taken down!' he ordered Watkin.

'No, Father.' The dung-collector got to his feet, his great ham fists hanging by his side. 'The crucifix is ours, Father, it's in the nave. The nave belongs to the people.'

Athelstan groaned. Watkin was right. The friar took a secret oath that never again would he expound on Canon Law for his parishioners: by ancient custom, the sanctuary belonged to the priest but the nave, and all it contained, was the property of the people.

'I said take it out!' Athelstan ordered again.

'The cemetery's ours.' Pike spoke up. 'God's acre belongs to the people too. You did say that, Father.'

Athelstan just glared at him. He felt like taking the crucifix and putting it in the sanctuary but Watkin, despite his bulk, moved more speedily. He removed the crucifix from the wall and, lifting it up like a standard, solemnly processed out through the church porch and down the steps, the crowd following him.

'Father, let them have their way,' Benedicta declared. 'Don't act hastily.'

'I'm sorry, I must be going.' Alison extended her hand, offering a silver coin.

Athelstan shook his head. 'I buried your brother as an act of charity,' he replied.

The young woman stood on tiptoe and kissed Athelstan on both cheeks. 'I'll be staying at the Silver Lute until this business is finished.' She smiled at Benedicta. 'I will collect my things.'

Athelstan watched her go. 'Shouldn't you be with her?' he asked.

'I have a seamstress working at home,' Benedicta replied. 'She will let her in. What are you going to do about this, Father?'

'What can I do, Benedicta? You know these people better than I do. The supernatural is as real to them as the sun, wind and rain. Demons stand round their sickbeds; demons slay the newborn child; they grimace in corners and lurk behind every tree.' Athelstan rubbed his face. 'At night, if Watkin is to be believed, evil spirits rumble about his house; they bump on the roof and creak in the rafters. Devils howl in the wind, strike cattle down in the meadows, cause riverbanks to burst.' He pointed to the parish coffin which stood in the transept. 'A brother told me how, at Blackfriars, a parishioner pulled a nail from a rotting coffin then drove it secretly into a bench. Whoever was the first to sit on that bench suffered the same disease from which the corpse in the coffin had died.' He smiled thinly at Benedicta. 'My point, Oh most faithful of parishioners, is that my people see devils and demons and evil all around them. It's only natural they also see miracles and God's intervention: angels swooping from heaven, relics which cure the most dreadful diseases and crucifixes which bleed.'

The door was suddenly flung open.

'What in the devil's fart is happening out there?' Cranston swept into the church. 'Brother Athelstan, have your

125

noddlepates gone mad? They are setting a shrine up in the cemetery!' Cranston took off his beaver hat and slapped it against his leg. 'Those noddlepates,' he continued 'believe a crucifix is bleeding. They are building their own altar and are charging a penny for people to pray before it. They have got candles lit, they even tried to make me pay! I told them a kick up the arse was all they'd get from the King's coroner!' Cranston grinned at Benedicta, swept her into his arms and kissed her juicily on each cheek.

'You are well, Sir John?' she asked breathlessly.

'Bloody awful.' The coroner stamped his feet. 'Come on, Athelstan, I need you. Leave your parishioners. They've got more maggots in their heads than mice in a hayrick.'

'I should really stay,' Athelstan replied.

'Nonsense!' Cranston bellowed. 'Come on, Brother, let them have their run.'

'Sir John speaks the truth, Brother,' Benedicta added softly. 'Go with him. I'll tidy up the sanctuary and the house, then I'll camp out in the cemetery.'

Athelstan closed his eyes to pray for guidance. He knew both Sir John and Benedicta were right. If he stayed, he'd only fret or interfere and Watkin was not only built like an ox, he was as stubborn as one.

'Shall I take Philomel?' he asked, opening his eyes.

'No, forget your horse,' Cranston replied. 'I came by river. Moleskin's waiting for us at the steps near Pissing Alley.'

Athelstan followed Sir John out on to the porch and stared in disbelief across the cemetery. Watkin had moved quickly: in the far corner a calvary had been formed, a mound of earth and rocks. On the top was the crucifix with candles glowing beneath it. The word had also spread: people were thronging into the cemetery, paying their coins to Pike and Tab whilst Watkin and the ditcher's wives strode up and down. They were both armed with ash cudgels and glared ferociously at anyone who dared approach their shrine without proper payment.

'If Father Prior hears of this,' Athelstan murmured, 'he'll have my head.'

Cranston stopped. 'Then you'd better not tell him, had you?' He tugged at the friar's sleeve. 'Come on, Athelstan, Moleskin's waiting and I'm hungry.'

Athelstan hastened across to his house to get his writing bag, then he and Sir John walked down the narrow alleyway towards the riverside. They paused outside Merrylegs's cookshop where Sir John bought a pie and bit into it as they walked; he smacked his lips and murmured how Merrylegs should be knighted for his services to the stomach.

'You are in good spirits, Sir John?' Athelstan hurried beside him. 'You slept well?'

'Like a little pig,' Cranston replied. 'But that's not because of the evening I had, Brother.' He described Ollerton's death and his confrontation with the Vicar of Hell.

'I've heard of him,' Athelstan exclaimed. 'They say he dresses all in black and that his face is disfigured by scars.'

'Nonsense!' Cranston replied. 'He's a merry rogue who can out-argue a lawyer, outwit a trickster and outlie the devil. He's been responsible for more villainy than I'd like to mention. The Guildmasters have a hundred pounds sterling reward posted for his capture, dead or alive. No one has come forward to claim it. He loves the ladies, does our Vicar of Hell, and they love him. Any man who betrayed him to the authorities would not survive for long.'

'But you say he knew about our clerks of the Green Wax?'

'And more.' Cranston finished the pie. 'Mistress Broadsheet told me that Alcest did business with Drayton.'

'A rich pottage,' Athelstan replied.

He paused to stare at a beggar crouching on the corner of the alleyway. The man was humming, rocking himself backwards and forwards. On a sack before him lay a whalebone.

'Taken from the side of Leviathan!' the fellow screeched. 'The great beast who lives in the sea. Touch it for a penny!'

Athelstan walked forward and tossed a coin on to the sack.

'Thank you, Brother, thank you. I've got more whalebones!' the man shouted.

Athelstan shook his head and turned back to the coroner. 'So, we have Mistress Broadsheet confessing that Alcest did business with Drayton whilst the Vicar of Hell knows about the deaths amongst the clerks of the Green Wax.'

'We also know,' Cranston added, 'that, according to Dame Broadsheet and her girls, none of the clerks left the Dancing Pig the night Chapler was killed. We also have this apparent wealth. How could Alcest afford such a sumptuous banquet? Finally, there's Ollerton's death. The assassin must have been in the chamber when the clerk drank the mead.'

'And the riddle?'

'My second is the centre of woe,' Cranston declared. 'And the principal mover of horror.'

Athelstan shook his head in disbelief. 'It makes no sense. Nothing makes sense, Sir John. Why have the clerks been killed? Why the riddles? Who is this mysterious young man, cloaked and spurred, who has been seen round the city?'

They walked down to the quayside.

'So where are we going, Sir John?'

'Back to Drayton's house,' Cranston declared. 'Yesterday evening the Regent had me taken to the Savoy Palace.' Cranston stopped and sucked in the river air. 'Oh, he wined and he dined me. Clapped me on the shoulder and called me Honest Jack. But he wants his money back, Athelstan: the silver taken from Master Drayton. Gaunt needs it urgently. So it's back to Drayton's house.'

They went down the slippery steps to where Moleskin's boat was waiting. The leather-skinned wherry man welcomed them as graciously as if he was captain of a royal man-of-war. He sat them in the stern, untied the rope and briskly pulled at the oars, taking his wherry across the sun-dappled river. Moleskin knew that Cranston would keep silent, whilst Brother Athelstan never told him about the business they prosecuted. Nevertheless, the friar could tell from the knowing gleam in Moleskin's eyes that the news of the great miracle at St Erconwald's had already reached him.

'Before you ask,' Athelstan declared, 'I know about the miracle, Moleskin, or the so-called miracle. Yes, I am angry. I am also puzzled, but it will wait, and that's all I'm going to say on the matter!'

Moleskin looked at him glumly and heaved his oars, guiding his boat across to Dowgate next to the Steelyard. Cranston and Athelstan disembarked. The friar saw the wisdom of Sir John's words in not taking his horse because the streets were packed: the traders, costermongers and journeymen, taking advantage of the good summer weather, roared and bellowed whilst the crowds swirled like shoals of fish from stall to stall. They made their way up into Cheapside where a mob jostled round an enterprising cook who had opened a stall in the centre of the marketplace to sell toasted cheese and wine. Children ran through the crowds. The beggars, mountebanks, cunning men, foists and pickpockets hovered, looking for prey. The mummers and the quacks were waiting sharp-eyed for a 'coney', someone to trap and separate from their wealth.

On the steps of St Mary Le Bow, a monk of tatterdemalion appearance was preaching in harsh tones, stabbing the air with his raised fist; he was prophesying the imminent end of the world and the advent of the Anti-Christ. Athelstan and Cranston, because of the crowd, were forced to stand and listen to his speech. How the Anti-Christ had recently been born to a wicked woman in a certain province of Babylon. This child, so the ragged monk asserted, had the teeth of a cat and was abominably hairy; on the occasion of his birth, horrible serpents and other different monsters had rained down from the skies whilst the child had been able to speak when only eight days old.

'Heavens above!' Cranston whispered. 'When you meet rogues like that, Athelstan, the Vicar of Hell becomes an angel of light!'

They crossed Cheapside and made their way up the tangle of narrow alleyways to Drayton's house. A city beadle on guard outside broke the seals, unlocked the door and let them in. Cranston and Athelstan went along the narrow passageways and down into the counting house; its great iron-studded door still lay against the wall. They made an immediate search of the scrolls and ledgers of the dead moneylender, going through the transactions for the last few days before Drayton's murder. Cranston ran one stubby finger down the pages, gave a cry of triumph and called Athelstan to come over. Athelstan did so, gingerly stepping over the dark, wine-coloured bloodstain on the floor.

'Look!' Cranston cried.

He jabbed a finger and Athelstan read the entry.

'Alcest came here,' the friar exclaimed. 'Two days before his great banquet at the Dancing Pig, but he didn't ask for a loan, he was changing gold for silver pieces. Now why should Alcest do that, eh?'

Athelstan stared at the door. 'Sir John, do you think Drayton could have been murdered by our clerks? Could this be the source of their newfound wealth?'

'It's possible,' Cranston replied. 'But, there again, it wouldn't explain the deaths amongst them.'

'But what happened if they were all thieves together,' Athelstan wondered, 'and what we are witnessing now is the falling out?'

Cranston scratched his chin. 'I'd like to get my hands on the Vicar of Hell,' he answered. 'There's not a mischievous mouse in London which moves without his permission: he could throw some light on this. However, let's visit our noble clerks and see what Master Alcest has to say.'

Chapter 7

Cranston and Athelstan were about to leave the counting house when the friar paused in the doorway. He stared up at the rafters, the whitewashed walls on either side and then the one at the far end.

'What's the matter, Brother?'

'It concerns me, Sir John. I have been in rooms and houses all over the city, so have you. Have you ever seen a room like this, a perfect square? The walls stand at right angles, as if the chamber was designed by some mathematician.'

'So?'

'Well, if you go through the rest of the house it's shabby, dirty; the rooms are long and narrow, the ceilings sag, the floorboards rise. Here it's all different, stone-floored, perfectly shaped. Have you noticed something else, Sir John? The walls have been freshly whitewashed.'

Cranston, mystified, followed Athelstan back into the counting house. Sir John gazed around: a bleak chamber, chests, a desk, chairs, a stool and a bench, but no hangings on the wall. Nothing to offset the sharp whiteness.

'Would Drayton have kept his monies here?' Athelstan asked.

'Knowing the little I do,' the coroner replied, 'I doubt it. He would keep some ready silver but he'd probably store his ill-gotten gains in the vaults or ironbound chests of the Genoese or Venetian bankers. Everyone would know that. Only, occasionally, as on the day he died, would Drayton ask for monies to be moved here.' Cranston smacked his forehead. 'And that reminds me: when I was at the Savoy Palace, the Regent assured me that the money was delivered to Drayton. The Frescobaldi would never dream of stealing the silver. It would only give John of Gaunt the pretext for seizing everything they have.'

Athelstan had moved across to the far wall and was tapping at the plaster. 'Sir John, can I borrow your knife?'

The coroner handed it over and the friar began to chip away at the plaster. At last he gouged a long scar on the wall, raising small clouds of dust. Athelstan cleared the area of plaster with his fingers and scrutinised the red brick beneath.

'What are you doing, Brother?'

'Never mind.'

Athelstan moved to the other wall. This time, when he cleared the plaster, the brickwork underneath was a dull grey. The same occurred on the wall behind the desk. Athelstan handed the dagger back and wiped his hands.

'Sir John. *Quod est demonstrandum.*'

'I beg your pardon?'

Athelstan pointed to the far wall. 'That's solid brick but it was built much later than the rest. The brickwork is new but Drayton took great care to ensure it was plastered and painted like the other two walls. He also positioned it carefully so this chamber became a perfect square.'

'And how does that solve his murder? Could there be a secret entrance?'

'Perhaps. Here we have a miser who, I supposed, hated spending money. So why should he build another wall but cover it so carefully? What I want you to do, Sir John, is to tell Master Flaxwith to get some of your burly boys here. Have them meet us later on.'

Cranston went across to the desk, seized a piece of parchment and a quill and scribbled a note.

'Now.' Athelstan smiled. 'Let's go and visit Master Alcest!'

–

At the office of the Chancery of the Green Wax, Cranston and Athelstan saw Alcest by himself in a small downstairs chamber off the main passageway. Alcest had lost a great deal of his arrogance. He was watchful and wary, more respectful to the plump coroner and the little friar who seemed to accompany him everywhere.

'Why do you wish to see me alone, Sir John? Do you have news of my companions' killer?'

'No,' Cranston answered cheerfully. He took a swig from the miraculous wineskin. 'But I do want to know why you visited Master Drayton days before he was found dead in his counting house. If I were you, young man, I would be prudent and tell the truth.'

Alcest sat down on the stool opposite.

'You know we had our festivities at the Dancing Pig?'

'Oh yes. We know about that,' the coroner replied. 'I have had a long talk with Dame Broadsheet and even managed a few words with the Vicar of Hell.'

Alcest flinched; try as he might, he found it difficult to hide his unease.

'You seem troubled by that?' Athelstan asked. 'Dame Broadsheet I understand. But what would a high-ranking royal clerk have to do with the Vicar of Hell?'

'We swim in the same pond, Brother,' Alcest replied cheekily. 'We work here by day but what we do by night...'

'Associating with outlaws and wolfsheads,' Cranston remarked sweetly, 'is a crime in itself.'

'I don't associate with them, Sir John, I merely said we swim in the same pond: alehouses, brothels and cook-shops. The Vicar of Hell is notorious,' Alcest continued. 'His name has appeared upon the Chancery Rolls under different aliases as the law tries to arrest him for this or that.'

'Have you and your companions ever met him? Sat down and shared the same table?' Athelstan asked.

'Never.'

The reply was too quick. Alcest looked away hurriedly.

'Ah well, back to Master Drayton,' Cranston said. 'You went down to see him, did you not?'

'Yes, I went down to change gold pieces for silver: the coin Dame Broadsheet demanded to be paid in.'

'Why there?' Athelstan asked. 'Why not some tradesman or one of the banking houses? Was there something wrong with your gold?'

'No, there was not. I obtained the coins from Master Walter Ormskirk, a vintner in Cheapside.'

'You bank with him?'

'The little I have, yes, Brother. We took it in turns to pay. On that particular night,' he hurried on, 'it was my turn. With Dame Broadsheet your purse has to be full. Money has to be divided. You cannot do that with two gold pieces.'

'But why not ask for silver from Master Ormskirk?' Athelstan insisted.

Alcest coloured and shuffled his feet.

'Why go there out of your way?'

Alcest breathed in. 'I was assured of getting a better coin from Drayton. You can't trust some London merchants. The coins they hold, some are counterfeit, others have been recast.'

'Come, come.' Cranston tapped the young man's knee. 'Master Alcest, I may look like a madcap to you with my red face, bristling whiskers and protuberant stomach but I'm not a fool: there must have been another reason.'

'I had confidence in him,' the clerk replied.

'Did you often go there?'

'Yes I did. Sometimes, in my earlier days at the Chancery, Drayton would give me a loan or change money.'

'And the day you visited him. What happened?'

'I was there only a short while and then I left.'

'And you noticed nothing untoward?'

'Nothing, Sir John, and before you put your accusation into words, I couldn't care whether Drayton lived or died and the same applies to Chapler. When he was killed, I was roistering at the Dancing Pig.'

'Ah yes, with young Clarice.'

'I was with her all night,' Alcest replied. He got to his feet. 'And now, unless you have further questions?'

'Why do you think your colleagues have been murdered?' Athelstan asked abruptly. 'And why the puzzles?'

'Brother Athelstan, if I knew that I would tell both you and Sir John immediately.' Alcest walked out. They heard him climb the stairs.

Cranston patted his stomach. 'Some refreshment, Brother? Let's collect our thoughts. Sit upon the ground and make an account of what has happened.'

Athelstan also felt hungry. He had not yet broken his fast. So he joined Sir John at an adjoining tavern, the Golden Goose, a spacious eating house on the corner of Shoe Lane and Farringdon Ward. The taproom was singular in that customers were able to hire small booths; these were closed off from the rest by a small door, with benches which faced each other across a large oaken table. They took one of these: Sir John ordered brawn soup, capon pies and two blackjacks of ale. Once the dishes had arrived, Cranston took his horn spoon from his wallet and ate with relish. Athelstan knew any sensible conversation would be impossible until the coroner declared himself refreshed, sat back, the blackjack of ale in his hands, eyes half closed and murmured his thanks to God for such a delicious meal. Once they had both finished, the coroner, demanding his blackjack be refilled, tapped his fleshy nose and smiled beatifically at the friar.

'Come on, Athelstan, get that quill and parchment out. Let's make an account of all these murders.'

Athelstan did so, sharpening his quill and smoothing out the piece of vellum with the pumice stone. He sighed in exasperation when he found his inkhorn almost empty, but the landlord had one to hire.

'I am ready, Sir John.'

The coroner put his blackjack of ale down.

'Primo.'

Athelstan began to write.

'Master Drayton, an avaricious moneylender, is found brutally murdered in his counting house. The bag of silver he was preparing to hand over to the Regent is stolen.' Cranston paused. 'Along with other items including the two gold pieces Alcest allegedly brought to change. Secundo, Drayton's corpse is found in a locked chamber. The door was bolted and secured from the inside. There are no secret entrances. So how did the murderer kill him with a crossbow bolt and steal the silver? Tertio, the rest of the house was found locked and barred, except the window used by the clerks to break in the following morning. Quarto, the two clerks Flinstead and Stablegate have a hand in this villainy but they can prove that they were elsewhere. Even if they were formally accused, we could not explain how the murders were carried out. Anything else, Athelstan?'

'Quinto,' the friar quipped back. 'Alcest visited Drayton days before he died. He wanted to exchange gold for silver. We also know there's some connection between Alcest and Drayton but it's tenuous and the clerk's explanation is not convincing. I believe Alcest used the gold pieces as a pretext to visit the moneylender but we were right not to pursue this matter: we have no proof to the contrary and Drayton's dead.'

'There's the question of the gold.'

'True, Sir John, but possessing two gold pieces is not a crime for a clerk of the Green Wax. Alcest claims it was his turn to pay, the others will corroborate that and his explanation makes sense: the young ladies would have to be paid, not to mention the landlord of the Dancing Pig.' Athelstan put his quill down and rubbed his fingers. 'So far, Sir John, the only firm suspicion we have is that the far wall in Drayton's chamber might hold a clue to how our moneylender was brutally killed.' He sighed. 'But I could be clutching at straws.'

Cranston's face became glum. 'The way things look, Brother, we will not arrest our murderers and the Regent won't get his silver. Now, let's move to the clerks.' He waved his hand despondently. 'You list what we know.'

Athelstan sat back. 'First, we know Chapler was murdered just after sunset. He visited St Thomas à Becket's chapel on London Bridge. The murderer knew he'd be there. He struck Chapler on the back of the head then tossed his body into the Thames where the Fisher of Men found it. Secondly, all those who knew Chapler appear to have been elsewhere. The clerks were roistering at the Dancing Pig. Master Lesures did not join them. However, I doubt if our noble Master of the Rolls had the strength to strike anyone, let alone lift a young man's body over the rail of London Bridge. The only other person who knew Chapler was his sister Alison. She was in Epping, about to leave for London because of her concern about her brother. Thirdly...'

'Thirdly,' Cranston intervened, 'we have the death of Peslep. He was killed sitting on a latrine. We know he was followed by this mysterious young man, cloaked, cowled and spurred. Fourthly,' the coroner continued, 'there's Ollerton's death. Now,' Cranston held up his hand. 'It was well known that Chapler liked to visit St Thomas's chapel. Peslep always broke his fast in that tavern at that particular time whilst it was customary for the clerks of the Green Wax to drink a cup of malmsey late in the afternoon. Therefore, whoever murdered these three men had intimate knowledge of their habits and customs.'

'I agree,' Athelstan replied. 'There's also the question of the riddles. Alcest's companions apparently loved to pose each other riddles for the rest to solve. The assassin knows this and, so far, we've had three. The one about a king fighting his enemies but in the end both victors and vanquished lying together in the same place. The second, how does it go, Sir John? My first is like a selfish brother, whilst the one delivered after Ollerton's death declares:

"My second is the centre of woe and the principal mover of horror".' Athelstan abruptly clapped his hands, alarmed at Sir John's heavy-lidded look. 'Come on, Sir John, concentrate with that brain as sharp as a razor, that wit as speedy as a swooping hawk.'

'I was just thinking, Brother,' Cranston replied crossly. He sat up. 'What would happen if Father Prior told you to leave St Erconwald's?'

Athelstan's heart sank. 'Now come, Sir John, that's not the matter in hand. Have you sent that note to Flaxwith?'

'Yes, yes, I did.' The coroner shifted on the bench. 'I paid a chapman a penny before we met Alcest.'

Athelstan got to his feet. 'Then, Sir John, no brooding! We have murderers to seize, and the King's justice to be done.' He poked the coroner in the ribs. 'And the Regent's silver to get back!'

By the time they returned to Drayton's house, Flaxwith had arrived with two bruising individuals, each carrying a huge mallet.

'Right, my lovely lads!' Cranston growled. 'I want you to knock a wall down.'

The house was unlocked and they went down the gloomy passageway into the counting house where, at Cranston's command, both men set to with gusto. They smashed their mallets against the wall, the sound echoing like drumbeats through the room which soon filled with dust that tickled the nose and throat.

'Despite the sound, it's not solid,' one of them shouted, standing back and resting.

Cranston, his muffler up over his mouth, went to inspect. 'You are not even through yet.'

'Sir John, you grasp villains by the neck and, I wager, you can see one across a crowded room. I know walls: there's something behind this.'

Athelstan, who had been carrying out another fruitless scrutiny of the door, came over to join them. 'What do you mean?'

'There's a small chamber behind this, Brother. This wall's new.'

'Could there be any secret door or gate?' Cranston asked.

The burly labourer laughed. 'No, Sir John, the wall's solid. Well, at least until we are finished with it!'

They set to again, giving a cry of triumph as the first bricks fell loose. The labourer picked one up, pointing to the mortar. 'This wasn't done by a mason, Sir John, but someone who knew a little building. The mortar is thick, slapped on. That's why whoever built this wall covered it with plaster and whitewash.'

Cranston peered through the gap into the darkness. 'I can't see anything,' he murmured.

The labourers returned to their task. More bricks fell away. An entrance was formed. Athelstan took a battered tallow candle from its iron spigot, Sir John struck a tinder and they went into the secret chamber. The dust-filled darkness made Athelstan shiver as he protected the flame by cupping his hand. He held the candle up and exclaimed in surprise. In the far corner lay a skeleton. He hurried across, followed by Cranston and the labourers. Athelstan, silently praying, crouched down by the grisly remains. In the glow of the smelly candle he carefully studied the skeleton which sat half propped up against the wall. The bones were still white and hard; tattered clothing still clung to it. Athelstan could tell by the dusty shreds that the skeleton belonged to a woman. He continued his examination, ignoring the exclamations of the labourers. He put his hand out, felt round the skeleton and picked up a battered pewter cup and platter.

'In sweet heaven's name!'

He took the candle and searched the rest of the chamber but found nothing. Chilled by the silent, eerie atmosphere, he walked back into the counting house.

'Who do you think it is?' Cranston asked, following him out.

'Well, the house has always belonged to Drayton,' Athelstan replied. 'No one could wall up another human being without his knowledge so it's logical to deduce that he was responsible, therefore those might be the poor remains of his wife. She clearly didn't leave Drayton. I suspect she baited and taunted her husband until he grew tired of her. He probably gave her drugged wine, brought her down here and walled her up alive. God rest her!' he breathed. 'She must have taken days to die.'

Cranston thanked and dismissed the labourers, giving each a coin. The coroner then shouted for Flaxwith. The bailiff came hurrying down, his dog loping behind him, though Samson had the sense to stay well out of Cranston's path.

'What's the matter, Sir John?'

'There's a skeleton in there.' The coroner jabbed his thumb over his shoulder. 'Have it removed. Tell the vicar of St Mary Le Bow the city will bear the cost of its burial. Don't look so frightened, Henry, she's been dead for years. Now, do you have news for me?'

'Oh yes.' Flaxwith stared distractedly over Sir John's shoulder as if he expected the skeleton to come walking out of the room towards him.

'Well, come on, man!'

'First, Sir John,' Flaxwith gabbled, 'we are keeping Dame Broadsheet's house under strict guard and she does not suspect it. We have heard little rumours that the Vicar of Hell is much smitten by little Clarice there.'

'And?'

'Stablegate and Flinstead were seen carousing the night Drayton was murdered. According to witnesses, they drank until they were stupid. They never returned here. The same goes for those clerks at the Dancing Pig. Mine host says that after they retired to the upper chambers, he saw neither hide nor hair of them till dawn. Finally, Sir John,' Flaxwith spread his hands, 'I have a friend who works in the muniment room at the Tower.'

'Oh yes.'

'We checked the subsidy rolls of 1380 for Epping in Essex. They list Edwin and Alison Chapler. Edwin is described as a clerk, Alison a seamstress. Apparently both are quite wealthy.'

'Very good.' Cranston clapped him on the shoulder.

'Oh, before you go,' Athelstan called out. 'Sir John, perhaps we could have a small mummer's play?'

A bemused Cranston and Flaxwith followed Athelstan back into the dusty counting office.

'Now,' Athelstan began, 'I'll pretend to be Drayton.' He held up his writing bag. 'This is the Regent's silver. Sir John, how am I killed?'

Sir John pointed to Athelstan's chest.

'Right,' Athelstan replied. 'I'm dying. I fall to the ground. In my death throes, in my guilt, I remember the woman I have walled up alive, so I crawl towards the hall, praying for forgiveness. That explains why we found Drayton in the position he was, but the problem remains. If the two clerks killed Drayton, how did they get out of the chamber?' Athelstan pointed to the door. 'Locking and bolting that from inside? If Drayton had locked himself in,' Athelstan continued, 'then how could the clerks enter the chamber and kill him?'

'We've been through all this,' Cranston grumbled.

'No, listen, Sir John: we now know the only way into this room is through the door.'

'Yes, yes, I know,' Cranston said irritably. 'And it was locked and bolted.'

'Sir John, Master Henry, if you would oblige me.'

Athelstan walked towards where the huge door lay against the wall. 'Is it possible for you to hold that up?'

Swearing and grumbling under their breaths, both men obliged, pulling the huge door away from the wall. Athelstan approached it. He pulled down the small trap to look through the eye grille; he stood there for a while then looked round the door.

'Can we put this bloody thing down?' Cranston gasped.

'Yes, Sir John.'

Both men pushed the door back against the wall.

'Well, Brother?'

'I don't know,' Athelstan replied. 'I'm not sure, Sir John. Master Flaxwith, do you know a good carpenter?'

'Aye, there's Laveck in Stinking Alley.'

'Bring him here,' Athelstan ordered. 'I want this door examined from top to bottom, the grille, the locks, the bolts, the bosses, everything. I don't care what damage is done.' He nudged Cranston in the ribs. 'Tell him the city will pay the costs. If it doesn't, the Regent certainly will. Provide him with ale and bread, but he is not to leave this house until his task is finished and both I and Sir John have returned to question him.'

Flaxwith undid the rope which held Samson tethered and hurried down the passageway.

'What do you hope to achieve, Brother?'

'Trickery, Sir John. The world is full of trickery and deceit. Everything is a riddle. Clerks are killed when no one is about. A moneylender is found dead in his locked counting house, whilst in Southwark,' he added bitterly, 'crucifixes drip with real blood.'

'You don't believe that, do you?'

'No I don't, Sir John. But my parishioners do. John, you know the villains and the cunning men of the under-world. How could they do that?'

Cranston sighed. 'I have knowledge of it,' he answered. 'But usually they are fairground tricks, Brother. The blood is wine or paint.'

'This was real blood,' Athelstan replied.

'The men I have arrested,' Cranston continued, 'used secret levers or mechanisms.'

'I don't think that's the case here,' Athelstan said. 'The crucifix was bleeding when no one was holding it.'

'What about Huddle?' Cranston asked.

'A cunning, subtle painter. What he can do with a paintbrush is beyond me. But why this, eh, Sir John?' He linked his arm through Cranston's as they walked down the passageway. 'As I keep pointing out to you, my Lord Coroner, I am a Dominican. My order, to its eternal shame or credit, has the reputation of being the Domini Canes.'

'The hounds of God!' Cranston translated. 'The Inquisition?'

'Precisely, Sir John. It is their duty to investigate so-called miracles, question self-confessed prophets. In our library at Blackfriars, there is a book, a record of such investigations. Now, Laveck is coming to examine this door and I have no desire to return to Southwark, so what I propose, Sir John, is that we visit Blackfriars.' He nipped Cranston's arm. 'Don't worry, I have just remembered, Father Prior is on a brief pilgrimage to St Thomas's shrine at Canterbury.'

Cranston stopped, a stubborn look on his face.

'Our mother house also has a new cook,' Athelstan added slyly. 'A man who can perform miracles with a piece of beef or roast pheasant. Even His Grace the Regent tried to tempt him into the kitchen of the Savoy.'

The coroner clapped Athelstan on the shoulder. 'Brother, if you weren't a Dominican, you'd make a very good tempter. The spirit is willing, but the flesh is very weak. Accordingly, my only answer to such temptation is yes.'

–

Robert Elflain, clerk of the Green Wax, left the Chancery Office and made his way up Holborn towards Fleet Street. It was Wednesday and Elflain was determined that he would spend some part of the day away from the cloying, suspicious attitude of his comrades. Everything had gone wrong. Alcest had sworn that in the end they would have nothing to fear but Elflain was worried. He did not like the fat coroner whilst that sharp-eyed friar seemed to sense something was wrong. Alcest had demanded that they stay together, that no one should wander off, but this was Wednesday and, at Dame Broadsheet's, Laetitia would be waiting: those soft eyes and even softer skin, that long, sinuous body! Elflain was tense – he needed to burrow his face into her swanlike neck and embrace her body.

He passed Newgate and tried not to look at the scaffold: that would reawaken his fears. If only Chapler had been more accommodating, everything would have gone smoothly! Elflain loosened the collar of his shirt and cursed as he slipped on the offal dripping along the cobbles from the butcher's stall. On the corner of an alleyway he turned and stared back: was anyone following him? The crowds milled about, grouping round the stalls, haggling with the traders. Elflain heaved a sigh and continued on his journey. When he glimpsed the front of Dame Broadsheet's house, he felt a glow of satisfaction in the pit of his stomach. He hurried along until he reached the door. Naturally, it was closed and bolted because Dame Broadsheet only had a licence to sell ale in the evening. Elflain groaned. There would be the usual tarrying as he explained to a suspicious porter who he was and why he had come. Dame Broadsheet was ever suspicious of some bailiff or tipstaff trapping her and bringing a charge against her of conducting a house of ill repute.

Elflain banged on the door. Silence. He knocked again. 'Elflain!'

He turned and stared at the hooded, cowled figure which had appeared like a ghost behind him.

'What the...?' Elflain stepped forward but it was too late.

The catch of the small arbalest was sprung and the barbed bolt took him full in the heart, smashing through flesh and bone. The clerk staggered back against the door, writhing in pain. He glimpsed the cowled figure drop a small parchment scroll at his feet and then he died, even as the door swung open.

Chapter 8

When Sir John Cranston left Blackfriars, his stomach was full of capon pie, but his mind was totally bemused by what he had read in the library. As he and Athelstan reached Ludgate, the coroner took his hat off and shook his head.

'Heaven knows, Brother,' he exclaimed. 'I have seen villainy enough in the city: how quickly and easily people are gulled. But what I read there is beyond all human understanding.' He ticked the points off on his podgy fingers. 'A goblet in which wine miraculously appears. Statues which move and cry. A cloth which is supposed to have wiped Jesus Christ's face suddenly becoming blood-soaked. A rock on which Jesus stood that glows in the dark. Straw from the manger at Bethlehem which smells of some heavenly perfume.' He laughed. 'And that's before we get on to the people! Was there really a man in Salisbury who dressed in goatskin, ate ants and honey and pretended to be John the Baptist?'

'Oh yes,' Athelstan replied. 'The human mind is a great marvel, Sir John: people are only too quick to believe. Go into any great church. I know of at least ten which claim to have the arm of St Sebastian; five which contain the dorsal fin of the whale that swallowed Jonah.' Athelstan's smile faded. 'But, there again, nothing about a crucifix which drips blood.'

'Do you think it could be real?' Cranston asked.

'I'd love to believe it, Sir John, I really would. I'm no different from the rest of humankind. I have a hankering for signs and wonders, but there's something...' Athelstan chewed his lip. 'I don't trust Watkin and the same goes for Pike the ditcher. But, talking of trickery, Master Flaxwith and Laveck must have arrived at Drayton's house. I am eager to learn what they may have discovered.'

They made their way through the crowds, Cranston, full of good humour as well as capon pie, doffing his cap to the ladies of the town and answering their witticisms like with like. When they arrived at Drayton's house, the small, nut-brown carpenter Laveck had been very busy. The door had been gouged, rows of the great iron studs being removed. Flaxwith sat in a corner, one hand round the ever-vigilant Samson who licked his lips and growled when he saw Cranston.

'Keep your dog under control,' the coroner warned. 'Now, Master Laveck, what have you found?'

'At first nothing, Sir John. The hinges are sound, the keys and locks are good.' The man's bright eyes grinned up at the coroner towering above him. 'Master Flaxwith,' he continued, 'told me what this was all about. I knew Drayton. He was a mean old bugger.'

'Yes, yes, quite,' the coroner replied. 'But what have you found?'

'Nothing much, Sir John.' Laveck picked up one of the great iron studs which fitted into the outside of the door. 'This was held in place by a huge screw on the inside. It's been loosened.'

'What do you mean, loosened?' Cranston gazed threateningly at Flaxwith. 'I thought you examined the door?'

'No, no, let me explain,' Laveck intervened quickly. He was eager to keep the goodwill of the bailiff who had assured him he would be paid good silver for this day's work. 'When this door was constructed, the carpenter gouged holes in the wood then inserted these great iron studs facing outwards. They are held in place by a clasp or screw on the inside.'

'Why is that done?' Athelstan asked. 'I know.' He smiled at Laveck. 'You can see them on any strongroom door but why?'

'Because if someone tried to break in, Brother, these iron bosses outside take the force, protect the wood they do. It's very, very difficult to remove them but, in this case, one has been. Here, in the second row beneath the eye grille. What seems to have happened is this.' Laveck shuffled sideways to give them full view of the door. 'The clasp on the inside was loosened, the bolt taken out.' Laveck held up one of the iron bosses. 'Look at that, Sir John. Clean as a whistle. It's been removed, polished and greased. This,' he picked up another one, 'is all dark around the edge. Now, from what I can gather, a bolt was removed and greased then put back in again.' He shrugged. 'Is that of any help?' He picked up the clasp or screw. 'This held it from the inside. Notice again.' He held it up. 'How the rim has also been cleaned and oiled. Very clever indeed!'

'Anything else?' Cranston asked.

Laveck shook his head. 'Do we put it back?'

'Yes, yes,' Cranston answered, glancing over his shoulder. Athelstan was lost in some reverie. 'Is there anything else, Brother?' he asked.

Athelstan was about to reply when there was a pounding on the stairs and Sir Lionel Havant came striding down the passageway.

'Do you have the Regent's silver yet, Sir John?'

'No, I bloody well don't! Surely you haven't come down to ask me that?'

'No, Sir John, I haven't!' The young knight slapped his leather gloves against his thigh. 'His Grace the Regent is now more concerned about his clerks at the Chancery of the Green Wax. Another one has been killed outside the house of Dame Broadsheet: a crossbow quarrel straight through his heart. According to the porter there was no one in the street, certainly no one from Dame Broadsheet's. Elflain died immediately. He tried to speak but nothing came from his mouth except a stream of blood. Naturally, the Regent is anxious...'

'Naturally,' Cranston repeated.

'Oh.' Havant handed across a greasy piece of parchment. 'This was found near the corpse.'

Cranston undid the scroll, read it and handed it to Athelstan.

'My third is like Fate,' the scrawling hand had written.

'What does it mean?' Havant asked.

'Heaven knows.'

'Well,' the knight replied. 'You know as much as I do. Elflain has been killed, a riddle left by his corpse. The Regent has lost another clerk, not to mention his silver. He is not in the best of moods, Sir John.'

'In which case you'd best tell his Grace that at least we have something in common,' Cranston snapped back.

Havant hurried off.

Athelstan told Laveck to put the bolts back, then he joined Sir John further down the passageway.

'Four clerks dead,' Cranston murmured. 'Each with a riddle left by his corpse. *My third is like Fate.*' He paused. 'No, that's strange, isn't it, Athelstan?'

'Sir John?'

'Well, four clerks have been killed; Chapler, Peslep, Ollerton and now Elflain. However, no riddle was left by Chapler's corpse whilst the assassin apparently regards Elflain as his third not fourth victim.'

Athelstan tweaked the coroner's cheek. 'My Lord Coroner, like a swooping hawk! The poppets should be proud of their father.'

John beamed, then his smile faded. 'Why is it important, Brother?'

'Because, Sir John, you are correct: the killer draws a distinction between the murders of Peslep, Ollerton and Elflain and that of the first, Chapler.' Athelstan sat down at the foot of the stairs, his chin cupped in his hand. 'Sir

John, could those clerks of the Green Wax be involved in some villainy?'

'Such as what?'

'Forgery, theft, blackmail?'

Cranston scratched his chin. 'What they do, Brother, is draw up licences and letters. The seal itself is held by Master Lesures. I doubt if he would be involved in such wickedness.'

'Could they forge a seal?'

Cranston raised his eyebrows. 'It's not unknown, Brother. We should go down to the Chancery.'

'It would be a fruitless journey.' Athelstan tapped his sandalled foot. 'I am sure Masters Alcest and Napham will have very good explanations of where they were. I also wager a jug of wine that it was well known that Master Elflain visited Dame Broadsheet's on a certain day at a specific hour. Yes, we would be wasting our time. I am more concerned about these riddles. Let's have them again.' Athelstan closed his eyes. 'My first is like a selfish brother,' he recited. 'My second is the centre of woe and the principal mover of horror. My third is like Fate.' He glanced up at Cranston. 'What's the centre of woe, Sir John?'

'No claret,' the coroner replied.

Athelstan grinned. 'The centre of woe: does it mean the word itself? Of course it does.' Athelstan got to his feet. 'O is the centre of the word "woe" and, without it, horror as a word would not exist. Now that was found beside Ollerton's corpse. And what is Fate, Sir John?'

'The finish...' the coroner stammered. 'The end of life.'

'Fate also ends in an E, the first letter of Elfiain's name. Peslep's riddle's a little more difficult, isn't it? Like a selfish brother: what begins with P, Sir John?'

Athelstan, fully immersed in the riddle, began to walk up and down. 'Like a selfish brother,' he repeated. 'The riddle definitely refers to a P. The first letter of Peslep's name.' Athelstan paused. 'That's it, Sir John. A selfish brother's the first to pity but the last to help: "pity" begins, and "help" ends with a P. But why the letters? These clerks have apparently been killed according to sequence P, O, E.'

'Poe?' Cranston asked. 'No such word exists.'

'Ah, we've not finished have we, Sir John? There's Napham and Alcest. Add N and A and what do we have? There's no such name as "poena" but in Latin *poena* means punishment.'

'Punishment!' Cranston exclaimed. 'The assassin is playing a game with his victims. The first letter of each of their names is hidden in these riddles and the killer believes he is carrying out a punishment. But for what?'

'One thing is clear,' Athelstan replied. 'The murderer believes all these clerks are guilty but, as you say, guilty of what? And two other questions warrant our attention. Why isn't Chapler's name mentioned? He worked with these young men. Secondly, was he innocent of any crime?'

'How do we know Chapler's dead?' Cranston asked.

'Oh, Sir John, don't be stupid!'

'I'm not being stupid, monk!' Cranston snapped. 'A young man is fished out of the Thames, and only by the contents of his wallet do we know he is Edwin Chapler.'

'But Mistress Alison, his sister, recognised the corpse as that of her brother.'

'No, no.' Cranston shook his head and leaned against the wall. 'What happens if Chapler is not dead? He knew the habits and customs of his companions. He knew they liked riddles. Perhaps he and his sister are waging their own private war of vengeance, God knows for what reason.'

'It's impossible,' Athelstan murmured. 'Mistress Alison was not in London when Peslep was killed; she was in Southwark when Ollerton died and the second riddle delivered. We know Havant viewed Chapler's corpse whilst the poor clerk was last seen alive near the very place where he probably died.'

Athelstan stared down at the corridor where Flaxwith still stood with the carpenter Laveck. 'It's like any puzzle, isn't it, Sir John?' he continued. 'There are many answers but only one is correct. I may have the riddles wrong. Chapler could well be alive. Moreover, we must not discount Master Lesures: he must know what is going on in his own Chancery Office. And there's the other little strand we've picked loose: your good friend, the Vicar of Hell, seems to know a lot about our beloved clerks. Perhaps he has a score to settle? He can move round the city like a will-o'-the-wisp. Finally...' Athelstan paused, wiping some dust from his sandal.

'Yes, Brother?'

'We must not be carried headlong by the force of our own logic. Here we are suspecting everyone of murder but there are others, besides Lesures, we must not forget. Napham and Master Alcest, in particular. How do we know that one, or both, might not be the assassin? Was there some quarrel amongst the clerks? Peslep might have been born wealthy but all these young men do seem to have a lot of money.'

'So, a visit to the Chancery of the Green Wax may not be fruitless?' Cranston asked.

'It might be very rewarding, Sir John.'

'And this business here?'

'Well, the remains of Drayton's wife have now been removed. Master Laveck has told us what he knows about the door. However,' Athelstan stared around, 'is that enough to accuse the two clerks? How did they really kill Drayton? It's possible that in the days preceding the murder they distracted Drayton and worked one of those bolts loose. But how did they kill their master and how could they enter and leave the house without leaving some door or window loose?' Athelstan picked up his writing bag. 'The day draws on, Sir John. Let's visit Master Lesures and his clerks. Then I'm back to Southwark to see what fresh miracles have occurred.'

They walked out of the house and almost bumped into Mistress Alison. She was breathless and for a while just stood, hands on her chest, panting for air.

'Oh, Sir John, Brother Athelstan.' She smiled. 'I am sorry. I made inquiries at the Guildhall. They told me you were meeting your bailiff here.'

'That's right. Why, what's the matter, girl?'

'Nothing. It's just that I'm leaving London, Sir John.' She leaned up and kissed him on both cheeks and did the same to Athelstan. 'I could not go without saying goodbye. I want to be on the road before the sun sets. Oh,' she continued in a rush, 'Brother Athelstan, I went back across the bridge. I had forgotten something at Benedicta's. Your crucifix is still bleeding and the crowds are fair flocking there.'

Athelstan closed his eyes and groaned.

'But Benedicta sent a message.' Alison closed her eyes. 'Er, Wat...'

'Watkin,' Athelstan intervened.

'Ah yes, Watkin has everything under control. I must go.'

'I am afraid you can't.'

Athelstan looked at Cranston in surprise. The coroner hunched his great shoulders. 'Mistress Alison, we are hunting your brother's murderers.'

'But you surely could send a message out to Epping? I am more than prepared to return. I don't like it here.' Tears sprang to her eyes. 'Go ask mine host at the Silver Lute. Last night and today I've had a visitor, Brother Athelstan. He was very similar to the young man you described who was in the tavern where Peslep died. The landlord remembered him well: he was cowled and hooded, spurs jangling on his boots.'

'Have you seen him yourself?' Cranston asked.

'No, Sir John, I have not. However, I remember you describing such a man when I first met you in the Chancery Office.' Alison moved a loose hair away from her face. 'I am afeared.'

'Tell me.' Athelstan took her gently by the hand and stroked her fingers. 'Mistress Alison, you came into London to see your brother?'

'Yes.'

'Did you do that often?'

'Not as much as I would have wished. When the weather changed and the rains and snow clogged the trackways, no. But in summertime as often as I could.'

'You came this time because you were concerned?'

'Yes, I told you. Edwin fell suddenly ill. He was vomiting, his bowels were loose. Some contagion of the belly.'

Athelstan studied her closely. 'This illness?'

'It was sudden,' Alison replied. 'One afternoon at the Chancery. Edwin suspected his drink had been tainted.' She pulled a face. 'But there's no proof for that and Edwin was so agitated.'

'Did he say about what?'

'Never!'

'Did he have other friends in London?'

'I think he talked of Tibault Lesures, Master of the Rolls.'

'Any young women?'

Alison laughed. 'If he did, he kept it a great secret. But Sir John,' Alison turned back to the coroner, 'I want to go.

I should go, I have no business in London. My brother is buried. I have a trade in Epping, property to look after.'

'Go back to the Silver Lute,' Athelstan offered. 'Pack your baggage, and come and stay with Benedicta.'

Alison looked down at the ground.

'You'll be safe there,' Athelstan insisted. 'No one will hurt you.'

'I agree,' she replied.

'Good.' Athelstan patted her on the shoulder. 'I'll meet you there.'

Athelstan watched her go then, half listening to Sir John's chatter, he followed the coroner through the afternoon crowds, past Newgate and down Holborn to the Chancery of the Green Wax. As they passed the old city gate on to the Holborn road, Cranston stopped, a hand on Athelstan's arm. The coroner stared fixedly at the mouth of an alleyway.

'What's the matter, Sir John?'

Cranston scratched his chin and took a swig from his miraculous wineskin. Athelstan followed his gaze. There were a few stalls; children played with an inflated pig's bladder near a drunken juggler who was trying to ply his tricks much to the merriment of some labourers.

'One of your villains, Sir John?'

'Oh yes,' Cranston breathed. 'Lovely lad, lovely lad! William the Weasel. I know him of old. There's not a window he can't climb through. Show him a crack in a wall and he'll slither through as swiftly as a river rat.'

'But I can't see him.'

'No, no, you won't, Brother. He's gone in the twinkling of an eye. William was not up to villainy, he was watching me. The Weasel is one of the Vicar of Hell's most ardent parishioners and, if young William's watching me, that means the Vicar of Hell is very interested in where I go and what I do. So Flaxwith's story is correct. Our Vicar must be greatly smitten by young Clarice. I think it's only a matter of time before he rises to the lure.'

'But he'll know you'll have Dame Broadsheet's house watched?'

'Yes, yes.' Cranston gnawed on his knuckle. 'I'll have to think about that. But come, Brother.'

The Master of the Rolls met them in a small chamber at the back of the office of the Green Wax. He sat on a bench to one side of a table, Cranston and Athelstan sitting opposite.

'Master Tibault, you seem agitated?' Athelstan began.

The Master of the Rolls scratched an unshaven cheek and rubbed one red-rimmed eye. 'All these deaths,' he wailed. 'Brother Athelstan, this is an important office of state. The Regent, the Chancellor, even the King himself has sent messengers down.'

'The dead clerks have been replaced?'

Master Tibault pulled a cloth from the cuff of his robe and mopped his brow. 'Oh Lord save us, yes. There's no shortage of skilled men.'

'We have come to talk about Chapler,' Athelstan continued. 'Master Tibault, describe him to me.'

The Master of the Rolls did and both the coroner and his secretarius recognised the young man who had been fished out of the Thames. Athelstan raised his eyes heavenwards as one theory crumbled to dust.

'Why?' Tibault asked, playing with the rag.

'Oh nothing,' Athelstan replied. 'Sir John and I wanted to be sure: apart from his sister, no one identified the corpse taken from the Thames. However, the man you describe fits Chapler's description exactly, from the colour of his hair to the small mole on his right cheek.'

'Yes, yes, that's so.'

'What was Chapler like? As a person?'

'Very shy, very secretive. He kept himself to himself. He did not carouse with the others.'

Athelstan watched the bead of sweat form on Lesures' upper lip. You are lying, he thought. You are not just flustered because your clerks have been killed: there's some great secret here.

'So you know nothing about his private life?' Athelstan asked.

Lesures shook his head.

'And nothing happened untoward, before Chapler's death, which would account for his murder?'

Again the shake of the head.

'Not even Chapler's sickness?'

Lesures gulped, his Adam's apple bobbing up and down.

'He was sick, wasn't he?' Athelstan continued. 'A slight contagion of the belly, so his sister told me: vomiting, a flux in the bowels.'

'Oh yes, yes,' Lesures gabbled. 'He was ill for a few days.'

'Did he fall ill suddenly?' Athelstan grasped the old man's hand: it was cold and clammy. 'Master Lesures, you are wasting our time. I am becoming very suspicious about the doings of your clerks in the Chancery of the Green Wax.'

Athelstan glanced sideways at Cranston, who sat dozing, eyes half closed.

'Would you please answer our questions?' Athelstan insisted. 'Either here or in the Tower.'

Lesures licked his lips. 'I'm just frightened,' he whined. 'That is all, Brother Athelstan. My mind is clogged, my wits numb. I go home and lock myself in...'

'You live by yourself?' Cranston opened his eyes.

'I am a bachelor, Sir John.'

'And you do not join your clerks when they carouse the midnight hours away?'

'Sir John,' Lesures simpered, 'I may be a bachelor, but I am also quite vulnerable.'

'We were talking about Chapler's illness,' Athelstan intervened. 'He became ill here, didn't he?'

'Yes, yes, he did.' Lesures swallowed. 'After I had served the malmsey, Chapler suddenly fell sick: clutching his stomach, he ran down to the privy in the small garden.'

'And no one else showed similar symptoms?'

'No.'

'And you didn't think that was suspicious?'

'I...'

'Come, come, Master Tibault.' Cranston hammered on the table. 'A healthy young man takes a cup of malmsey like the rest, but only he has gripes in his belly.'

'I thought it was suspicious,' Lesures bleated. 'But the clerks are always playing tricks upon each other. They did not like Chapler,' he continued in a rush. He put his face in his hands. 'Some madcap scheme. I asked Peslep but he just laughed.'

'I wish you had told us,' Athelstan replied. 'How do you know, Master Tibault, it was some witless trick? Chapler could well have been poisoned. Sometimes the poison works but if you are fortunate, depending on your belly, the body can expel it. It would leave you weak but not dead.'

Lesures' face went as white as a sheet.

'What is happening here?' Cranston asked softly. He gripped Lesures' wrist. 'Master Tibault, you are one of the Crown's principal clerks, yet you shake like an aspen leaf. What do these young rapscallions know about you? You should be their master, but look, you sit here more like their minion. Bring down the seal,' Cranston continued.

'I don't need to bring it down.' Lesures unbuttoned the cords of his gown.

Athelstan glimpsed the chain and the small round box on the end. Lesures took this off, opened the clasps and handed the seal across. Cranston held it as if it was some holy relic: dark green in colour, on one side it showed the young King Richard II on horseback, sword in hand; on the other a crown and the arms of England, France, Scotland and Castile quartered on a shield.

'Sir John, what are you hinting at?' Lesures asked, taking the seal back. 'You know no one holds that seal except me. No one can use it to impress a document except me.' Lesures made to rise as if to walk off in disgust.

'We haven't finished,' Athelstan remarked. 'But you may go and ask Napham and Alcest to join us. We have something to tell them.'

Lesures hurried off. He returned with the clerks. Both men look subdued, pale-faced, not a touch of their old arrogance and swagger.

'Did you like Chapler?' Cranston began abruptly.

'No, we did not,' Alcest retorted. 'I've told you, he was not one of us so we let him be. He came to work here then he went home. We knew nothing about him except that he had a sister in Epping.'

'How long did Chapler work here?' Athelstan asked.

'Two years,' Lesures answered from where he stood nervously by the door. 'He came highly recommended from a merchant in Cambridge.'

'And he was the last to join you?'

'Yes, yes, he was,' Alcest replied. 'He came a stranger and remained as one.'

'Is that why you tried to poison him?' the coroner asked.

Napham sat back as if a crossbow bolt had hit him in the chest.

'You did try to poison him or someone here did? A few weeks ago, he drank some malmsey...'

'We didn't poison him,' Alcest retorted. 'That was Peslep's idea of a joke. He put a purgative in Chapler's cup. Peslep thought it was amusing. We did not.'

'You have no proof of that,' Athelstan said sharply.

'I have spoken the truth.'

'Ah yes, the truth,' Cranston remarked. 'Pilate also asked what is the truth. Brother Athelstan, tell him what we have already learnt.'

Athelstan explained the three riddles and how each of them was a reference to the first letter of the surname of the murdered clerks. Alcest and Napham became even more subdued, especially as Athelstan explained how there was little connection between the murder of Chapler and the other three clerks.

'This makes us wonder,' Athelstan concluded. 'We have Peslep, Ollerton, Elflain: P O E. If we add the first letters of Napham and Alcest the word *poena* is formed, the Latin for punishment. Now,' Athelstan leaned his hands on the table, 'what have you five clerks done to deserve such punishment?'

Napham began to shake but Alcest abruptly got to his feet and, taking his Chancery ring off, threw it on the table.

'Pray, sir, what's the matter?' Cranston barked.

'I'm a royal clerk in the Chancery of the Green Wax,' Alcest declared. 'I work for the Crown. I am being threatened. Accordingly, unless we take the appropriate measures, both I and Master Napham will also be brutally killed whilst you, Sir John, fumble around!'

'And so?' Athelstan played with the Chancery ring lying on the table.

'Sir John will tell you the custom.' Napham also took his ring off. 'In times of great danger royal clerks can demand the Crown's protection.'

'Of course!' Cranston breathed. 'And where will you go, sir?'

'To the Tower, of course.'

Alcest picked up both rings and slipped them into his pouch. 'I will go to the Constable of the Tower and demand that we be housed there.' He jabbed a finger at Cranston. 'Until you, the coroner of this city, discovers who the assassin is!'

Alcest, followed by Napham, walked to the door. 'We will both stay in the Tower from where we will petition the Regent for his protection and complain about the bumbling doings of a drunken coroner!'

Cranston sprang to his feet. 'And you, sir, can go down to hell and ask the Lord Satan for protection. If you seek it in the Tower, then go! Yet you have still not answered our questions.' The coroner continued. 'Why are you and your companions being hunted and killed? What have you done to merit such terrible punishment?' He smiled bleakly. 'My Lord Regent will be interested in your reply, as will I.' He glanced at the Master of the Rolls. 'Lesures, will you join them?'

'No, no, my post is here!'

'Good,' Cranston breathed. 'Master Alcest, you will be in the Tower by the morning, yes? I can visit you there.'

The two clerks were already pushing their way out of the door, slamming it behind them. Cranston took out his wineskin and swallowed a generous mouthful.

'They should be careful,' Athelstan warned. 'They are not yet in the Tower and the assassin still hunts them!'

Chapter 9

Athelstan left Cranston in Cheapside. The coroner was growing tired, rubbing his face and murmuring about Lady Maude and the poppets. The day was drawing on. The market bell was tolling and already carts and barrows were being refilled as peasants prepared to leave the city before sunset. The air was ripe with rotting fruit and vegetables as Athelstan made his way along the streets. A beggar boy, for a penny, took him to the Silver Lute tavern, a broad-fronted hostelry with a small gatehouse which dominated its spacious cobbled yard. Athelstan walked into the taproom. The taverner, a great leather apron round him, came hurrying up, a cheerful, merry-eyed fellow.

'Yes, yes,' he declared, scratching his bald pate. 'Mistress Alison Chapler is here.'

A tapster was sent to fetch her.

'I'll have a pot of ale,' Athelstan requested. 'And a few moments of your time, sir.'

The taverner brought him a quart but shook his hand at the proffered coin. 'No, Brother, remember me at Mass. Now, what do you want?'

Athelstan described what Alison had told him: the taverner scratched his cheek.

'It's true,' he replied. 'Mistress Alison asked me to keep an eye for anyone who came to the tavern asking for her, especially a young man, cowled and cloaked, with spurs on his boots. She seemed fearful of him.'

'And you saw such a person?'

'Well, yes. Once today and once yesterday. My counting house overlooks the yard so I can keep an eye on anyone who comes in under the gateway. I saw this young man twice. If Mistress Alison had not asked me to watch, I would not have noticed him at all.'

'Do you know who he was or where he came from?'

The taverner shook his head. 'The first time I didn't mention it but after I saw him today, I told Mistress Alison. She became frightened. She said she was leaving and asked me to present my bill, which I have done.'

'Yes, she's leaving with me.' Athelstan smiled. 'She's going to stay with a friend in Southwark.'

The taverner was about to question him further but Alison and the tapster, carrying bulky saddlebags, came downstairs into the taproom. She and Athelstan made their farewells, the boy taking them out to the yard. He saddled a gentle-looking palfrey, across which Athelstan threw the baggage. Alison wrapped the reins round her hand and they left in the direction of London Bridge.

At first they walked in silence. Alison seemed fascinated by the different sights: a woman accused of scolding standing in the thews; two sorry pickpockets standing nearby, their fingers clasped in the stocks, their hose round their ankles. A legion of beggars of every description, some genuine, others fraudulent. A group of mailed horsemen rode by, forcing everyone into the doorways of shops and houses. These were followed by an elegant young man with a hooded falcon on his wrist; two verderers followed swiftly behind. On the rods over their shoulders hung the gutted corpses of hares, pheasants and quail.

'Some lord returning from the hunt,' Athelstan observed. He watched the horsemen retreat in a jingle of harness. 'This man you saw,' he continued, 'the one who wore spurs and was seen when Peslep was killed. Do you think he is hunting you?'

Alison stopped and stroked the muzzle of her horse who snickered and pushed at her. She took a small apple out of her pocket; the palfrey greedily seized it, shaking his head in pleasure. They moved on.

'I asked you a question, mistress.'

'I don't know what to say,' she replied. 'Edwin did not talk very much about the other clerks. I don't think he liked them: he considered Peslep a lecher, Ollerton a glutton.'

'And Alcest?'

'Ah, that's what frightened me, Brother. On one occasion I am sure Edwin called him a fop who liked to wear spurs on his boots for effect.' She glanced sloe-eyed at Athelstan. 'Has he ever, since this business began, worn spurs?' She glimpsed the surprise in Athelstan's face. 'I thought Lesures or one of the others would remark on that.'

Athelstan paused. 'Are you sure?'

'Brother, I simply repeat what I heard.'

Athelstan stared around. Across the lane was a small alehouse. He told Alison to wait and went over. The owner, a small, wiry-haired man, recognised him.

'You are thirsty, Brother?'

'No, no.' Athelstan paused. 'Er...'

'Haman.'

'Ah yes, Haman. I wonder if you would do me a favour?' Athelstan's hand went to his purse but Haman gently knocked it away. 'I wonder if you, or one of your boys, would go to the house of Sir Jack Cranston. You know where he lives?'

The ale-keeper nodded.

'Tell him to search out Master Tibault, he'll know what I mean. He must ask Tibault which of the clerks liked to wear spurs.'

Haman looked perplexed. Athelstan made him repeat the message until he had it by heart. Then he rejoined Alison.

'Was that important, Brother?'

'Yes, yes, it was but...' The friar touched her gently on the elbow. 'Not enough to hang a man.'

'Someone will hang,' she replied. 'Won't they, Brother? All those dreadful deaths: Ollerton poisoned; Peslep killed on a latrine with his hose about his ankles.'

'And Elflain,' Athelstan added. 'Earlier today he was killed by a crossbow bolt.'

He crossed himself and they continued on. At the corner of Lombard Street, near the Cornmarket, Athelstan stopped and stared back.

'What's the matter, Brother?'

'Nothing,' he replied but he was unsure. When he had crossed over to see Haman, Athelstan was certain he had glimpsed a figure behind him. He shook his head.

They went down an alleyway which led out to Gracechurch Street and London Bridge. The houses on either side towered over to block out the sunlight; the runnel was gloomy, filled with offal. The contents of chamber pots stained the walls on either side, the stench reminding Athelstan of the city ditch near Cock Lane. The palfrey became skittish, picking its way daintily over the bloated corpse of a dead cat. Alison took out a nosegay and held it to her face. Athelstan was about to apologise, bitterly regretting taking this short cut, when two figures stepped out of a shabby doorway. They were dressed like rifflers, the masked footpads who preyed on the unwary in the warren of London's alleyways. One was short, the other tall; battered leather masks covered their faces and their heads were concealed by pointed hoods. Each carried a stabbing dirk in one hand, a cudgel in the other.

Alison stopped. Athelstan patted her on the arm and, plucking up his courage, walked forward.

'I am Athelstan, priest of St Erconwald's in Southwark. This young lady and myself have little wealth.'

'Stay where you are!' the taller of the two ordered, his voice gruff behind the mask.

'Why do you stop us?' Alison shouted.

'Keep your tongue still, pretty one,' the smaller one replied in a high, reedy voice.

Athelstan peered at the diminutive footpad. He recalled Cranston's words to him earlier in the day.

'You are William the Weasel, aren't you? One of the parishioners of the Vicar of Hell.'

The little man backed away as if Athelstan had slapped him. The taller one was disconcerted, coughing and muttering behind his mask.

'Sir John would not be very pleased,' Athelstan took another step forward, 'to hear that William the Weasel dared to rob the coroner's secretarius and friend.'

'We are not here to rob you,' the little man screeched back.

Athelstan smiled; these two would-be footpads were not as terrifying as they appeared. 'Well, why are you here?' he snapped. 'How dare you stop a priest and a young lady going about their proper business!'

'Tush, tush, Brother!' the taller man replied. 'We would ask you to give Sir John a message from the Vicar of Hell.'

'What message?'

'The Vicar of Hell is angry. He has an affair of the heart with young Clarice. He objects to Sir John keeping Dame Broadsheet's house under strict surveillance. My Lord Coroner should be careful.'

'I'll tell him to be so,' Athelstan responded. 'But, as you know, Sir John does not frighten easily.'

'We bring other messages.' There was now a note of desperation in the Weasel's voice.

'Then you'd better hurry: we haven't all the time in the day to stand in this stinking alleyway.'

'Tell the Lord Coroner,' the Weasel was almost pleading, 'that the Vicar of Hell sends his compliments and that he had no hand in the dreadful murders at the Chancery of the Green Wax.'

Athelstan sighed. Sir John was right! There was some connection between the Vicar of Hell and these clerks. Now London's most famous outlaw was trying to distance himself from the horrid murders taking place.

The two figures disappeared. Athelstan came back and patted Alison on the shoulder. He was pleased the young woman was not shaken by the encounter. 'You do not frighten easily, mistress?'

'No, Brother, I do not.'

They walked on down to London Bridge. City guards were already taking up their positions, chatting merrily to Robert Burdon, the little gatehouse keeper. He was busy combing the hair of three severed heads laid out on the table before placing them on pikes which would jut out over the river.

'I like things to be tidy and neat,' he shouted as Athelstan passed by. The friar sketched a hasty blessing and hurried on.

In the middle of the bridge Alison stopped and stared across at the small chapel dedicated to Thomas à Becket. Tears filled her eyes and she bit her lip. 'If only,' she whispered, 'if only, if only I'd been there, Brother.'

Athelstan gently led her on, trying to cheer the girl with his chatter. They entered Southwark, now coming alive as the sun began to set and the stallholders set up their evening market. One of the traders called him over.

'Come, buy something, Brother Athelstan, needles, pins, a bit of cloth. A new leather bridle for your horse?'

'I'm in a hurry,' Athelstan replied.

'Oh yes, of course. Everyone's heard of the great miracle at St Erconwald's. I've been there myself and paid a groat. Tell your parishioners I've lovely things to sell, cheap at the price.'

'They are not his to sell,' Athelstan murmured as they walked on. 'Oh, they are not thieves, Mistress Alison. As Sir John Cranston often remarks, it's just that they find it difficult to tell the difference between their property and everyone else's!'

As Alison and Athelstan threaded their way through the alleyways of Southwark, Thomas Napham, clerk of the Green Wax, was also hurrying home. Napham was highly anxious. He did not trust Alcest but he recognised that he was in great danger. That little friar whom they had mocked was as sharp as a razor, and someone was killing his colleagues, hinting that he knew what they were guilty of. Napham had given in to Alcest's urging. He would leave the Chancery, collect a few belongings and make his way downriver to the Tower. He'd be safe there and, by all that was holy, he would never leave that narrow, well-guarded place until the assassin was caught. He paused in the entrance to his lodgings and peered through the gloom. Was someone there? A door opened further down the passageway; another tenant emerged, a journeyman apprenticed to a clothier in Cheapside.

'Have you been here all day?' Napham asked abruptly.

'Why, yes, I have, working on my master's accounts.'

'Has anyone come here inquiring after me?'

'Not that I know of but, there again, I am a journeyman not the doorkeeper!'

Napham unlocked the door to his chamber and pushed it open. He failed to see the scrap of parchment nailed to the wall above the door. Instead, he stopped and savoured the sweet smell from the herb pots placed around the room. 'You have nothing to fear,' he whispered.

The door had been locked. No one had forced an entry. Napham walked into the darkness. He took his tinder out and lit a candle on the table. The shutters on the window flapped in the evening breeze. Napham froze. The window had been shuttered before he left this morning! He lifted the candle up, but could see nothing disturbed. The shelf containing his books, the small coffers and pieces of parchment on the table beside his bed: everything was as he had left it. He walked across to pull the shutters open and allow in the light whilst he packed a few belongings. Napham's foot caught something hard. There was a snap followed by the most excruciating pain. Napham screamed. The pain in his right foot shot up his leg like a sudden spurt of fire. He collapsed to the floor, and the lighted candle, as if it had a life of its own, rolled away from him. Instead of the flame going out, it now burnt greedily as it caught the dry rushes. Napham didn't care. The pain in his foot was so intense! He pulled himself up and saw the great iron-toothed caltrop hidden amongst the rushes had bitten through his soft boot, gripping his foot. The blood now poured out like wine from a cracked jug.

Napham screamed, yelling for help. He turned round, his terror increasing as the flames raced along the rushes, catching the cloth of the bedstead. Sobbing and gasping, Napham tried to push himself towards the door. If he could only reach it, take himself and his pain beyond the fury of the growing fire. He pulled himself two, three paces but the agony was intense. He fell into a dead swoon even as the fire licked the dry cloths of the small four-poster bed and roared greedily towards the ceiling.

—

Athelstan sat in his kitchen. Even though the rays of the setting sun streamed in through the open shutters, the friar was cold with rage at what he had witnessed in the cemetery. Bonaventure, sitting on the table, studied his little master with his one good eye. The cat sat motionless as if he knew there was something wrong. Athelstan smiled and gently caressed the tangled remnants of Bonaventure's damaged ear.

'It's not you, great cat,' he murmured. 'But you should have seen that great fool Watkin! He was striding up and down with a tin pot on his head, a basting spoon in his hand, guarding the gateway to the cemetery! And the others! Tab the tinker, Pike, Pernell, even Ranulf the rat-catcher, organising the visitors now streaming into St Erconwald's to pray before their miraculous crucifix.'

Athelstan rose and paced up and down. Bonaventure solemnly followed. 'It's not right,' Athelstan murmured. 'Crucifixes don't bleed!'

He paused, the great tom cat almost crashing into his legs. There was something wrong. Watkin was belli-cose, Pike and the rest were screeching about their rights. Athelstan could see the figure on the crucifix had been bleeding again, the blood glistening in the light of the many candles which had been placed beneath it.

Athelstan glanced down at the tom cat. 'What happens if it wasn't a miracle, Bonaventure, eh?'

The cat winked and yawned.

'Exactly,' Athelstan rejoined. 'Miracles don't happen in Southwark!'

'They happened in Bethlehem!'

Athelstan whirled round. The tall, lean-visaged Dominican stood just within the door, hidden in the shadows.

'Why, Brother Niall!'

Father Prior's lieutenant and messenger walked into the kitchen. He and Athelstan embraced each other and exchanged the kiss of peace. Athelstan stared at the pale face and green eyes under the shock of red hair.

'Welcome to St Erconwald's, Brother Niall. *Pax tecum.*'

'*Et cum spiritu tuo.*'

'Some wine, Brother?'

Athelstan's visitor nodded. 'And if you have some bread and cheese?' he called out as Athelstan went into the buttery. 'I decided to fast today but the journey exhausted me. The good Lord will understand.'

'Man does not live by bread alone,' Athelstan retorted.

'That's why I asked for the cheese as well,' Niall quipped back.

Athelstan brought back food and drink for himself and his visitor as well as a pannikin of milk. Bonaventure, if not distracted, would only join in and take the food literally from his visitor's mouth.

They sat down. Brother Niall took out a small knife, cut himself a piece of cheese and popped it into his mouth. He stared appreciatively around. 'The house is clean and sweet-smelling, Athelstan. The bread and cheese are soft and fresh.'

Athelstan shrugged. 'Nowhere in the Gospel does it say you have to be dirty to be saintly.'

Niall laughed, covering his half-open mouth with his hand. 'You were always quick, Athelstan.' His face became grave. 'I've been in the cemetery. I've seen the crucifix.'

'It's nothing to do with me,' Athelstan snapped back. 'And don't tell me you're here on a pilgrimage!'

Niall shook his head. 'How long have you been here, Brother?'

'Almost three years.'

'Athelstan, Athelstan.' Niall shook his head. 'You were one of the best scholars in the schools. Your love of mathematics and sciences were well known. And then…'

'And then,' Athelstan finished, 'I wrecked it all three years before my final vows by going off with my brother Francis to the wars.'

'Why did you do it?'

'My brother and I were always close.' Athelstan half closed his eyes. 'Two peas out of the same pod, Niall. Oh, he was a merry soul, his eyes and heart were full of joy. He could charm the birds out of the trees. He didn't want to kill – he saw himself as a knight errant. He begged me to join him. Perhaps, for the last time in our lives before I became a Dominican, we'd share something together, come back laden with glory. So I went.' Athelstan fought to keep his voice steady. 'Francis was killed and I saw the glory of war: mangled corpses, widows and orphans. I committed a great sin before God and my parents. I broke their hearts and the rule of St Dominic. I returned to Blackfriars, took my vows and spent three years cleaning the latrines, kitchens and corridors.'

'Yes, yes, I know,' Niall interrupted. Athelstan was on the verge of tears.

'Then Father Prior sent me here to work amongst the poor. I fell in love with these ordinary people who lead such extraordinary lives. They can't read, they can't write. They are taxed and they are pushed around, but they have a joy, a courage I have never seen before.' Athelstan closed his eyes. 'And sometimes they are stupid. God knows what lies behind that mummery in the cemetery!'

'And Cranston?'

'Sir John is my brother. A fat, uncouth, curmudgeonly coroner but brave as a fighting cock, innocent as a child.

A good father, a loving husband, a man of deep integrity. He likes his wine and his food but there's not a shred of malice in that huge frame. Anyway, why has Prior Anselm sent you?'

'He thinks you have worked here long enough. Our house in Oxford requires a Master of the Natural Sciences, a man with your logic and love of study...'

'Nonsense!' Athelstan retorted. 'It's the Regent, isn't it? John of Gaunt, Duke of Lancaster. He doesn't like me. Ever since that business at Westminster when I investigated deaths amongst the knights of the shires! He knows that I am aware of his subtle schemes and clever plots.'

'His Grace admires you immensely,' Niall argued, putting his knife down. 'But I can't lie, Brother. He fears you. He fears that you know the truth but, above all, he fears the way you are loved and respected here in Southwark. Summer's dying, autumn is coming and the harvest is due. Outside in the shires, the peasants meet and plot. Gaunt fears an uprising. Armies marching on London. He does not want some friar whipping up the mobs of Southwark!'

'As if I would!'

'I know that, you know, Father Prior knows, but John of Gaunt doesn't.' Niall got to his feet, brushing the crumbs from his robe. 'Father Prior is minded to move you, and that business in the cemetery might prove to be the last straw.'

Athelstan sighed and got to his feet. 'Then tell Father Prior,' he declared, 'that I am a loyal son of the order. I will do what he says but if I am moved then, for the third time in my life, my heart will break. So plead for me, Niall.'

They embraced, Niall opened the door and slipped out into the gathering dusk. After he had gone Athelstan sat, face in his hands, and cried quietly. Eventually he wiped his face and breathed in deeply.

'I'm going to have a goblet of wine,' he declared to Bonaventura but the cat, busily finishing off the remains of Niall's bread and cheese, just swished his tail. Athelstan filled his goblet and sat: sleep would be impossible. He put the wine goblet down and pushed it away. He knew the dangers of that: too many priests on their own drinking and brooding, unleashing the demons in their souls. He picked up his writing bag, took out a scrap of parchment and placed his inkhorn on the table.

He forced himself to concentrate on the day's events. He drew a rough sketch of the door in Drayton's room and tried to envisage how the old miser had been murdered and the money taken. Perhaps, he reasoned, if he found the Regent's silver, John of Gaunt might be persuaded to speak to Father Prior. How, he wondered, had the man been killed in a locked and barred chamber? He recalled those iron bolts on the door and the two clerks Flinstead and Stablegate. Were they both guilty? Or just the one? If it *was* one... Athelstan closed his eyes and concentrated: it would be as difficult for one person to carry out such a crime as it would be for two. Athelstan stared at his own door.

Pretend, he thought, pretend you are Drayton. People can only get into this room if you allow them! And if they leave? I have a crossbow bolt in my chest so how can I possibly have the strength to lock the door behind them? Why spend so much precious energy bolting the stable door when the horse has gone? He stretched over and stroked Bonaventure. 'Which reminds me, I must pay a visit to our good friend Philomel.' Athelstan went back to his reasoning. One or two killers? Did it matter? He smiled then clapped his hands, making Bonaventure jump.

'Of course it does!' he shouted. 'There had to be two, that's the only way it could be done!'

And the house? How could they leave? Athelstan rubbed his face: the oldest trick in the book. They took poor Flaxwith to a locked window. It doesn't mean that at the moment the bailiffs broke in every other window was locked and barred! Athelstan stretched across to the wine cup and sipped from it. He put his pen down and looked at the goblet. And Chapler's death? And the murders of those other clerks of the Green Wax? Athelstan was sure that Alcest was somehow involved. Was he the young man with the clinking spurs? It would have been so easy for him to follow Peslep to that tavern. Athelstan chewed his lip. There was something about Peslep's murder… something he had learnt. Something that had been said. What was it?

Alcest, Athelstan concluded, Alcest could have put that poison in Ollerton's cup. Alcest knew where Elflain was going. Alcest visited Drayton before he was killed. But Chapler? The night that young man was murdered, Alcest, according to witnesses, was tucked up in bed with a young whore. Or was he? Was Clarice telling the truth? And the Vicar of Hell? Why was he so determined to tell Sir John that the murders amongst the clerks of the Green Wax had nothing to do with him? Why was it so important to send as messenger a ruffian like William the Weasel? Finally, Lesures, the Master of the Rolls. He had been sick with fear. Was he guilty? What was he trying to hide?

Athelstan picked up his pen again. *Alcest and Clarice*, he wrote, underlining their names. If he could disprove Alcest's story, everything would fall into place. Athelstan stretched, yawned, then jumped at a knock on the door.

'Go away, Watkin!' he shouted. 'I am saying Mass tomorrow and then I'm off to see Sir John.'

The door opened. A white-faced Benedicta, followed by Alison, equally pale, came into the kitchen.

'What's the matter?' Athelstan exclaimed. 'Come, sit down. You want some wine?'

Both women shook their heads.

'I was at home,' Benedicta began, unhitching her cloak. 'As you asked, Brother, I took Alison to my own house. She went upstairs to prepare for bed.'

'Yes.' Athelstan smiled. 'I saw you flee before my confrontation with Watkin.'

'I was sitting in my parlour,' Benedicta continued. She picked up Athelstan's wine cup and sipped from it. 'I heard a sound outside, in the small alleyway which runs along the side of my house.'

'What do you mean? What sound?'

'I was working on a piece of embroidery but, I'll be honest, my mind was busy with Watkin and his miraculous cross. At first I didn't take any notice but then there was a clink as if someone wearing spurs was walking up and down. I looked out, it was dusk, the alleyway seemed empty. I called out: '*Who's there?*' but there was no reply. I closed the shutters and went back to my embroidery. A few minutes later I heard the clink of spurs again. I called up to Alison to ask if she was well. She replied she was.' Benedicta took a deep breath. 'I admit I was frightened so I…' She looked down at the table. 'Oh, Athelstan, have you had a visitor?'

'Oh, just a messenger from across the city.' Athelstan pulled the platter across. 'But go on, tell me about this.'

'I went upstairs and asked Alison if she'd heard anything.'

'I had,' Alison intervened. 'I thought it was my imagination. I told Benedicta not to go out, but she said that if I came with her…'

'We went downstairs,' Benedicta continued. She took a small scroll of parchment from the cuff of her sleeve and handed it to Athelstan.

'"My last,"' he read. '"The one behind it all; the first and the last will always be discovered at the centre of a maze."'

'What does it mean?' Benedicta asked.

'We are hunting a murderer,' Athelstan replied. 'Someone who kills and always leaves a riddle on the corpse of his victim. But for the first time,' he smiled thinly as if echoing the words of the riddle, 'one has been found before any crime has been committed.' He paused. 'No, that's not true. There was no riddle found on Chapler's corpse. Anyway,' he continued, 'we know that the other riddles spell out the first letter of the surname of each of the murdered clerks. However, this appears to be different. You'll leave it with me?'

Benedicta nodded.

'And you are going back to your house?'

'Yes, yes, I am,' Benedicta agreed. 'I have had a word with Watkin. He's going to send Beadle Bladdersniff with two others to watch my door.'

'Ah yes,' Athelstan replied. 'Sir Watkin, knight of the basting spoon.' He smiled at both women. 'Are you sure you won't stay any longer?'

They both made their excuses and left.

Athelstan returned to his study of the scrawled riddle.

'The last,' he murmured. 'What's discovered at the centre of a maze? Of course, a rood: a crucifix above a rose bower?' He chewed on his lip. 'But what does that mean? Another word for maze is labyrinth: R is its central letter.' Athelstan paused. R the first and the last. He was certain the murderer was exposing his motive: *revenge*!

Chapter 10

Sir John Cranston sat in the small chancery at the top of his house in Cheapside. He stared through the unshuttered window watching for the first rays of the rising sun. As always, Sir John had woken early. The Lady Maude lay beside him lost in her dreams whilst, in the adjoining chamber, the two poppets, dressed in their linen night-gowns, sprawled on their cot beds. They looked so much alike: thin blond hair, apple-red cheeks, the firm chin and mouth of their father.

'Lovely lads!' Sir John had breathed and smiled as he noticed how they even snored in unison. He had tiptoed further down the gallery, quietly praying under his breath that the poppets would not awake. If they did, and knew Sir John was about, they'd rouse the entire house with their shouts. This was going to be a busy day for Sir John; he had gone down to the kitchen where he had washed, shaved and quickly dressed in the fresh apparel the Lady Maude had laid out the night before. A meat pie in the buttery kept savoury in a linen cloth, and a small jug of watered ale, served as breakfast. Sir John had then knelt and, closing his eyes, said his morning prayers before going up to his chancery.

He now sat with the Coroners' Roll in front of him though his gaze strayed to the thick manuscript lying to his right: Cranston's famous treatise, 'On the Governance of London'. Sir John leaned back on the cushioned chair. He had reached a new chapter, 'On the keeping of the streets, alleyways and runnels free of all filth'. Cranston had recommended the building of public latrines, strict laws against filling the streets with refuse and the contents of chamber pots. The open sewers would be moved beyond the city limits whilst the dung-collectors would be organised into a guild.

Sir John sighed and returned to more mundane matters, the first entry on the Coroners' Roll:

> On Thursday, the morrow of the feast of St Joachim and St Anne, Richard Crinkler sat on a latrine high in his tenement in a house owned by Owen Brilchard on the corner of Bore Street. The said latrine did break and the aforementioned Richard fell to his death which was not his proper death.

Sir John scratched his cheek. Why did his clerk use such convoluted phrases? And how could a man fall to his death down a latrine? Cranston closed his eyes and recalled the old, rotting mansions in Bore Street.

'Ah yes,' he murmured.

He could visualise what had happened to poor old Richard Crinkler. Those great houses had small cupboards which served as stool rooms built into a shaft which ran the whole length of the house. Crinkler had either been half asleep or drunk. The wooden latrine board had broken and so Crinkler fell to his death.

'Heaven be praised!' Cranston whispered. 'We all have to die but sometimes the Good Lord does call us in rather strange ways.'

He started as he heard the bell of St Mary Le Bow begin to toll, the sign that the night curfew was over. He put his quill back in its box and blew out the candle. Grabbing his war belt and cloak, he hurried down into Cheapside. The broad thoroughfare was still deserted. Any beggars, night-walkers or whores who had been lurking in the mouths of alleyways soon disappeared once they heard the news that the Lord Coroner was on the streets. Cranston walked down towards St Mary's. The beacon was still alight in the steeple. Cranston studied the cavernous doorway to the church and smiled as he glimpsed Henry Flaxwith with the ever-vigilant Samson.

'Good morning, Sir John,' the bailiff called, grasping the rope holding Samson more tightly.

'Is everything ready?' Cranston asked and looked in surprise as a small side door opened and Athelstan came out. 'Lord, Brother, what are you doing here?'

'Praying, Sir John, I've been praying!'

Athelstan had washed and shaved and wore a new robe but his eyes looked as if he had slept badly or not at all.

'Is everything well?'

'Everything, Sir John. I said a very early Mass not long after midnight, when the tumult in the cemetery had died down. I'm too angry with my parishioners to meet them.' Athelstan breathed in. 'They can spend a day without their priest.'

'Don't judge them too harshly.' Cranston patted Athelstan on the shoulder. 'God knows why they are doing it.'

'Did you get my message?' Athelstan asked, abruptly changing the subject.

'Yes,' Sir John replied. 'I went to see Master Lesures: timid as a rabbit, crouching in his chamber. According to him, Alcest sometimes acted the fop and insisted on wearing spurs to his boots.' Cranston whistled through his teeth. 'And I want to question Alcest further. There's been another death: Napham.'

'I thought there might. How did he die?'

'A caltrop had been hidden amongst the rushes in his chamber, a huge, jagged affair...'

'A caltrop, Sir John?'

'They are used against armoured knights,' Cranston explained, seeing the puzzlement in Athelstan's face. 'Steel man-traps, often placed on roads when planning an ambuscade or used to defend a dry ditch during a siege. Simple but terrible, like a rat-trap. The horse or the man puts his foot in and the trap is sprung.'

'A terrible death,' Athelstan remarked.

'It almost severed Napham's foot,' Cranston continued. 'However, in his agony he must have knocked a candle over. It fired the rushes and bedstead in his chamber. The poor man burnt to death. Another tenant noticed the flames and the fire was put out. The chamber was on the ground floor and the floor was made of stone, so the fire did not spread too quickly. I went to view Napham's corpse.' Cranston shook his head. 'Nothing more than burnt meat, the horrible caltrop still buried in his foot.'

'And the assassin?'

'Probably got in through a downstairs window,' Cranston replied, 'to place the caltrop, which can be bought at any ironmongers or armourers.'

'And the riddle?'

'Oh yes, Napham didn't see this when he went into his chamber: it was pinned on the wall above the door. My next,' Cranston closed his eyes to recall the riddle, 'my next is like the flesh on the tail of a stag.' He opened his eyes. 'N, of course, is the last letter of venison.'

Flaxwith broke in. 'Sir John, we must be going. The scrimperers will be waiting.'

'The what?' Athelstan exclaimed.

'The scrimperers.' Cranston grinned. 'My lovely little boys from Rat's Castle. I'm going to catch the Vicar of Hell.'

'In which case,' Athelstan said, 'we can talk as we walk.'

And the coroner, striding across Cheapside, listened attentively as Athelstan told him, not only about William the Weasel's message, but also of the strange occurrence outside Benedicta's house the previous evening.

'Devil's futtocks!' Cranston stopped. 'Devil's futtocks!' he repeated.

'My sentiments exactly, my Lord Coroner,' Athelstan replied. 'But perhaps I wouldn't use your words. I've been wondering, Sir John, why the Vicar of Hell should be so keen to distance himself from the murders amongst the clerks. I also wonder where Master Alcest was last night and why he's now so interested in Mistress Alison.'

'Devil's futtocks!' Cranston repeated.

'Sir John?'

'I forgot my miraculous wineskin.' Cranston flailed his hands. 'I knew there was something...'

'Sir John!' Athelstan felt like roaring in exasperation. 'Have you heard what I said?'

'Of course, dear monk.'

'Friar, Sir John.'

'Precisely. The Vicar of Hell has sent me a message. You think Alcest is the murderer and he now has an interest in Mistress Alison. I, however, have forgotten my bloody wineskin! Anyway, do you think Alcest is the murderer?' Cranston asked, hurrying on.

'I do. I also know how Stablegate and Flinstead killed their master!'

Cranston stopped again; this time Flaxwith and Samson almost crashed into him. The coroner grasped Athelstan by the shoulders and kissed him on each cheek.

'Marvellous monk!' he bellowed, then hurriedly stepped aside as a window opened and the contents of a chamber pot came spluttering down. The filthy contents narrowly missed them. Cranston shook his fists. 'I'll have you arrested!' he roared.

He hurriedly grabbed Athelstan and pushed him forward as the shutters opened again and another chamber pot was emptied, this time spattering poor Samson who stared up and growled his defiance.

'The scrimperers?' Athelstan asked.

'Wait a minute.' Sir John stood aside as a huge dung cart piled high with the previous day's rubbish made its way down the alleyway.

'The scrimperers,' Cranston explained, 'are a group of very small men. Really, they are dwarves. They live in a house in that mean tangle of alleyways near Whitefriars. I call them the "Lords of Rat's Castle". Now, they're the most godforsaken of people. No one trusts them, no one likes them. Now and again they are hired by some lord or a travelling mummers' troupe as acrobats or jugglers.'

'Like Master Burdon on London Bridge?'

'Oh no.' Cranston shook his head. 'These are even smaller.'

He jingled his purse. 'They are not averse to a little housebreaking, stealing through gaps where others cannot get. For some strange reason they like old Jack Cranston and he likes them.'

'Of course,' Athelstan conceded as they finally stopped on the corner of the alleyway leading up to Dame Broadsheet's.

'Now you remember.' Cranston grinned. 'Every year, on the feast of St Rahere, Lady Maude and I entertain them to a small banquet in our garden...'

'And you're going to use them to catch the Vicar of Hell?' Athelstan asked.

'Oh yes.' Cranston jabbed a finger towards Flaxwith. 'Faithful Henry here has had Broadsheet's house watched day and night. Clarice, the love of our villain's life, never leaves, yet the Vicar of Hell never comes.'

'So?'

'I don't believe it,' Cranston replied. 'The Vicar of Hell eats lambs' testicles and drinks Spanish wine. He's as lecherous as a boar in rut. He's been and gone but I don't know how.'

'And the scrimperers?' Athelstan asked.

Cranston stared longingly down at Dame Broadsheet's placid-looking house.

'I'm sure the bugger's there,' he growled. 'Henry, are your men on guard?'

'Yes, Sir John.'

'Where are the scrimperers?' Athelstan asked.

'Where Dame Broadsheet and the Vicar of Hell least expect!'

'I'm glad we came here,' Athelstan declared. 'I want to have words with young Clarice. I don't believe Alcest spent the entire night with her when Chapler died.'

'First things first,' Cranston murmured.

They must have stood for at least a quarter of an hour. Cranston's unease became apparent; he shifted from foot to foot, cursing under his breath and patting his cloak where the miraculous wineskin should have been. The streets started to fill. Traders and journeymen; shopkeepers setting up their stalls; heavy-eyed apprentices carrying out merchandise from the storerooms. Debtors, released from the Fleet prison, to spend the day shackled together, begging for a pittance for themselves and others in the debtors' hole. Two Abraham men danced by, naked as they were born, except for a loincloth, their faces and bodies covered in charcoal dust. They sang and danced. One bore a metal dish with burning charcoal on his head. He announced, to any who would listen, that he and his companion were Gog and Magog and they were going to Sodom and Gomorrah to carry out God's judgement.

'You know where that place is?' one of them screeched at Cranston. 'Do you, Brother, know the way of the Lord?'

'Yes, go straight down Cheapside and turn left at the stocks,' Cranston growled. 'Now piss off and leave me alone!'

The two Abraham men danced by.

'Sir John Cranston! Sir John Cranston! God bless you! God bless you and all that's in your breeches!'

The beggar stopped short as Cranston raised a ham-like fist. 'Not now, not now, Squirrel Head!' he snarled.

Squirrel Head deftly caught the coin Cranston threw and disappeared into a nearby pie shop. Cranston looked down the alleyway and stiffened as the doorway opened. A court gallant swaggered out, the door slamming shut behind him. Others followed: a servant carrying buckets, a young lady, her hips swaying provocatively. Athelstan was beginning to despair when suddenly the door swung open again and he gaped at the spectacle that unfolded. An old woman tried to rush out into the street, what appeared to be children hung on to her dusty skirts and plucked at her cloak as she dragged them along. Suddenly the old woman slipped, the grey wig falling off her head.

'It's the Vicar!' Cranston roared. 'Flaxwith!'

Already the bailiff had released Samson, who sped like an arrow to join the pandemonium. The Vicar of Hell, his disguise now thrown, was desperately fighting off the scrimperers, who buzzed about like flies. Samson gripped his ankle: the Vicar yelped with pain. He slipped on a clod of mud and disappeared in a welter of bodies. Samson, apparently believing his task now done, went for the ankle of one of the bailiffs running to assist. Windows were opened and a crowd began to gather as Cranston and Athelstan hurried down. Flaxwith was wielding his staff. Samson, lured by the sweet cooking smells from Dame Broadsheet's, had now sped indoors looking for more juicy morsels. Cranston laid about with the flat of his sword until order was imposed. The Vicar of Hell, slightly ridiculous in his ragged dress, his face covered in white chalk, was manacled and bound between two bailiffs. Now and again he would wince at the pain where Samson had bitten him or glower at the scrimperers.

'We caught him,' one of the little men shouted, jumping up and down, his wizened face bright with pleasure. 'Sir John, we caught him creeping downstairs. I sees him kiss the girl. I've never seen a beldame kiss like that!'

Cranston, ignoring the Vicar of Hell, congratulated the scrimperers who danced around, clutching at the coins he tossed into their outstretched hands. Athelstan gazed in astonishment. The scrimperers had nut-brown faces, bright eyes, but their features seemed out of joint, like children wearing masks at some mummers' play. Their dress only emphasised this: motley rags, small leather boots, each armed with dirk or poniard no bigger than a man's hand.

'You're a clever bastard!' the Vicar of Hell bawled.

Cranston grinned. 'It was the only way, sir. Get the scrimperers through the cracks and into the house. They broke in through a window at the back.'

'We watched the stairs and passageways,' one of them shouted. 'No one ever noticed us.'

'And if they had,' another added, 'we'd have been gone before they caught us.'

'Went in early this morning before dawn. A busy house, Sir John, a molly shop if there ever was one. Young girls coming and going, footsteps in the gallery, cups of wine and squeals of laughter.' The leader of the scrimperers beat his little glove against his thigh, raising small puffs of dust.

'But now you are finished,' Cranston declared proudly. 'It's to the Guildhall for all of you. Seek out the chief beadle. He'll also give you coins, some provisions. Here…' He took one of the small seals he always carried in his purse and handed it to the man. 'Just show that and all will be well.'

The scrimperers disappeared, shouting and laughing as they went. Cranston snapped his fingers. Flaxwith pushed the Vicar back into the cavernous taproom of Dame Broadsheet's house. The atmosphere was sombre. Dame Broadsheet stood at the foot of the stairs, one hand covering her mouth. Behind her the girls had gathered, gaping at this great coroner and his illustrious prisoner. Scullions and tapsters appeared from behind doors. Cranston, enjoying himself, strode into the centre of the room.

'A cup of your best claret, Dame Broadsheet. I mean your best, no droppings from the vat.'

This was brought in the twinkling of an eye. Cranston toasted the Vicar of Hell. 'How many years is it, sir, three or four since I tried to lay you by the heels? It's Newgate for you, my lad, and then before the King's Justices at Westminster. You,' Cranston grinned evilly at Dame Broadsheet, 'and your accomplices. It is a felony to harbour a known criminal.'

'They didn't know I was here,' the Vicar of Hell retorted.

'What's your name?' Athelstan asked, coming forward.

'I have no name, Father. Once, like you, I was in Holy Orders. Now I'm a leaf on life's stream and, by the looks of it, soon washed up. Father, intercede with Sir John. These good ladies have nothing to do with me.'

'Not even Clarice?' Athelstan asked. 'I had a visit from William the Weasel. I know you are moonstruck over the girl.' He stepped closer, his voice dropping to a whisper. 'Why were you so eager to distance yourself from the murder of the clerks of the Green Wax?'

The Vicar of Hell looked away. 'Not here, Father.' His lips hardly moved. 'There's a time and place.' He glanced up, his eyes full of mischief, so boyish that Athelstan's heart warmed to him. 'I may even throw some light on the great miracle at St Erconwald's.'

'But not here?'

'No, Father, not here.'

Athelstan looked over his shoulder at Cranston, who nodded.

'Take him away!'

And the Vicar of Hell, head held high, was pushed out into the street. Cranston clapped his hands and called Dame Broadsheet over. 'I want to talk with one of your girls, Clarice.'

The pert little girl came over, all coy and simpering. Cranston gestured at Athelstan. 'You have questions for our young lady?'

Athelstan stared into the girl's beautiful blue eyes. She reminded him so much of Cecily the courtesan, he could have sworn they were twins. Dame Broadsheet hovered anxiously behind her.

'Do you remember?' he asked. 'That night with the clerks at the Dancing Pig?'

Clarice nodded.

'Remember what you told me? How the young man you were with, Alcest, never left your bed the whole night through. You were lying, weren't you?'

Clarice looked over her shoulder at Dame Broadsheet.

'Answer, girl!' Cranston thundered. 'Or I'll have you and this whole establishment in the common room at the Fleet!'

The mention of one of London's worst hellholes sent Dame Broadsheet and all her girls aflutter.

'I woke up,' the young girl replied. 'I saw Alcest put something in my drink, so I spilt it on the rushes. I pretended to sleep. He left me, dressing quickly, and went out through a window. Our chamber was at the back of the Dancing Pig. Alcest climbed down. He must have been gone an hour and a half, then he came back; that's all I know.'

'And that's all we need to know.'

Athelstan stepped back. 'Sir John, what happens to these ladies and their house is a matter for the law, but young Clarice has been most helpful.'

Cranston thrust the wine cup back into Dame Broadsheet's hands. 'I shall think about matters,' he declared sonorously. 'I shall reflect and ponder, Dame Broadsheet. I shall have words with our young Vicar of Hell and then I'll make a judgement.'

Dame Broadsheet sank to her knees, hand clasped. 'Sir John, you have a heart as big as your frame. My house and all that is in it,' she simpered, 'are forever at your disposal.'

'Don't be so bloody stupid!' Cranston snapped. 'If the Lady Maude heard that, you and everything in this place would be put on board ship and sent to the Great Cham of Tartary.'

He glanced balefully round and, followed by Athelstan and Flaxwith, left the taproom. Once they were out of the alleyway, Cranston shook Flaxwith's hand.

'A good morning's work, Henry. Good man! The Vicar of Hell arrested. Dame Broadsheet knows the difference between right and wrong whilst Master Alcest is in for some interesting questions.' He stretched till his muscles cracked. 'Now, be a good lad, Henry, and go back to the Guildhall. There's a chest in my chamber; the key is in the corner under the statue of the Virgin and Child. Unlock it and bring my second wineskin.' He looked at Athelstan. 'Where to now, Brother?'

'Master Drayton's house,' Athelstan replied. 'Perhaps Henry and two of his burliest boys could call on Flinstead and Stablegate? They, too, have questions to answer.' Athelstan looked up at the sky. 'But in the meantime, Sir John, I would like to have words with Master Tibault Lesures.'

The Master of the Rolls was even more agitated than last time when he came down the stairs. 'Oh, Sir John!' he wailed. 'I have heard about Master Napham's death and Alcest is in the Tower!'

'He can bloody well stay there.'

Cranston pushed the Master of the Rolls into the chamber. Once inside, Lesures, his hands outstretched, gazed beseechingly at Brother Athelstan. 'I have committed no crime,' he said, but the friar glimpsed the calculating look in his eyes.

'Come, come, Master Tibault.' Athelstan walked over. 'You know more than you admit. Master Alcest, what mischief did he get up to? And, more importantly, sir, how did he become cock of the roost here?' Athelstan stared into Lesures' old shrewd eyes. 'To do evil, sir, is not just a matter of committing a sin: it's also turning your head and pretending you don't see.'

'I don't know what they did,' Master Tibault stuttered.

'What I am more interested in,' Athelstan persisted, 'is how they made you turn your head. Now, you can answer here or, perhaps, accompany us to the Tower. We're going there to interrogate Master Alcest. He doesn't know it yet, so it's best if we kept it a secret.'

Tibault breathed in. 'Two years ago,' he began, sitting down, 'Alcest found out my little secret. There's a house in Cross Street,' he smiled bleakly at Cranston, 'within bowshot of the priory of St John of Jerusalem. It's beyond the city limits. You can drink there with…'

'With young men?' Athelstan asked.

'Yes, Brother, so tactfully put.'

'And Alcest found out?'

'Yes, Alcest found out. He did not threaten me, he just said it was our little secret.'

'And in return?'

'In return nothing, Brother.' Tibault grasped Athelstan's hand. 'I swear,' he declared hoarsely, 'I know nothing of what they did.'

'But you had suspicions?'

'Oh yes. Now and again, during the day, Alcest would leave. He would meet with different people in this tavern or that.'

'How do you know?'

'On one occasion I followed him. Sometimes, when the clerks thought I was gone, I would eavesdrop on their chatter. They would talk in whispers.' Lesures gabbled on. 'Once I heard Alcest and Peslep having angry words with Chapler: he was indignant about something. Afterwards, they kept well away from him. On another occasion, when the doors had been left slightly ajar, I came upstairs in my slippers. Chapler was absent because of the gripes in his stomach. The clerks were gathering together at the far end of the room. They were discussing money matters. Alcest seemed to be defending himself.'

'Did you learn anything else?'

'They appeared to be accusing Alcest of keeping monies due to them, but the matter seems to have been resolved.'

'And did they mention any names?'

Lesures closed his eyes.

'Come on, sir!' Cranston barked.

'Once I heard them talk of the Vicar of Hell.'

'And you,' Cranston poked him in the chest, 'know who the Vicar of Hell is, sir. A well-known outlaw.'

Tibault's face was as white as wax.

'You'd best confess all,' Athelstan murmured.

'I also heard them mention the usurer who was murdered.'

'Drayton?'

'Yes, that's the one. Alcest knew one of his clerks, a man called Stablegate.'

Chapter 11

Sir John and Athelstan stood in the parlour of Drayton's house. The coroner kept looking over his shoulder, waiting for Flaxwith's arrival.

'Lesures is still hiding something,' Athelstan remarked.

'Oh, I am sure he is, Brother,' Cranston replied. 'Whichever way he jumps he's in trouble. The Master of the Rolls is supposed to exercise better control over his clerks. A corrupt man,' he continued. 'Soft and treacherous. Lesures likes to have his cake and eat it. I intend to return to the matter in due course. Now, Brother, you have a solution to this matter?'

'I think so, Sir John, but I am going to need the cooperation of our two clerks. Which of them do you think is the more amenable?'

Cranston pulled a face. 'Stablegate's as hard as steel.'

'Then the stage is set,' Athelstan rejoined. 'Come on, Sir John, let's walk on to it!'

They went down the gloomy passageway, the smell of mildew and corruption stronger than ever. Athelstan paused and stared into the darkness.

'This is a cold and dismal place, Sir John. It reeks of evil. What will happen to this house when we are finished?'

'The property of the Crown,' Cranston replied. 'The Regent will sell it and make a profit.'

'It needs to be exorcised and blessed,' Athelstan murmured. 'Ghosts still linger here.'

The door of the counting house had been rehung but Athelstan noticed how an iron stud just beneath the grille had been loosened. The bolt on the inside was quick to the touch and easy to turn. He beckoned Sir John in and closed the door. Athelstan pulled down the grille and stared through it as if searching for something.

Cranston heard a sound and sighed. 'Here comes Flaxwith with my miraculous wineskin. He's also brought our guests.'

Athelstan opened the door. Flaxwith, hot-faced, thrust the wineskin into Sir John's hand. Behind him the two clerks stood sullen-eyed. Athelstan studied them carefully. Sir John was right: Stablegate was obdurate but Flinstead's lower lip quivered, eyes constantly blinking. Athelstan made his decision.

'Henry, take Master Stablegate back to the parlour and keep him there. Flinstead can stay with me for a while.'

Flaxwith beckoned. Stablegate was about to refuse but Samson, who had been sniffing further up the gallery, now made his appearance; he growled at the clerk who hastened to obey. Once they had gone, Athelstan beckoned Flinstead forward.

'A clever murder, eh, master clerk?'

'Brother Athelstan,' he spluttered. 'I don't know what you mean!'

'Oh, yes you do,' Athelstan replied. He winked at Cranston who stood, wineskin in one hand, watching him intently. Athelstan took Flinstead by the arm and led him to the iron-studded door. 'Now, sir, look at this: here's a door to match all doors. Strongly hinged...'

Flinstead kept looking over his shoulder at the damage done to the far wall.

'Oh, don't worry about that,' Athelstan declared. 'This room had secrets, Master Flinstead. No hidden passageways or oubliettes but it did have secrets known only to Master Drayton and, of course, you and Stablegate.'

'I don't know what you mean!'

'Then let me explain. Drayton was a miser, a usurer, a hard taskmaster. He kept you under the whip. Most of his monies were kept out of this house well away from greedy fingers. However, you and Stablegate heard that the Lombards were bringing down a bag of silver, thousands of pounds. So you laid your plans. How could you murder Master Drayton and yet scream innocence of any crime? If you secretly filched it and Drayton lived, how far could you flee? If you openly stole it, and Drayton died, you'd be cast as outlaws who would never get as far as Dover. So you plotted very carefully. In the days before the arrival of the silver,' Athelstan continued, walking to the door, 'you worked at one of these bosses. The sharpened pieces face the outside but you noticed that the door's one weakness is that these bosses are screwed in by clasps on the inside.'

Athelstan pointed to one just beneath the grille. 'You worked at this. Whenever Drayton was away from his office, you strove to loosen the clasp on the inside. It wouldn't take long. The clasp was loosened and the steel boss could be removed. You then cleaned it, coating it with oil so that it no longer stuck into the wood and could be moved in and out whenever you wished.' Athelstan paused and stared into Flinstead's face, white as a sheet and covered in a sheen of sweat. 'Ah, Master Flinstead,' he whispered, 'I have the truth of it – your face tells me all.'

'I, I...' Flinstead stuttered. 'I don't know what you mean, Brother.'

'Yes you do, you little pudding bag!' Cranston hissed.

'Now,' Athelstan continued, 'on the night in question everything was prepared. During the afternoon you removed the clasp from the inside. Drayton wouldn't notice because the metal boss was still stuck in. In the evening, just before you left, the robbery took place. Drayton would not be expecting you. One of you came into this counting house, took the bags of silver, threatening Master Drayton with a knife, crossbow or whatever. Bloodthirsty threats, perhaps even promises to return. The robber then left. Drayton, all agitated, locks and bolts the door. He doesn't raise the hue and cry: the robber might be waiting. He has lost his silver and he's fearful lest he lose his life. Now, our criminal clerk has fled.'

Athelstan paused, then shut the door, drawing the bolts over. 'And this is where the horrible beauty of this crime occurs. The other clerk, pretending all innocence, comes hurrying down. "Master," he would wail, "what is wrong?" Whatever he says, he brings Drayton to the door and the grille is opened. Our poor miser thinks he is speaking to an innocent man who is loud in his condemnation of his criminous colleague. Drayton presses close to the door, full of concern…'

'Wouldn't he open the door?' Flinstead interrupted.

Cranston came over, his wineskin in one hand. 'Of course not, you little liar. Drayton had just been robbed, pushed back in his room. He wasn't too sure what was happening. He'd do what any sane man would do, lock and bolt the door lest the outlaw return to kill him. Now he hears a tap on the door, cries of concern. Whatever has happened, Drayton knows he is safe as long as he doesn't open that door.'

'Which we shall now do,' Athelstan declared.

He opened the door and beckoned Sir John to step outside. Then he closed the door and pulled down the grille, staring through it.

'Drayton's all anxious,' he continued. 'One of his clerks is a felon but the other is acting quite innocent. Drayton's too astute to open the door but at least he'll stand by the grille and gabble, perhaps ask him for help. What he fails to realise is that the clerk on the other side of the door has carefully and silently removed the metal boss. He's also brought a small arbalest, the bolt already in the groove. Drayton has his body pressed against the door, there's now a sizeable hole which exposes his body. The assassin on the other side of the door releases the catch and the bolt is fired. Drayton takes it in his chest and staggers back, falling to the ground. In his death throes he has only one thought, to reach the far wall, to seek forgiveness for another more ancient sin.'

Athelstan saw the puzzlement in Flinstead's face. 'Oh yes, sir,' he went on, opening the door to let Sir John in and closing it behind him, 'there's more to this chamber than meets the eye. A place of evil but for you, sir, the perfect crime. The silver has gone. The door is locked and bolted, Drayton is dead within. Who can blame you? You place the metal boss back in the hole and rejoin your accomplice.'

Athelstan studied the door again. 'I hadn't thought of that,' he murmured. He opened the door, removed the boss, knelt down and peered through. 'Even if Drayton had not come to the door,' he sang out, 'a crossbow, a small arbalest, could be used against him anywhere in his counting chamber.'

Flinstead wetted his lips.

'Now, to perfect your crime,' Athelstan continued, 'you lock and bolt the front door then steal out through one of the windows, making sure no one sees you. After that, it's heigh-ho to one of the taverns. The following morning you return to the house and make sure you are standing outside when Master Flaxwith makes his rounds. You are all concerned. Flaxwith, the honest bailiff, tries to assist. You explain what has happened and lead poor Flax-with by the nose. You go round the outside of the house. You deliberately ignore the window through which you left the previous evening but, instead, break in through one properly secured.'

'Once you were in the house,' Cranston remarked, coming up and poking Flinstead in the chest, 'you were safe. Flaxwith, all distracted, eager to find out what happened to Master Drayton, is brought down to the counting room. I am sure one of you slipped away and properly secured the window through which you left the night before, making it look as if the entire house had been properly secured and locked.'

'Now we come to this door,' Athelstan declared. 'Locked and bolted but with the grille down. Flaxwith knows it's secure. He peers through the grille but, in the gloom, cannot see much. After a great deal of commotion, the door is forced. Everyone throngs into the room. There's no suspicion about the door, it's locked and bolted and there's a bloody corpse on the floor. While the bailiffs bustled around, you or Stablegate put the clasp back on the metal boss on the inside. It could be done in a few seconds: cleaned and greased the clasp can be spun on and, if necessary, tightened later. The perfect crime, eh, Master Flinstead?'

'This is ridiculous!' he sputtered. 'You can't prove it!'

'Oh, yes I can,' Cranston retorted. 'The carpenter who examined the door will swear how the metal boss beneath the grille has been loosened, removed, greased and reclasped. It's the only solution, Master Flinstead. And, again, there's no real mystery about how you left the house.' Cranston took a swig from his wineskin then stretched till his muscles cracked. 'So, it's Tyburn for you, my lad.'

'A perfect crime,' Athelstan declared. 'You knew the silver was coming: you loosened the boss, you knew which one, eh? How many times have you and Stablegate seen your master peer through the grille?'

Flinstead just shook his head.

'Of course,' Athelstan continued, 'something might have gone wrong. However, your master had no kith or kin, you had all night, and some of the next day, to put it right.' He shrugged. 'Or even flee. As it was you committed a crime which you thought no one could lay against you. Well, at least till now.'

Flinstead slid down the wall, putting his arms across his chest as if feeling a draught of icy air. Cranston crouched down beside him.

'Do you want a drink, lad? It will warm your belly and feed your wits.'

Flinstead shook his head.

'Now for robbery and murder,' Cranston spoke quietly as if discussing the weather, 'you just hang. But the silver you stole belonged to the Regent. His Grace John, Duke of Lancaster. That's treason. So it will be no quick death. The executioner will wait until you are half dead, then cut you down from the gallows, slice your body from neck to crotch and pull your heart and entrails so you see them before your eyes close. Afterwards, he'll cut you up like a butcher does collops of meat. Your head will be fixed over London Bridge. Your quarters? Well, heaven knows where they will go. One to Temple Bar, perhaps the rest to the ports, Dover and Southampton, all nicely pickled in a bucket.'

Flinstead's head sagged.

'Take him out!' Athelstan declared. 'Sir John, put him in another room in the house. Well away from Stablegate.' He winked. 'Haven't you read the Book of Daniel, Sir John?'

Cranston caught his drift. He hauled Flinstead to his feet and pushed him out of the counting house. Athelstan stood, arms crossed, staring down at the floor. He felt excited yet cold, as he always did when he trapped a murderer. Excited because he had resolved the mystery, cold at the terrible evil he had witnessed. On the one hand, Drayton's blood cried to heaven for vengeance but, on the other, Athelstan knew that Cranston's words were no empty threat. Flinstead would stand before King's Bench, the Justices would convict and the young clerk would suffer a horrifying sentence. Athelstan closed his eyes.

'O Lord,' he prayed quietly, 'don't hold their blood to my account. You, the searcher of hearts, know that I am innocent of any desire for their lives.'

He opened his eyes as Cranston pushed the arrogant Stablegate into the room.

'Sir John, what is this?' the clerk protested.

'Shut up!' the coroner bawled. He pointed to a stool. 'Sit down!' Cranston came across to Athelstan, his face red with excitement, whiskers positively bristling, blue eyes popping. 'What now, my little monk?' he whispered.

'Friar, Sir John!'

'Bugger that! Are you going to tell him the same story?'

Athelstan plucked Cranston by the sleeve and, looking round the portly coroner, stared at Stablegate. The young man gazed flint-eyed back.

'Have you ever been in the presence of a demon, Sir John?' Athelstan murmured. 'Well, if not, count this the first time. Stablegate will tell us nothing.'

'So what do we do?'

'Silence, Sir John.'

Both the coroner and Brother Athelstan waited. Now and again the friar would walk towards the door and ostentatiously begin to undo the clasp. He glanced over his shoulder at Stablegate who just watched him, narrow-eyed.

'What am I doing here?' the clerk protested. 'Sir John, if you are to arrest me then swear out the warrants. If not, let me go.'

Athelstan screwed the clasp back on more tightly. 'Is this some game?' Stablegate scoffed.

He froze as Sir John abruptly whipped out his broad stabbing dirk, walked across and grabbed him by the hair, pressing the dagger into the soft flesh of his neck.

'In my long eventful life,' the coroner rasped, 'I have killed good men. God be my witness, I am sorry, but I took their lives in battle. They were warriors. They fought for what was right as I did. I regret every spot of blood I have split. Each day I pray for their souls. I have given money to the almshouses but you, sir, are nothing but a bag of corruption, a thief, a swindler, a murderer, a lying toad from hell!'

Stablegate remained unabashed and Athelstan secretly marvelled at the iron-hard malice of the man.

'Cut me or cut me free,' Stablegate retorted.

'Oh, I'll cut,' Sir John breathed, resheathing his dagger. 'A thousand cuts and a thousand more. Brother, how long do I have to have the stench of this turd in my nostrils?'

'Take him away now,' Athelstan ordered. 'Put him back with Master Flaxwith and bring Flinstead here.'

Sir John pulled the clerk to his feet and pushed him out. Flinstead returned drying the tears on his cheeks. Athelstan waved him to the stool.

'You may well weep, sir,' he began. 'I have sung the same song to Master Stablegate as I did to you.'

Flinstead glanced up.

'He's confessed, you know. He claims that he stole the silver, but you killed Drayton.'

'That's a lie!' Flinstead screamed, jumping to his feet. 'It was Stablegate! His idea from the start! When Drayton used to keep us waiting outside, Stablegate would study that bloody door. At night, in the tavern, he developed his scheme. It took a week to loosen that boss: I would take the accounts into Drayton and distract him whilst Stablegate worked on the clasp.' Flinstead held up his hands. 'God be my witness, I stole the silver. I told Drayton I had knocked Stablegate unconscious and that there were footpads in the house who were bent on slitting his throat. I ran down the passageway with the silver. Drayton locked the door and began screaming. Stablegate then went back. He was pretending to be hurt. "Master," he croaked. I heard him whilst waiting in the shadows. "Master, Flinstead has struck me! It is me. Master, look!"'

'Was it dark in the passageway?' Athelstan asked.

'Oh yes. Stablegate had removed the boss. He then loosed the crossbow.' Flinstead shrugged. 'The rest is as you described. We went out of a window which we carefully closed behind us. Stablegate insisted that we spend the evening being well seen by other people. The next morning, we came back. We knew Flaxwith would be doing his usual rounds. We broke in through a window and while Stablegate took him down to the strongroom, I locked the shutters we had opened the night before.'

'And then Master Flaxwith organised the door being broken down?'

Flinstead nodded.

'And Stablegate secured the boss he'd removed the previous night,' Athelstan added. 'He'd coated it with a glue so that when the door was broken down it held fast and, in the confusion, one of you simply replaced the clasp on the inside.'

'Yes,' Flinstead moaned. 'We practised it so many times. Stablegate even had a piece of wood made containing a boss and clasp. He showed me how it could be done: a crossbow bolt is only an inch across, the hole is at least twice that. He said Drayton would come to the grille; at such a close distance, any wound would kill. Drayton would be dead by morning...' His voice trailed off.

'And the silver?'

Flinstead slumped down on the stool. 'Sir John, I don't know. Stablegate took it off me. He says he's hidden it.'

'Do you know where?'

Flinstead shook his head. 'Heaven be my witness, Sir John, I was so agitated, so nervous after…'

'Drayton had been murdered.' Athelstan finished his sentence.

'Well?' Cranston asked. 'Surely you must know? You are his companion in crime.'

'Stablegate said that he didn't fully trust me. I was too nervous but at the right time we'd take the silver with us.'

'Where did you plan to go?'

'Stablegate was sure that, although we might be suspected, nothing could be proved. We'd leave the country, go across the Narrow Seas.'

'Ah.' Athelstan sighed and crouched down beside the young man. 'Listen, look up!'

Flinstead lifted his head.

'You may be nervous,' Athelstan continued. 'But you are also a killer. You slew a man in cold blood and stole what was not yours. Stablegate was right. It would be very hard to prove that you were the killers. It would have remained a mystery if it hadn't been for that door.'

'Come to the point, Brother!' Cranston snapped, standing behind him. 'The day is long and we have other business to do.'

'Oh, Flinstead knows my point,' Athelstan replied. 'Much suspected, nothing proven, eh? But you know, Sir John, any attempt by these two lovelies to leave the kingdom, particularly if they were suspected of stealing so much silver, would have been carefully scrutinised. You need a licence to go beyond the seas. That's why Alcest, the clerk from the Chancery of the Green Wax, came down here, wasn't it?'

'I think so,' Flinstead mumbled. 'Stablegate said he would take care of that.'

Athelstan tapped him under the chin. 'Oh, I am sure he would, Master Flinstead, he would have also taken care of you. A knife in the back and another corpse is pulled from the Thames, eh?' Athelstan got to his feet. 'I think it's time for Stablegate.'

The second clerk had hardly entered the room when he looked at Flinstead and realised what had happened.

'You snivelling bastard! You caitiff! They have trapped you, haven't they? I told them nothing.'

He would have lunged at Flinstead if Flaxwith, standing behind, had not given him a firm rap across the shoulder with his cudgel. Stablegate, wincing with pain, fell to one knee. Flaxwith dragged him back to his feet; nevertheless, the clerk was still defiant.

'You fat, red-faced bastard!' he sneered at Cranston. 'You and your little mouse of a friar. Well. I don't mind. Drayton was a hard-nosed, avaricious bag of turds. Life is hard. It's only a short dance at Tyburn.' His face became contorted with rage. 'As long as Flinstead dies beside me, I couldn't give a fig!' He shook his fist at Cranston. 'You can tell that to the bloody Regent! He'll never get his silver!' Stablegate stopped and smiled maliciously. 'Of course...' His voice had fallen to a whisper.

'Where's the silver?' Cranston took a step closer. He took his dagger out and pressed the tip into Stablegate's chin.

Stablegate stretched out his hands. 'What is it, Cranston? A journey downriver to the Tower? The King's torturers? Do you think I'd give up the silver then? And if I die, what will His Grace the Regent say to that, eh?'

'You are an evil young man,' Athelstan accused.

'Piss off, priest! Sir John knows what I'm talking about. Don't you realise, Flinstead,' he raised his voice, 'there's hope yet. Now you can see why I hid the silver. You'd have blabbed all.'

'What do you want?' Cranston asked.

'Sanctuary,' Stablegate demanded. 'Sanctuary for me and Flinstead. The right to flee to Mary Le Bow. We'll stay there forty days.'

'And then you'll abjure the realm,' Cranston said. 'You'll be taken to the nearest port, thrown on the first available ship and if you set foot in England again, you'll hang.' Cranston rubbed his chin. 'The Crown will post a reward on your heads,' he added. 'One hundred pounds dead or alive. You can beg, across the Narrow Seas, but set foot in any English port and every harbour reeve looking for a quick profit will have your name and description.'

Cranston took Stablegate by the arm and marched him across to the counting desk. 'Sit there,' he said. 'Take a quill.' He pointed to a scrap of parchment. 'Write down where you have hidden the silver. Then both of you can flee. Don't be stupid! Don't try and get beyond the city walls. We'll ride you down. Flaxwith here will ensure you take sanctuary in St Mary Le Bow.'

Stablegate struggled but Cranston's grip was vicelike. 'You are a horrible young man,' the coroner snarled. 'And if that silver isn't where you say it is, I'll go across and, sanctuary or not, I'll pull both of you out and watch you hang, be disembowelled and quartered! I'll even do it myself!'

Stablegate sat down. Sir John moved away. The room fell quiet except for the squeaking of Stablegate's quill.

'Oh, by the way,' Cranston called out. 'If anything happens to Flinstead before you leave England, you will have violated the law of sanctuary and you can be killed on the spot.'

'As the Book of Ecclesiastes says, Sir John,' Stablegate scoffed over his shoulder, 'there's a season and a time under heaven for everything.'

'And the clerks of the Green Wax?' Athelstan asked. 'What business did you have with Alcest?'

'Safe passage from the kingdom, but ask him yourself!'

Stablegate got to his feet, the parchment now crumpled into a ball. 'I have your word, Cranston?'

'You have my word. Drop that parchment on the floor. You and Flinstead can flee. Flaxwith will follow.'

Stablegate threw the parchment on to the ground. He made a rude gesture at Sir John and ran for the door; Flinstead needed no second bidding but followed. The coroner and the friar stood and listened to their feet pounding down the passageway, the front door being opened and slammed shut behind them.

'Is that just?' Flaxwith asked.

Cranston grinned evilly.

'You can't break your word, Sir John.' Flaxwith's eyes rounded in alarm. 'Holy Mother Church is most zealous about the law of sanctuary.'

Sir John picked up the parchment and tossed it from one hand to the other. 'Oh, they can stay forty days in St Mary Le Bow on bread and water. Then I'll have the two bastards marched down into Queenhithe. Now, Henry, you may think I'm a bastard, but I have a friend, Otto Grandessen, half merchant, half pirate, a *real* bastard. Otto owns a cog which does business in the Middle Seas, sailing to Aleppo and Damascus. He'll take those two beauties aboard. By the time Otto's finished with them, they'll wish they had died at Tyburn. He'll put them ashore at Palestine. There's not much mischief they can do in the desert surrounded by Saracens who would love to take their heads.' Cranston opened the piece of parchment. 'Go on, Henry, find where they have gone.'

The bailiff hurried off.

'Well?' Athelstan asked.

'The insolent…!' Cranston looked up. 'Oh, he's told us where the money is: they never took it out of the house. It's buried in the cellar.'

Athelstan made to follow him out, but the coroner waved him away. 'No, sit there, Brother, I'll find the bloody silver! If I know this house correctly, the floor will be beaten earth. When Henry comes back, tell him to join me.'

Cranston marched off and Athelstan sat down. He felt pleased: Stablegate and Flinstead were evil men. Whatever Drayton's crimes, he died a miserable death and Sir John's agreement to the criminals was more than just. Athelstan leaned back and closed his eyes. He felt a small glow of satisfaction and realised that, in their own way, he and the coroner had done God's work, as necessary and demanding as preaching and ministering to the parishioners of St Erconwald's. Athelstan's eyes flew open. Any feeling of goodwill disappeared as he recalled Watkin marching up and down.

'God knows what trickery they are up to,' Athelstan declared. 'But how and why?'

'I beg your pardon, Brother?'

Flaxwith stood in the doorway.

'I'm sorry, Henry, I'm just speaking to myself. Our two felons?'

'Headed into the porch of St Mary Le Bow like rats down a hole.'

'Good. Sir John wants you in the cellar.' Athelstan smiled. 'Yes, that's where they hid the silver. Stablegate must have put it there, planning to return at his own convenience. You'd best hurry.'

Athelstan cocked an ear at the string of colourful oaths he could hear from below. Flaxwith left and, for a while, Athelstan wondered how he could deal with the miraculous cross of St Erconwald's. He thought of Alison. She must be allowed to leave soon, Athelstan concluded. Sir John could not keep her here for ever. His mind wandered further: he recalled what Stablegate had said about the clerks of the Green Wax. Athelstan was now certain that Alcest, his companions and possibly Chapler had been involved in some subtle trickery, forging licences and letters. A very serious crime: the Vicar of Hell would have known about it, and any wolfshead or outlaw who needed a letter or an official writ would pay a heavy price. Alcest probably had a forged seal. Lesures might well suspect it but because of Alcest's blackmail, he dared not investigate or protest. But why the killings? Athelstan scuffed at the floor with the toe of his sandal. All the clerks involved had died grisly deaths, starting with Chapler. Was it a question of thieves falling out? Had Alcest become greedy and decided to keep their ill-gotten wealth for himself? He heard Cranston's voice in the corridor. The coroner, specks of dirt on his robe, strode into the counting room with two mud-covered sacks which jingled as he shook them.

'To those who knock, it shall be opened, those who seek shall find.'

'The Regent's silver?'

'Precisely. Those impertinent villains had buried it deep beneath an old chest. Do you know who found it?' Cranston shook the sacks as if they were bells. 'Samson, he started sniffing and scuffling...'

'That's why I have him,' Flaxwith announced proudly, coming in with the other valuables. 'Now, Sir John, surely the dog deserves a small stipend, or a juicy bone or a piece of meat?'

Cranston thrust the sacks into Flaxwith's already laden arms. 'The Corporation hires donkeys so why not dogs, eh, Henry?'

The bailiff looked puzzled. Cranston crouched down and patted the dog on his head. Athelstan was sure that, if dogs could smile, Samson did.

'Right!' Cranston got to his feet. 'Henry, get your burly boys and take that silver, the gold pieces and the candlesticks down to the Bardi in Leadenhall Street. Tell them Sir John has sent it. They are to count it, weigh it and send it under guard to the Regent at the Savoy Palace.' He pointed to the seals round the necks of the grubby sacks. 'It's all there and don't worry, the Bardi wouldn't dream of stealing a penny from John of Gaunt. Then go to the Guildhall and draw on the common purse.' He clapped the bailiff on the shoulder. 'You may take Samson to the Holy Lamb of God,' he added in a reverential whisper. 'And ask that good alewife for two blackjacks of ale and an onion pie for yourself as well as a nice piece of goose for the dog. I'll pay.'

Cranston watched as Flaxwith strode down the corridor as if he had just been anointed whilst Samson, who'd paused to cock his leg, wobbled behind as pompously as any Justice at Westminster.

'There goes a satisfied man,' Cranston murmured. 'Well, Brother, where to now? A word with Master Alcest?'

'In time, Sir John. However, I believe the Vicar of Hell might be partial to one of your agreements, so a visit to Newgate wouldn't be out of order.'

'It's Hanging Day there,' Cranston warned darkly.

'Good,' Athelstan replied. 'It will help concentrate the Vicar's mind, won't it?'

'You think Alcest is the assassin, don't you?'

'Yes, Sir John, I do. I believe he definitely killed Chapler, then, for his own obvious reasons, turned on his companions in crime.'

He and Sir John walked down the corridor and out of the house. Athelstan slammed the door and, stepping back, looked up at the dirt-covered windows.

'*Avaritia, radix malorum*, Sir John: the love of riches is the root of all evil. Or is it?' he added as if to himself. 'And is it the case now?'

Chapter 12

Athelstan crossed himself and murmured a silent prayer, as he always did when he approached the main gateway of Newgate prison. He and Sir John had just forced themselves through the press as the crowd assembled for Hanging Day. Six footpads who had preyed upon travellers along the old Roman road were now being dispatched as quickly as rats by a farmer. Newgate was a foulsome, horrid place. Athelstan could never decide which was the more offensive, the filth and dirt in which the prisoners were kept or the fawning attitude of the jailers and bailiffs: these smiled falsely and wrung their hands whenever Cranston appeared. Sir John had his own thoughts on the matter. Whenever he entered the prison, the coroner never drank, joked or bothered to pass the time with any of its officials.

'If I had my way,' he growled as they followed the jailer across the great cobbled yard to the cells, 'I'd burn this place to the ground, rebuild a new prison and put it under the governance of a good soldier. I'd certainly put an end to that.' Sir John pointed to an unfortunate who had refused to plead before the Justices; he was stripped, ready to be pressed under a heavy, oaken door until he agreed to plead either guilty or not guilty.

They left the yard and entered a mildewed corridor which ran past cells, veritable hellholes. The air was gloomy and the stench made Athelstan gag. Paltry sconce torches fought against the murky air and Athelstan tried to ignore the terrible din, the oaths, rantings and ravings of mad prisoners and the filthy abuse hurled at the jailer going ahead of them. They passed cell chambers; in one the corpses of executed felons lay like slabs of meat upon a butcher's stall. These would be placed in iron cages and taken out to be gibbeted along the roads leading into London. In another the corpses of executed criminals who had been hanged, drawn and quartered were being boiled and pickled before being given a coat of tar and placed over the gates of the city.

'Never come here!' Cranston warned. 'This is truly the abomination of the desolation. Every time I do,' he added in a whisper, 'I pray God will send fire from heaven to consume the place.'

They entered a large room where bailiffs and beadles were drinking or playing checkers or hazard.

'Good morning, Sir John.' A pox-faced beadle, one eye hidden beneath a patch, waved them over. The man pointed to the chessboard. 'Would you like a game, Sir John? King against king, bishop against bishop?'

Cranston shook his head. 'Some other time and certainly not here.'

They were about to follow the jailer down another narrow passageway when Athelstan stopped.

'Brother?'

'Sir John, the first riddle about a king defeating his enemies but, when the battle is over, both victor and vanquished lying in the same place: it describes a game of chess.'

Cranston told the jailer to wait. 'Of course!' he breathed. 'A game of chess! What does it prove, Brother?'

Athelstan rubbed his face. 'I don't know, Sir John. I think our assassin sees the murders as a game and, at the same time, is clearly proclaiming that he will play the game, even if he has to end up in the same place as the vanquished.'

'And that's the grave,' Cranston replied. 'It makes sense, Brother. If Alcest is our assassin, there's no doubt that he'll die as well.'

'But why should Alcest be prepared to put his own life at stake?'

'That I don't know, Brother.' They continued down the passageway until the jailer stopped at a door. 'At the heart of Newgate, Sir John.' His chapped, dirty face brightened with malicious glee. 'The Vicar of Hell deserves the best and the best he will get.'

He unlocked the door, swung it open and, going inside, fixed the sconce torch into a rusting clasp on the wall. The Vicar of Hell sat on a pile of straw in the corner; his ankles and wrists were loaded with chains which were clasped to iron rings in the wall. His face was covered in dirt and a large bruise darkened his right cheek, yet he still smiled cheekily.

'Sir John, I would rise and bow but...' He spread his hands in a rattle of chains. 'I suppose you've come to tell me that the Bishop of London has decided to reinstate me as a priest or the Regent has issued a pardon?'

'You'll hang, me bucko.' Cranston stood over him. 'Yet, when you've gone, I'll miss you.' He waited until the jailer closed the cell door behind him.

'Am I going to hang?' the Vicar asked softly and stared piteously at Athelstan. 'So many psalms yet to be sung. So much claret to be drunk.' He sighed. 'There again, I've seen the days and all good things must come to an end.'

Cranston stepped back to lean against the wall. Athelstan went over to the door and stared through the grille; the jailer, eavesdropping on the other side, scampered off.

'You are not a bad man,' Cranston continued. 'Not a really wicked soul. You are a rogue born and bred. You are attracted to villainy as a cat to cream.' He lifted a hand. 'But I swear, I don't wish to see you hang. Exiled from London, perhaps for two or three years.' Sir John paused and scratched his chin.

The Vicar of Hell was now all attention. 'And the terms, Sir John? What are the conditions?'

'The clerks of the Green Wax.'

'Oh, Sir John, you couldn't!'

'Oh, Sir John, I can,' Cranston quipped back. 'What's so special about them? Most of them are dead and have been replaced, whilst we know enough about Alcest to send him to do the hangman's dance at Tower Hill or Tyburn.'

'Agreed.' The Vicar of Hell sat back in the corner. 'If I tell you, Sir John, these chains are loosed?'

'If you tell me,' Cranston replied, 'you'll be a free man by dusk. However, if you are caught in the city again, it's summary justice: down on your knees, neck against a piece of wood and off goes your head!'

'It's like this, Sir John,' the Vicar began. 'People like myself have to – how can I put it? – move around. Go to this city or that. Travel beyond the seas. Or, when the fire becomes too hot, seek retirement by gaining a position in some merchant's household. To do that I need letters, warrants and licences. Now, what am I going to reveal will mean the closing of a loophole much loved by us villains. Tell me, Sir John, if I want such a letter or a licence what have I to do?'

'Well, you can apply to the mayor, sheriff or Corporation of London.'

'Yes, yes, Sir John, but you know me, as the good shepherd knows all the black sheep of his flock. So where else can I go?'

'You could apply to the Chancery, but such letters are only written at the behest of the Chancellor.'

'And it takes time,' the Vicar of Hell snapped. 'So what we do is this, Sir John. We take the name of a dead person. We then get a clerk like Alcest to petition the Chancellor on our behalf...'

'Of course,' Cranston interrupted. 'And if the petition has the recommendation of a clerk then it goes ahead and there'll be no delay.'

'Precisely, Sir John.'

'So,' Athelstan said stepping forward, 'if Philip Stablegate wishes to leave the country with a considerable amount of silver, he approaches Alcest. The clerk will then go through the records and extract the name of someone long dead. Let's call him Richard Martlew. The petition goes to the Chancellor, who will undoubtedly grant it because it's got a recommendation. Alcest will not even wait for the Chancellor to reply: he will draw up the document, Master Lesures seals it and the letter is issued. There are no forged seals.'

'In a word, yes,' Cranston replied. 'Now, let us say this Martlew decides to leave England by one of the Cinque Ports. The reeve or harbourmaster probably can't even read. He doesn't give a fig if Martlew is Stablegate, but he is trained to examine the seal. False seals can soon be detected but, if it's genuine, he won't even dream of stopping the person concerned.'

'Isn't a record kept?' Athelstan asked. 'I mean, the petition itself and the Chancellor's reply endorsing it? And what happens if someone can prove that Richard Martlew is long dead?'

The Vicar of Hell clapped his hands in a crash of chains. 'What's the use of that, Brother? Can't you see the subtlety of the scheme? It was the Chancery Office which authorised the letter to be written, not Alcest or Lesures. Moreover, Alcest could easily prove that he thought it *was* Martlew and that he didn't even dream anything was wrong. He simply received a petition which he endorsed and sent to the Chancellor. Such requests are never refused: the letter, licence or warrant is drawn up and sealed. That's what Alcest did. And who is going to betray him? To do that would be sealing your own death warrant.'

'But stop! Surely,' Athelstan asked, 'there would be a discrepancy over the date? I mean, it's issued almost immediately.'

'No, Brother,' Cranston retorted. 'I can now see what our good friend means by a loophole. Let's say you petitioned the Chancellor to travel to Calais: you put the petition in through Alcest, he would recommend or not recommend. He would also ensure the wrong date, perhaps ten days later, is put on the petition and dispatched to the Chancery Office. The Chancellor doesn't see it, some clerk in his office simply writes "approved", or the Latin *placet*, "it pleases", and then it's sent back. Alcest, meanwhile, has drawn up the licence, perhaps adding another two days on. Accordingly, a petition which looks as if it was drawn up on the tenth of August and issued, let's say, on the twenty-second, really only took a day or two. It's been done before, everybody abuses the system. What Alcest did was not just accept pennies, as other clerks have done for approval of a petition: he knowingly arranged for letters and licences to be issued to wolfsheads, outlaws and counterfeit men. Most clerks would certainly baulk at that. Alcest didn't.'

'And that was the source of their wealth?'

'Of course!' the Vicar of Hell scoffed. 'And no one dared betray Alcest. For the first time, Brother, people like myself could travel freely, and protected by the law thanks to him.'

He rattled his chains at Sir John. 'Alcest and his coven are for the dark, if they haven't gone there already. Our good coroner here will ensure the Chancery Office strikes hard and either closes this loophole or cuts it off. There will also be some interesting times when the Chancellor orders the scrutineers to go through past records. I certainly don't want it bruited abroad that it was I who betrayed Alcest. I may have my life, but Sir John has received very valuable information in return.'

'Aye, you're right,' Cranston sighed. 'And it would have gone on. Alcest's replacement would be approached and the offer of gold for a simple letter is very hard to resist.' He squatted down before the Vicar. 'Did Lesures know about this?'

'Oh come, come, Sir John! Lesures is well known for his love of a pretty pair of buttocks. Alcest would have known that.' He shrugged. 'Lesures had nothing to fear: there was no forged seal, so he just had to turn a blind eye.'

Athelstan crossed his arms and wondered if Lesures really was the plaintive old man he pretended to be. Or did he have a hand in these deaths? Had he grown tired of Alcest's blackmailing or did he wish to take over the counterfeiting for himself?

'And that's all you can tell us?' Cranston barked.

'Do I have my freedom, Sir John?'

'I'll leave instructions with the chief jailer. You'll walk free this evening.'

'You'll not let it be known what I told you about Alcest?'

'No. I'll keep it as if Athelstan heard it under the seal of confession. However, I don't want to see your pretty face in London for many a summer.'

'Oh, don't worry, Sir John.' The Vicar of Hell wetted his lips. 'I think it's time I travelled. Perhaps Clarice can join me. But I have your word I won't hang?'

Cranston agreed again.

'And mine,' Brother Athelstan added, turning to shout for the jailer.

'You are good men.'

Cranston laughed.

'You are good men,' the Vicar of Hell repeated, his face now serious.

For the first time ever, Athelstan could see this young man as a priest, celebrating Mass or speaking from the pulpit.

'I am a villain,' the Vicar continued, 'and the world is full of knavery, but neither of you are corrupt. What Alcest and the rest did, well, there's not a Crown Official who doesn't take a coin slipped under the counter, but you are different. You are honest as the day is long. So I'll give you two pieces of information free. First, that other clerk, the one who was fished from the Thames?'

'Chapler?'

'Yes, that's the one. He was like you, Sir John. He didn't take bribes. He never consorted with the whores. All my villains steered well clear of him. They did business with Alcest.'

'That is interesting,' Athelstan murmured.

'Aye, Brother, it is, and I've got something for you. I've heard about your miraculous crucifix. Even the cut-throats and footpads around Whitefriars are wondering whether to pay it a visit.'

'But you don't think it's a miracle, do you?'

'No, Brother, I don't. The Good Lord is too busy to visit Southwark. You're the next thing to Christ that lot will get!'

Athelstan sketched a bow in compliment.

'Now, if our good coroner lets me go before the curfew bell, I know someone who can help, provided he can enter and leave Southwark without arrest.'

'Who?' Athelstan asked.

'The Sanctus Man. There's not a false relic he hasn't sold, not one piece of subtle trickery he hasn't practised. Let Cranston release me and you be at your church when Vespers rings. If your crucifix is miraculous, the Sanctus Man will tell you.'

Cranston clapped his hands. 'Oh, what a day! What a day!' he crowed. 'The Vicar of Hell in Newgate and now the Sanctus Man is about to emerge. How I'd love to finger his collar!'

'No, Sir John, you must give me your word that he can come and go without fear,' Athelstan pleaded.

'Oh, you have my word,' the coroner replied. 'But the Sanctus Man is another rogue born and bred. He sold Christ's crown of thorns fifteen times. His ability to make people part with their money is a miracle in itself.'

'At Vespers then?' the Vicar of Hell insisted.

Cranston agreed. Athelstan sketched a blessing and they walked back through the cavernous passages of Newgate to the jailers' lodge. Cranston stepped into the keeper's small office and re-emerged smiling from ear to ear.

'Our Vicar is now free, Brother, or will be, within the hour.'

'Will he keep his word?' Athelstan asked.

'Oh yes, for such people their word is their bond. The Sanctus Man will be there. Now for Master Alcest...'

Cranston and Athelstan made their way along West-chepe, down Friday Street to where barges waited at the wharf. They clambered into one and the wherry men, straining at their oars, pulled the barge into midstream.

'Do you think Alcest will confess?' Cranston asked, making himself comfortable in the stern.

'Perhaps,' Athelstan replied. 'We know he is guilty of counterfeiting but whether he is an assassin or not...?' Athelstan sat back and closed his eyes.

'You are not going to sleep, Brother?'

'No, Sir John, I am not. We are approaching London Bridge and when we go under the arches my stomach positively dances.'

'O man of little faith,' Cranston quipped. 'Why are you so frightened of death?'

'I am not, Sir John.' Athelstan smiled. 'It's just drowning I fear.'

The coroner sat forward, however, and began to exchange pleasantries with the two wherry men, drawing them into good-natured banter. As they approached the bridge, Cranston's heart skipped a beat: the water was bubbling like oil in a pot as it gushed under the narrow arches of the bridge. The noise became like thunder. Cranston lost his wager with the wherry men for, as they shot through, narrowly missing the starlings or wooden partitions built to buttress the stone pillars, he closed his eyes as everyone did, not opening them until they were out into the quiet water near Botolph's Wharf. The pace of their journey slowed down. Eventually the barge turned towards the shore, going past the fish markets of Billingsgate, the air rank with the stench of herring, cod, brine and salt. They disembarked at the Woolquay. Above them soared the Tower with its sheer walls, bulwarks, crenellations and bastions. Even on that sunny day the huge fortress had a threatening and forbidding air. Athelstan disliked the place: he had visited it on many occasions, accompanying Sir John in the pursuit of some red-handed murderer.

'A narrow, cruel place,' he muttered. 'May St Dominic and all the angels take us swiftly in and out, for death and murder always lurk here.'

They crossed the drawbridge. Beneath them the moat was filled with dirty green slimy water which stank worse than any midden heap in the city. They went under the black arch of Middle Tower. The huge gateway stood like an open mouth, its teeth the half-lowered iron portcullis. Above them the severed heads of two felons, now rotting under the sun, grinned down at them.

'God defend us,' Athelstan prayed. 'From all devils, demons, scorpions and malignant sprites who dwell here!'

The gateway was guarded by sentries who stood under the narrow vaulted archway seeking shade from the sun.

'Sir John Cranston, Coroner!' Cranston bellowed. 'I hold the King's writ and this is my clerk, Brother Athelstan, who for his sins is also parish priest of St Erconwald's in Southwark. A place,' Cranston paused and grinned at Athelstan, 'where, as the Sanctus Man will show, virtue and vice rub shoulders and shake hands.'

In response, one of the sentries hawked and spat, narrowly missing Cranston's boot. The coroner advanced threateningly towards him. The fellow forced a smile, mumbled an apology and fairly skipped before them, up past Byward Tower. They turned left at the Wakefield, going through another fortified wall and on to Tower Green. Most of the garrison was assembled there: soldiers lying on the grass, their wives at the washtubs, children climbing over the catapults, battering rams, mangonels, huge iron-ringed carts and the other impediments of war. To their right stood the massive half-timbered Great Hall with other rooms built on to it. Here the soldier handed them over to a snivelling red-nosed groom who took them up into the Great Hall. Cranston patted the two rough-haired hunting dogs snuffling amongst the dirty rushes. One of them took this friendliness too far and was about to cock its leg against Sir John but ran off growling when the coroner lashed out with his boot. The hall itself was a vaulting, sombre room with a dirty stone floor and smoke-charred heavy beams. Against the far wall was a fireplace, broad and high enough to roast an ox. The midday meal had just been finished and scullions were clearing the tables on either side of the hall, throwing the pewter and wooden platters into a tub of greasy water which they pushed around on wheels. A group of men stood before the fireplace. The groom hurried over. One of the men, tall and lanky, red-haired with pink-lidded eyes, sauntered over, thumbs stuck into his broad leather belt. He forced a smile as he recognised Cranston and Athelstan.

'Goodmorrow, sirs!'

'Master Colebrooke, isn't it?' Athelstan asked, going forward to shake the man's hand.

'The same, now Constable of the Tower.' Gilbert Colebrooke preened himself. 'To what do I owe this honour?'

'Alcest,' Cranston snapped. 'Clerk of the Chancery of the Green Wax. He came here seeking shelter.'

'Oh yes, so he did.' Colebrooke scratched his chin. 'In a fair fright he was, demanding all his rights. I gave him a chamber high in the Wakefield. What's this all about, Sir John?'

'Look, sir, you know better than to ask and I'm too astute to tell. I want to see him now!'

Colebrooke pulled a face. 'Sir John, you know the rules of war. The Tower is under my direct authority. Any royal official who shelters here has my protection.'

'Of course, Master Gilbert, you can be present when we question him.' Cranston smiled. 'I still want to see him now. Or I can take a barge down to the Savoy Palace and tell His Grace the Regent that I am unable to carry out his commands, at least at the Tower.'

Colebrooke almost ran from the hall. He returned a short while later, Alcest trailing behind, and led Sir John and Athelstan down a corridor into a small, whitewashed room. Athelstan studied Alcest closely. The clerk was dirty and dishevelled; he looked as if he hadn't slept, whilst a muscle high in his right cheek kept twitching. Cranston waved him to a stool whilst Colebrooke slammed the door and stood with his back to it.

'You find it restful here, Master Alcest?' Cranston demanded.

'Yes.' The young man rubbed his eyes.

'You came here late last night?' Athelstan asked.

'I had to collect my belongings but, yes, I came just before the gates were closed.'

'Did you go to Southwark?'

Alcest shook his head.

'Are you sure?'

'I don't know,' Alcest mumbled.

'Neither do we,' Athelstan retorted. 'Because, sir, you are a liar. Your paramour, Clarice, tells us that on the night Chapler was killed you were not asleep with her all night but left and came back.'

'I...'

'What?' Athelstan declared. 'Are you going to confess that you put a sleeping potion into her wine which she did not drink? Quick of wit and sharp of eye is Mistress Clarice. Where did you go?'

Alcest licked his lips. He glanced furtively around as if seeking some bolt-hole.

'Where did you go?' Cranston demanded.

'I returned to my own lodgings. I forgot the silver. I needed to pay Mistress Broadsheet's girls.'

'You are a liar,' Athelstan declared. 'You slipped along the alleyways to London Bridge. Chapler was well known for going to the chapel of St Thomas à Becket. Lonely and deserted after dark, you went there, struck him on the head, pulled his corpse round to the rail and tossed it over, as easy as a leaf falling from a tree.'

Alcest's hands went to his face as his legs began to shake.

'You killed Edwin Chapler,' Athelstan continued remorselessly, 'because Chapler was a man of integrity. He knew about your subtle schemes, the issuing of licences and warrants to the villains and rogues of London's underworld. The use of false names...'

'Are you going to deny it?' Cranston asked. 'There are those like Stablegate and Flinstead who are more than prepared to buy their lives by sending you to the gallows.'

'Where is the money?' Athelstan asked. 'The vast profits you and the others made. Collected together, is it in one account? With which goldsmith?'

Alcest swallowed hard.

'When Sir John and I began our inquiries into this matter,' Athelstan continued, 'your companions panicked, didn't they? Was that what you intended? Did you make the rest hand over their monies to you for safekeeping? Did you object to sharing out your ill-gotten gains and that's why you plotted to kill them all?'

'No, no!' Alcest moaned.

'I believe you did,' Athelstan continued. 'You are like Stablegate and Flinstead who wanted to get forged licences and letters from you. You are consumed by avarice; the pleasures of the belly and the crotch are your only guiding lights, yet you wanted more.'

'But the riddles,' Alcest wailed. 'I wouldn't leave riddles!'

'Wouldn't you?' Athelstan replied. 'I thought you were skilled in the art of the riddle. Moreover, Master Alcest, look at the way these young men died. Peslep sitting on a jakes with his hose about his ankles.' Athelstan paused and stared at the light streaming through the arrow-slit window. Had he said something wrong?

'Brother?' Cranston asked.

'Yes,' Athelstan faltered. He didn't feel so sure any more. 'You followed Peslep to that tavern because you knew he went there every day. The same applies to the other murders. You knew their habits, their lifestyle. Did you send Napham back to his lodgings?'

'Well, no, he wanted to go…'

'Didn't you arrange to meet him before coming to the Tower?'

'No.'

'Why not? Or did you already know that Napham was going to walk into his chamber and have half his foot taken off by a caltrop? Were you busy in Southwark trying to terrify Mistress Alison, Chapler's sister? You act like a court fop,' Athelstan continued, 'wearing your cloak and spurred boots.'

Alcest put his arms across his chest and began to rock gently backwards and forwards on the stool.

'You do dress like that, don't you?'

Alcest nodded.

'So why did you stop?' Cranston asked.

'I became frightened,' the clerk said. 'When I heard that Peslep had been killed by a man wearing spurs on his boots...'

'So easy, wasn't it?' Athelstan insisted. 'The poison in Ollerton's cup just as you tried to poison Chapler.'

Alcest lifted his head.

'Oh yes.' Athelstan smiled. 'We know about that. Did Elflain tell you he was going to visit Dame Broadsheet? What next? Were you going to arrange some attack on yourself from which you would escape?'

'I'm no murderer!' Alcest retorted defiantly.

'You are a thief,' Cranston intervened. 'You are a felon and an assassin. Master Alcest,' the coroner intoned, 'I arrest you for petty treason, homicide, theft, sustaining and nourishing known outlaws and wolfsheads.' He walked over and, crouching down, stared into Alcest's face. 'I shall tell you something, Master Alcest: you will weep and bitterly regret entering this narrow place.' He winked at Athelstan. 'It was a mistake, wasn't it, Master Colebrooke?' Cranston asked, turning to the Constable.

Athelstan did not like the sneer on Colebrooke's face: he was staring at Alcest as a cat would a mouse. The Constable came forward.

'Master Alcest,' he declared. 'You are now my prisoner. You fled to the Tower and in the Tower you shall remain.'

'You see,' Cranston explained as Colebrooke dragged Alcest to his feet, 'according to ancient law and customs, a felon can receive sanctuary in a church but, if he is found in the royal presence, be it Westminster, Eltham, Sheen or the Tower, he can be arrested and summarily tortured. Master Colebrooke here will help you remember.'

The Constable was already dragging Alcest to the door, shouting for guards. Within a few minutes the hapless clerk had been bundled out of the room, Colebrooke ordering him to be taken to the dungeons.

'Is that really necessary?' Athelstan asked.

'He'll not confess,' Cranston replied. 'And we have to be careful, Brother. If Alcest left the Tower, he might flee to a church, seek sanctuary and, as a royal clerk, claim benefit of clergy.'

'In which case,' Colebrooke continued, 'he would demand to be tried by the Church courts. Brother Athelstan, I am afraid you have no choice in the matter. Sir John mentioned the Regent. He will insist that Alcest be closely questioned.'

'But why did he come here?' Athelstan murmured. 'Why jump from the pot into the fire?'

'Oh come, Brother.' Cranston went across to the table where the servitors had left their blackjacks of ale. He drank his in one gulp then picked up the one left for Alcest. 'Our clerk is arrogant; he acts like cock of the walk. He really believed he wouldn't be arrested.'

'No, no, that's not true.' Athelstan shook his head. 'Sir John, Master Colebrooke, can I be excused for a while? I need to think, reflect.'

And without waiting for an answer, lost in his own thoughts, Athelstan left the chamber and went down the stairs.

'Ah well,' Cranston sighed. He finished the second blackjack and picked up the third. 'Master Colebrooke, I do not want Alcest to die.'

The Constable grinned wolfishly. 'Sir John, he is a traitor and a felon. He has come to the dance floor and dance he must!'

Chapter 13

Cranston kicked his heels in the chamber. He dozed for a while then got up, threw open the door and went searching for Athelstan. He found him outside Wakefield Tower speaking to Colebrooke and one of the Tower scriveners. The latter listened carefully to what Athelstan was saying, nodded and hurried off.

'Brother, where have you been?'

'Sir John, I apologise. Master Colebrooke, thank you and goodbye.'

Athelstan slipped his arm through that of the irate coroner. 'Come, come, Sir John,' he said soothingly. 'I was just going about a little business.'

'What business?'

'In a while, my Lord Coroner, in a while, but the day draws on.'

They left the Tower, Cranston accompanying Athelstan along Tower Street to Eastcheap. At the corner of Greychurch street, the coroner stopped, drawing Athelstan into the door of an alehouse.

'Brother, I must return to Lady Maude and the poppets. There's business waiting for me at the Guildhall...'

'In other words, you are hungry so want a pie and a blackjack of ale at the Holy Lamb of God?'

Cranston grinned. 'You are a miracle, Brother, a reader of minds!'

'No, Sir John, your stomach's rolling like a drum.'

'Oh, so it is!'

'But you'll be in Southwark by Vespers, Sir John?'

'Of course, Brother.' Cranston rubbed his hands. 'I've always yearned to meet the Sanctus Man and I also want to study this precious relic of yours.'

'It's not mine,' Athelstan protested but Sir John was already striding off, raising his hand in farewell.

Athelstan watched the coroner waddling away like some fat-bellied cog making its way along the Thames. 'God bless you, Sir John,' he murmured.

Athelstan paused before continuing: a line of strumpets, their heads bald as eggs, had been caught soliciting within the city boundaries. They were now being led through the city, a bagpiper going before them, his screeching music silencing the din all around. The whores in their smocks, roped together, were escorted by a bailiff who carried a fish basket full of their scarlet or red wigs whilst behind them a boy beat a drum; a legion of urchins followed to see what mischief they could stir up. After that came other rogues: felons, nightwalkers, thieves and pickpockets, all lashed to the tails of carts, their hose pulled down about their ankles whilst a sweating bailiff birched them with thin strips of ash.

At last the sorry procession passed by and Athelstan went along on to London Bridge, making his way under the shops and houses built on either side. He paused at the chapel of St Thomas à Becket and entered its cool darkness. He sat just within the doorway, quiet as a mouse, staring at the huge crucifix which hung over the high altar. He was sure Chapler had been killed here. He must tell Father Prior that so the church could be reconsecrated and hallowed. He closed his eyes and said a prayer for Chapler and the other victims, as well as one for Sir John and himself. He just hoped that the Sanctus Man would help to clear up the mischief at St Erconwald's.

Athelstan left the chapel. He crossed the bridge and entered Southwark and made his way up through the maze of alleyways towards St Erconwald's. He'd prayed for a miracle, that Watkin and company might have come to their senses, but he found the situation worse than he even dared imagine. Booths had been set up near the steps of the church and other relic-sellers had made their appearance, their tawdry goods piled high on trays slung round their necks. Cecily the courtesan was talking to a sallow-faced young man just within the cemetery gates where Watkin and Tab the tinker stood guard.

Athelstan boiled with rage. 'Sir, can I have that?'

He turned to a surprised pilgrim who carried a long ash pole. The man blinked, opened his mouth to protest but Athelstan already had the pole and was striding towards the church, swinging it from left to right, sending the chapmen and relic-sellers scattering. The young man, busy with Cecily, caught the rage in Athelstan's face and loped like a greyhound for the mouth of the nearest alleyway; those waiting to be allowed into the graveyard thought again and stepped back nervously.

'Now, now, Brother.' Watkin pushed his chest out. Athelstan could see he had been drinking some of the profits. 'Now, now, Brother, fair is fair!'

'This is the house of God!' Athelstan shouted, throwing the staff which Watkin deftly caught.

'Keep the relic-sellers, and the rest who prey on human greed and weakness, well away from the porch of my church!'

'Father, you should bless our relic.'

'Oh, I am going to bless it.' Athelstan walked back, poking his finger at Watkin. 'Don't you worry about that. Make sure that you and the rest are here when the bell for Vespers tolls and that's all I'm going to say on the matter.'

He went to the stable where Philomel leaned against the wall, chewing as lazily as he always did. Athelstan chatted to him then went across to the priest's house; it was tidy and clean. Bonaventure had apparently gone hunting.

'Or to visit that bloody relic!' Athelstan murmured to himself.

He sat down on a stool and closed his eyes, breathing in deeply to calm himself. He drank a little ale, ate some bread and cheese, then went up into the loft where he sat on the edge of his bed reading through Richard of Wallingford's work, admiring the skilful sketches and drawings.

'When this business is over,' Athelstan declared loudly, 'I'm going to ask Father Prior for a little holiday. I'm going to St Albans to see Wallingford's clock.'

He closed the book and sighed. He dared not approach Father Prior: he was still deeply uneasy about Brother Niall's recent visit. There was something in the air, something was about to happen which would change his life. He lay down on his bed and thought of Alcest. Athelstan was sure he was a murderer, but guilty of which deaths? Athelstan, slowly but surely, went through all the circumstances. Something was wrong! He didn't need to write it down, he could list the problems in his mind. He had a solution, but did he have the proof?

'I'll have to wait,' he muttered. He felt Bonaventura, who had appeared silently from somewhere, jump on the bed beside him. 'Let's sleep,' he murmured. 'Let's sleep, at least for a while.'

Athelstan was woken by a loud knocking on the door and his name being called. Getting up, he wearily went down the steps and unlocked the door. Benedicta and Alison Chapler stood there.

'Come in! Come in!'

He sat them down at the table and served them cups of ale and some of the bread and cheese left over from what he had eaten earlier.

'Brother,' Alison began. 'I apologise but I've come to say goodbye.'

'You are leaving now?'

'No, early in the morning. I'm taking the road to Epping. My brother's murderer? You've apprehended him?'

'Alcest is under arrest at the Tower,' Athelstan replied. 'There are further questions he may be asked, but...' He smiled at her. 'Tomorrow morning you may go. I am sure Sir John will not detain you.'

'Watkin told us about your temper,' Benedicta intervened.

'Watkin is going to feel more of my temper,' Athelstan retorted. 'Benedicta, it may interest you, so stay until the Vespers bell rings. You, too, Mistress Alison. Perhaps you can tell the story in Epping. Will you stay there when you return?'

'Perhaps.' Her sweet face smiled back. 'Or perhaps I'll return to Norfolk.'

'What?' he asked, then changed the subject. 'Do you know about Master Lesures?'

'The Master of the Rolls!' Alison made a face. 'Edwin said he liked small boys. He was lazy and inefficient and didn't care very much. A frightened man, but Alcest ruled him and the rest like a cock rules the roost.'

'And he was right.'

Athelstan went across to the window and realised he had slept longer than he'd thought. For a while he sat with the women, with Alison chattering about Mass offerings for the soul of her dead brother.

Athelstan half listened. He felt tired, slightly weary, and started when Cranston burst through the door, bellowing greetings at Benedicta and Alison.

'Has the bugger arrived?' he roared, picking up the jug of ale and drinking from it.

'If you are referring to the Sanctus Man,' Athelstan said crossly, 'no, sir, he has not.'

'Well, he'll soon be here. Listen now!' Cranston took off his beaver hat and cocked his head. 'Any moment now, Brother.'

Sure enough, Athelstan caught the sound of the bells of St Mary Overy tolling across Southwark calling the faithful, and there weren't many, to evening Vespers. Benedicta and Alison caught the coroner's mood and, when the tolling stopped, sat up expectantly.

'He won't come,' Cranston moaned. 'I bet the Vicar of Hell is out of the city and into the woods.'

Athelstan looked towards the door and jumped. Somehow a figure had slipped through and stood standing on the threshold like a ghost.

'The Sanctus Man?' Athelstan asked.

He watched fascinated as his visitor, dressed completely in grey, hose, tunic and cloak, walked silently across to meet him, hands outstretched.

'Brother Athelstan.' His voice was low and caressing.

Athelstan took the soft hand and shook it.

'I am the Sanctus Man.'

Cranston gaped in astonishment at this legendary figure of London's underworld: a cheerful, cherub-faced man with crinkling eyes and rosy red cheeks.

'Sir John, you look surprised.'

Cranston gripped the man's hand: the Sanctus Man's grasp was surprisingly strong.

'Don't squeeze so hard, my Lord Coroner,' the Sanctus Man pleaded. 'My fingers are my trade.'

'Your fingers will lead you to the gallows one day,' Cranston replied gruffly.

'Now, now, Sir John, all I do is part rich fools from their money!'

'They still talk about your sale of the crown of thorns,' Cranston declared. 'I saw a set, even down to the blood-stains.'

'A work of art,' the Sanctus Man replied. 'A veritable work of art. After all, what is a relic? People want to see what they want and I am here. To help the faithful in their devotions,' he continued, 'to concentrate their minds on things supernatural.'

'As well as enrich yourself?'

'A labourer is worthy of his hire, Sir John.' The Sanctus Man now turned. 'And these lovely ladies?'

Athelstan made the introductions. He was scarcely finished when there was a knock on the door and Watkin staggered in.

'Well, Father, we're ready,' he announced, swaying slightly as if the floor was beginning to move. 'Who's this?'

'Good evening, Watkin.' Cranston brought his hand down on the dung-collector's shoulders. 'Don't you know your manners? Aren't we friends?'

Watkin belched noisily and squirmed in Sir John's grip.

'This is a friend of mine,' said Athelstan, bringing the Sanctus Man forward. 'He would like to see your miraculous crucifix.'

'It's not for sale.' Watkin glared at Athelstan's visitor suspiciously.

'Oh, I don't want to buy it, sir. But come on, the evening is drawing on and time is money.'

'Is the cemetery cleared?' Athelstan asked.

'It is, Father,' Watkin replied.

Athelstan led the way out, across the yard and in through the lychgate. The miraculous crucifix at the far end stood on a specially made altar of bricks and clods of earth; these were almost covered with lighted candles, placed there by the visitors.

'It looks the part,' Cranston murmured. 'You can even see the red streaks of blood above a sea of fire.'

The Sanctus Man walked forward and, before Watkin or any parishioner could stop him, he knocked a few candles aside, picked up the crucifix and brought it down.

'Put it back!' Pike the ditcher bellowed to a chorus of shouts and threats.

'Stand away!' Cranston warned.

The Sanctus Man studied the crucifix carefully. Athelstan glanced at the streaks of blood now covering the face and body of the Saviour. 'It is blood,' he declared.

'I'm sure it is,' the Sanctus Man replied.

'How did they do it?'

The Sanctus Man examined the figure and the cross itself. 'There is no secret lever or clasp,' he murmured. He tapped the figure. 'And this is solid. Good wood.' He glanced round the group. 'It's going to be a beautiful night,' he declared surprisingly and pointed up to the sky. 'A balmy evening.'

'What's that got to do with it?' Hig the pig-man shouted.

'I just said it was a very pleasant evening. However, if it had been raining or snowing...' He stared closely at the eyes of the crucified Christ carefully. 'Who carved this?'

Huddle the painter shuffled forward sheepishly, turning sideways as if he didn't want to meet Athelstan's eye.

'You are a very good artist.' The Sanctus Man smiled at him. 'But tell me, sir, would the miracle have occurred if it had been raining or snowing?'

'What nonsense is this?' Cranston asked.

The Sanctus Man handed the crucifix to Athelstan. He took a gold coin out of his purse. 'A fortune,' he breathed. 'More gold than you'll ever see in your life. It's yours, on one condition. Brother Athelstan...' He didn't turn but kept his hand outstretched. 'As I came here, I passed the Piebald tavern. This is what we'll do. I will put this crucifix into a vat of ice-cold water. The good landlord will have one. When it is taken out first thing tomorrow morning, the bleeding should have stopped. If I come back and it hasn't, this gold will belong to your parishioners. I shall also declare the relic to be one of the greatest in Christendom. I will pay,' his voice rose, 'five hundred pounds to make it mine. Well?'

Huddle shuffled his feet and looked away. Watkin and Pike the ditcher began to edge back into the crowd of parishioners. Their confederates and lieutenants, Tab the tinker, Hig the pig-man and Cecily, seemed to have lost interest.

'Come! Come!' the Sanctus Man cried. 'Are you saying the Good God would allow a great miracle to be stopped by a barrel of water and a dusty cellar?' He put the gold back in his pouch.

'What trickery is this?' Athelstan stepped forward and grabbed Huddle by his jerkin. The painter, his face pallid, looked over his shoulder, searching for Watkin. 'Tell your priest! Come on, tell your priest!'

'I shall tell you how it's done,' the Sanctus Man proclaimed. 'Let him go, Brother.' He pushed the crucifix into Athelstan's hands. 'Look at the eyes, Brother. You can't see it but there are very small holes. Inside each wound there will be such a cavity. Now the hole is covered up with a glaze of wax. The blood should really have dried, but Huddle mixed a potion to keep the blood slightly fresh.'

Athelstan nodded, quietly marvelling at the trickery.

'Now, if the crucifix had been hung in a cold church,' the Sanctus Man continued, enjoying himself, 'the wax would harden, and inside the cavity both the blood and the tincture would eventually dry. The longer it was left, the harder it would become.'

'The candles!' Athelstan exclaimed. 'When the crucifix was put up near the baptismal font, candles were lit. The iron spigots were on a level with the Saviour's body.'

'The heat would liquefy the blood and the tincture,' the Sanctus Man explained. 'And you have a crucified Jesus who bleeds.'

'But so much blood!' Cranston exclaimed.

'The cavities can always be refilled.'

Athelstan walked towards his now cowed parishioners. 'Why?' he demanded. 'Why this knavery? Are you so short of pennies? Must you cause such mischief, petty blasphemy, trickery!'

'Tell him,' Huddle cried at Watkin. 'Father,' the painter continued, 'I confess it was my idea. A painter in Genoa had done something similar. A sailor told me whilst I was dining in the Piebald tavern. I told Watkin...'

The parishioners stepped away from the dung-collector, who began noisily to protest.

'You always insist on being leader of the parish council!' Pike shouted treacherously. 'Tell Father the truth!'

Watkin stepped forward like a little boy. 'We did it for you, Father,' he declared, shrugging his leather-garbed shoulders. 'Oh, I admit, Father, I have spent some of the money on refreshments...'

'That's a crime!' Cranston bellowed.

Athelstan gestured for silence. 'Did you know, Benedicta?' he asked quietly.

She shook her head. 'I think you should ask them why. I have a faint suspicion.'

'We've heard you were leaving,' Watkin blurted out. 'Sir John here, in his cups at the Piebald tavern, was mourning the fact, after you and he had returned from that bloody business at Westminster.'

'And?' Cranston asked.

'We were going to give the money to you,' Watkin declared defiantly.

'I beg your...!'

'Oh, not as a bribe,' Tab the tinker added anxiously. 'We were going to ask you to take it to the Regent, honestly, Sir John, give it to him as a gift.' He wetted his lips. 'If not the Regent, the mayor, some alderman: anyone with influence with Father Prior.'

Athelstan confronted his parishioners. 'Don't lie,' he warned.

'We are not, Father,' they all chorused back.

'Do you all swear,' Athelstan raised his voice, 'that that was the reason you did it? Swear on the cross and the lives of your children?'

The parishioners now roared their assent.

'But you still did wrong,' Athelstan declared, shaking his head. 'You did very wrong and restitution has to be made.' He thrust the crucifix into Huddle's hands. 'Burn this!' he ordered. 'You will tell the curiosity-seekers that the candles caught the wood. God's fire burnt it.'

'I'll do it now, Father.'

Huddle loped off, the crucifix under his arm, to the small brick enclosure behind the church where Athelstan made a bonfire of materials no longer needed.

'Sir John will collect all the money,' Athelstan continued. 'Every single penny. He will keep it in trust and give it to one of the almshouses in the city. For the rest, I must thank...' He turned but the Sanctus Man had disappeared, going as quietly as he came.

'Sir John! Sir John!' Flaxwith, covered in sweat, came hobbling through the cemetery gates, Samson, tongue out, running beside him. 'You must come now, Sir John, to the Tower! The clerk, Alcest, he's had a seizure! Master Colebrooke says it was unexpected.'

Athelstan rapped out a few orders to Watkin and Benedicta.

'I'll take you across,' Moleskin the boatman volunteered.

Sir John accepted the offer and within a few minutes they were all hurrying along the alleyways of Southwark down to the waterside. They clambered into Moleskin's boat, Samson immediately going to stand in the prow, jaws half open, eyes closed, enjoying the cool evening breeze.

'I'm sure that bloody dog has a mind of its own!' Cranston murmured. He glared at Moleskin sitting opposite him, pulling at the oars.

'We meant well,' Moleskin replied. 'We did, Sir John. We can't let Brother Athelstan leave.'

'Silence now!'

Athelstan stared up at the darkening sky.

'Master Colebrooke appears to have been too hard.'

'No, no, I've heard it happen before,' Cranston replied. 'Alcest was a clerk. Sometimes it's the young and apparently strong who succumb, not to the physical pain, but the mental torture. Alcest will not be the first, and certainly not the last, to die of fear.'

Cranston and Athelstan sat back as Moleskin guided his wherry past grain barges, fishing smacks, and skiffs, some with lantern horns already hung against the gathering gloom. At last they reached the Tower. Moleskin, eager to please, took them along the quayside and promised he would wait for them. Cranston, Athelstan and Flaxwith clambered out but Samson refused to leave.

'Treacherous cur!' the bailiff whispered.

'I don't think so,' Athelstan replied. 'Moleskin always carries a sausage in his pouch and, if I can smell it, so can Samson.'

They made their way along the pebbled path and across the moat. The gates were closed but a sentry, carrying a torch, opened a postern door and then led them along the narrow lanes on to Tower Green. Colebrooke was waiting, sitting on the steps of the great Norman keep.

'You were too hard on him!' Cranston barked.

'Sir John, we'd hardly begun,' Colebrooke replied, getting to his feet. 'I had him manacled to a wall. The questioners applied a burning iron to his arm and suddenly he jerked like a doll, blood pouring through his nose. He's hardly conscious. I'll take you to him.'

Cranston told Flaxwith to remain outside as they followed Colebrooke down mildewed steps into the dark, sprawling maze of the Tower dungeons. They found Alcest in one of these, lying on a bundle of clean straw. Athelstan crouched down by the makeshift bed. He noticed a bruise high on Alcest's right cheek and the blood crusting around the nose at the corner of the mouth. The clerk's hands and feet were cold as ice. Athelstan felt for the blood pulse in the man's neck: it was slow and weak. The friar pointed to a tallow candle on the table.

'Light that!' he ordered.

Colebrooke did so, as well as the sconce torch on the wall above the door. He handed the candle to Athelstan, who let the flames burn for a while then blew it out, putting the wick under Alcest's nose. The sharp, acrid fumes made the clerk stir; his eyelids fluttered.

'Master Alcest,' Athelstan whispered into his ear. 'Master Alcest, you are very ill, perhaps even dying.'

'A priest,' Alcest murmured. 'Father, I have such pains in my head. God's judgement, such terrible pains! I have had them before. Sometimes at night,' he stammered. 'Father, I can't feel my feet or hands. It's so cold and dark.' His eyes closed. 'Shrive me, Father. Shrive me before I die.'

Athelstan looked over his shoulder. 'Leave us,' he ordered.

Cranston followed Colebrooke back along the passageway; they went out on to the green where Flaxwith was staring mournfully in the direction of the river.

'I'm sorry, Sir John,' Colebrooke confessed. 'But I've seen it happen before. Sometimes, even before battle, a blood pulse breaks in the head or neck; there's a loss of feeling in the lower limbs.'

'Do you have a physician?' Cranston asked.

'A leech but he's a drunken sot and at the moment is lying in his chamber. He could hardly open a door, let alone examine a man!'

Cranston walked across to study one of the heavy war machines. 'Where's Red Hand?' he asked. 'When I came here a few winters ago, I met him, a mad dwarf. He lived in the dungeons.'

'Gone the way of all flesh,' Colebrooke replied mournfully. 'Died of a fever last spring.' He pointed across to the little cemetery near the Tower chapel of St Peter ad Vincula. 'Buried there he is, at peace at last.'

Cranston and Colebrooke stood chatting about people they both knew. The coroner heard his name called as Athelstan came up the steps from the dungeons.

'You've shriven him?' the coroner asked.

'He'll die a better death than the life he's lived,' Athelstan replied. 'I don't think it will be long, Master Constable. There's no further need to question him. Give him some drugged wine, let him sleep. He'll slip away. Don't move him. The less movement, the less pain.'

Cranston went to thank the Constable.

'One moment, Sir John,' Athelstan intervened. 'Master Colebrooke, the scrivener?'

'He's still in the Byward Tower,' the Constable replied.

Athelstan promptly hurried off. A short while later he returned. Ignoring Cranston's questioning looks, he thanked Colebrooke and, with Flaxwith almost trotting before them, they left the Tower and made their way back to the quayside. Darkness was now falling. The clouds were building up over the Thames, gusted by a strong wind. Athelstan stopped and stared up at the sky.

'It will be a bad night for the stars, Sir John, but, there again, we've got business to do.'

'What business?' Cranston asked. 'Brother, what have you discovered?'

'I can't tell you that, Sir John. I can't tell anyone what I heard under the seal of confession.'

'But Alcest's the murderer?'

'Alcest is a murderer, as guilty as Judas.'

Athelstan made his way towards the steps. He grinned; his prophecy had been proved right. Samson sat in the boat, a piece of sausage dangling out of his mouth.

'Thank God you've returned!' Moleskin exclaimed. 'I was afraid that when he'd finished the sausage, he'd start on me!'

They all clambered in. Samson sat on his master's lap and began to lick his face. Moleskin pushed away and, straining at the oars, guided his wherry skilfully across the Thames. The swell of the river had become more noticeable in the evening wind, so everyone was pleased to reach the Southwark steps. Flaxwith wanted to return to the city but Athelstan asked him to stay.

'It's Lesures, isn't it?' Cranston asked, plucking at Athelstan's sleeve as they walked up an alleyway.

'Yes, yes,' Athelstan replied absent-mindedly. 'Master Lesures has a great deal to answer for.' He stopped as they passed the Piebald tavern and looked through a window. 'Stay there a moment, Sir John, you are not to come in. I won't be long.'

Before Cranston could protest Athelstan went through the doorway; when he returned, he was pushing something into his pouch. Cranston noticed how he held this carefully as if it was something precious.

They found the cemetery and the area around the church deserted. The air still bore the stench of burning and candle wax but the makeshift altar in the cemetery was now tumbled down and all traces of the 'Shrine of the Miraculous Crucifix' had disappeared.

'I hope Benedicta's here,' Athelstan murmured.

'I think she is,' Cranston replied. 'I can see candlelight through your window, Brother.'

They found Benedicta and Alison seated round the table. Cranston exclaimed delightedly at the huge earthenware pot of ale Benedicta must have brought from a nearby tavern. She carried in fresh tankards from the kitchen and laid out five traunchers, each with strips of dried meat, cheese and slices of apple. Samson, ears cocked, looked around him.

'Oh God!' Cranston prayed. 'Don't let Bonaventure come back, not now!'

'He won't,' Athelstan replied. 'He's a very intelligent cat and will know Samson's here. But, Henry, come here. I have a small present for you and your wife. It's upstairs in my bed loft.'

Athelstan ignored the curious looks from the rest and led Flaxwith up the ladder. A few minutes later the friar returned alone and sat down at the table. He blessed himself, dipped his fingers in a bowl of water, wiped them on the napkin provided, then sipped at his ale. Cranston began to speculate about a change in the weather, but Benedicta suddenly pulled at his hand.

'Shush, Sir John, listen!'

They all did.

'Oh no!' Cranston groaned, half rising to his feet. 'Do you hear that, Brother?'

The friar stopped eating.

'It's someone wearing spurs!' Benedicta exclaimed. 'He's outside the house!'

'It can't be Alcest,' Alison declared.

'Oh no, it's not Alcest, Alison.' Athelstan leaned over and clasped her hand. 'And although Alcest is a murderer, he's only guilty of one death, isn't he, mistress?'

'I beg your pardon, Father?'

'You heard what I said,' Athelstan replied. 'Mistress Alison, Alcest killed one clerk but you've slain four!'

Chapter 14

Alison would have sprung to her feet but Athelstan leaned across and pressed her back.

'What is your real name?' he asked.

'Why, Alison Chapler. I am Edwin's sister.'

Cranston, standing behind the girl, shook his head. Athelstan ignored him. Benedicta just sat with her mouth open. Flaxwith took Samson off and sat on a stool in a far corner; he pulled the dog on to his lap, stroking his ears.

'I went to the Tower,' Athelstan explained. 'In that grim fortress there's a muniment room with tax rolls going back decades. Interesting how tax-collectors are most assiduous in writing down details. They list people by tenement and occupation. Now, they list a family in Bishop's Lynn, Norfolk, for 1362. Father, mother, their son Edwin and his sister Alison, no more than a child of three years.'

'Well, you see, Father...'

'No, no,' Athelstan interrupted. 'I then asked the scribe to look at the tax roll for 1365. By then two of the family had died: Edwin's father and his sister Alison, who was described as mortua, dead. Now, if you want, I can always ask Sir John to send one of the King's cursitors to make careful inquiries into your background?'

Alison, her face drained of colour, just shook her head.

'Oh, by the way,' Athelstan remarked. 'The jingling you heard was a pair of spurs I borrowed from the landlord of the Piebald tavern. Master Flaxwith went upstairs, tied a bit of string round them and lowered them out of the window. He gave them vigorous shakes so it sounded as if someone wearing spurs was walking up and down. Last night you did the same at Benedicta's house. From the chamber above her parlour, you lowered those spurs out of the window, gave the string a vigorous twitch, but not before you had left the final riddle, as if it had been pushed under the front door.'

'I think you are mistaken.'

'Mistress, I am not. I was very intrigued how, in our discussion with the parish council, you knew all about a Norfolk legend, the "Kitsch Witch".'

'Edwin told me about it.'

'I don't think so, Mistress Alison. I have little proof of this, but with your art of being a seamstress, your knowledge of morality plays, as well as being so informed about mummers using fake blood, I suspect you are the daughter of travelling people. I believe Edwin met and fell in love with you.'

'Then why didn't we marry?'

'Oh come, come, Alison, or whatever your real name is. You and I know that royal clerks who are married, unless they are very senior in position, do not get the preferment they want. At the same time, I don't know why,' Athelstan paused and gathered the crumbs from the table, 'Edwin wanted to keep your past a secret, to give you a new identity. I wonder why?'

'Brother, I wasn't in London when some of these men were killed.'

'Let me start from the beginning.' Athelstan pushed away the trencher and sipped from his blackjack of ale. 'Edwin Chapler is born in Bishop's Lynn, Norfolk. His parents and sister died. I suspect he attended the Norwich Cathedral school; a very able and clever scholar, he was later sent to the Halls of Oxford or Cambridge. Which was it?'

'Cambridge,' the woman replied.

'Either there, or shortly afterwards, he met you. You became his sister. A quiet, industrious couple, you moved into the small Essex village of Epping. Edwin would come armed with letters of recommendation, possibly from a Master in Cambridge, and secured a benefice in the Chancery of the Green Wax. You stay in Epping, Edwin takes a paltry chamber overlooking the city ditch but, now and again, you come up to London to meet him. Am I correct, mistress?'

Alison refused to answer.

'Now, what should have been the beginning of a glorious career in the royal service,' Athelstan continued, 'turned into a nightmare. Chapler was a very honest man. He soon realised that, despite all the banter, the revelry and the riddles, Alcest and his companions controlled

Lesures through blackmail whilst they dabbled in trickery, selling writs and licences to the outlaws, wolfsheads and denizens of London's underworld. They invited Chapler to join them. Many a young man would have accepted such bribes joyously, but Edwin was different. He was a man of integrity.'

'He was a great man,' Alison interrupted, tears rolling down her cheeks. 'Never once did I see him lift a hand to hurt anyone but yes, Brother, he regarded Alcest and the rest as demons from hell: their gods were their bellies and their cocks!'

'Chapler told you all about them, didn't he?' Athelstan asked. 'He told you all their little customs and practices. How they dressed, what they drank, which brothel they attended. How they revelled in their wealth and their arrogance. Of course he had scruples, as any righteous man would: those clerks were committing a very serious crime and he, by his silence, was condoning it.'

Alison nodded as she wiped her cheeks with the back of her hand.

'I am not too sure what happened then,' Athelstan continued. 'But Edwin must have protested, perhaps even threatened them. Alcest and the rest responded with counter-threats and silence until one day they tried to poison him, putting a potion in his malmsey cup at the Chancery.'

'How did Edwin keep his relationship with Alison so secret?' Flaxwith, sitting in the corner, called out.

'As I've said,' Athelstan replied, 'they kept up the pretence of being brother and sister. Alison would travel to London in man's dress. A subtle enough game to fool the good people of Epping as well as anyone who knew them in the city. Moreover, it provided extra protection when she travelled. I've visited Chapler's lodgings: they were mean and simple and yet his salary was good.' Athelstan gestured round the kitchen. 'Everyone deserves a home: you and Edwin had another chamber, didn't you? As far away as possible from the Chancery of the Green Wax: beyond the walls at Holywell or to the west of Clerkenwell? However, when Edwin fell ill, you, dressed as a man, visited him in his lodgings. You then realised how serious the situation was: those clerks were going to kill Edwin. You begged him to resign, to leave the Chancery, but Edwin was stubborn and courageous. He recovered and returned to work, so Alcest and the rest decided to kill him. It was well known that Edwin Chapler liked to visit the little church of St Thomas à Becket on London Bridge. Alcest organised a revelry: food, wine, pretty whores, then, cloaked and cowled, he slipped out through the darkness to London Bridge. He lay in wait for Edwin. When the moment was right, Alcest killed him, smashing his skull and tossing his corpse into the Thames.'

Alison lowered her head, her shoulders shaking.

'The wheels of God,' Athelstan remarked, 'move in inexplicable ways. They thought they could kill a good man, that his death would not be laid at their door. They would all take the oath and have witnesses that when Edwin Chapler died, or at least on the night he disappeared, they were too drunk to walk, never mind kill.

They didn't count on Mistress Alison. You must have still been in London the night Edwin died and, when he didn't meet you the following day, you sensed what had happened. Your love is so great, isn't it?' Athelstan continued. 'You'd feel it in your soul and so you plotted your revenge.'

'But I only arrived in London,' Alison interrupted, lifting her tear-stained face, 'the morning you came to the Chancery of the Green Wax.'

Athelstan looked at Sir John, hoping the coroner would support him in his petty lie.

'I don't think so, mistress. Sir John here sent a messenger to Epping. We know you've been out of the village for some time. Ah no, you laid your plans very cleverly. On the morning we met, you'd already been busy. Edwin had told you about Peslep's daily habits. You went to the Ink and Pot tavern dressed as a young man, imitating and mocking Alcest by having spurs on your boots. Peslep went out to the jakes; the tavern was noisy, he was by himself and so you struck. You went across and stabbed him twice, once in the belly and once in the neck whilst his hose was still around his ankles. You knew that.'

Athelstan pushed a blackjack of ale towards her. She sipped from it, but her eyes never left his.

'When I brought you here to Southwark the night we met William the Weasel you remarked on how Peslep had died, stabbed with his hose around his ankles. How did you know that?'

'You told me.'

'No, we didn't, mistress,' Cranston interrupted. 'Brother Athelstan and I never tell anyone the exact details of a murder.'

'Then someone else told me!'

'No, no, they didn't.' Athelstan paused. 'You also made another mistake: the day I anointed Edwin's corpse in the death house, you talked not of one assassin but a group. You asked if "they" would be caught and punished. At the time, a slip of the tongue but, as more murders took place and we discovered the villainy of those clerks, I began to wonder.' Athelstan sipped at his ale. 'Anyway, you killed Peslep, returned to your private chamber, God knows where it is, changed into a travel-stained dress and made your way to the Silver Lute, as if you had just arrived in London. You then went to the Chancery of the Green Wax. The news of Edwin Chapler's death had reached there. The clerks informed you, comforting you. They saw you as they saw every woman, a pretty face and an empty head. You are, however, most skilful and sharp-witted, a veritable Salome dancing amongst the innocents.' Athelstan smiled grimly. 'Or perhaps not so innocent! You knew all about their little pots of malmsey; they let you wander round the chamber, perhaps hold Edwin's cup. At the appropriate moment you slipped a potion into Ollerton's cup. You were going to pay them back in similar coin.'

'Edwin had told you everything, hadn't he?' Cranston intervened. 'Particularly the clerks' love of riddles. So you concocted some of your own. Each riddle stood for a letter forming the word *poena*, the Latin for punishment. You would carry out punishment against these assassins.'

'I was in Southwark when they found the riddle after Ollerton died.'

'Oh come, mistress.' Sir John patted her on the shoulder. 'Do we have to make inquiries amongst the traders near the Chancery of the Green Wax? Some apprentice will surely recall a young man, hooded and cowled, spurs on his boots, giving him a note, paying him well to push it under the door of the Chancery at a certain time.'

'You planned to be elsewhere,' Athelstan added, 'by asking to leave the city. You never really would have left until this matter was finished.'

Alison closed her eyes.

'Elflain was easy,' Athelstan remarked. 'Off to see his pretty whore. For Napham you bought a caltrop, entered his chamber by a window and laid it on the floor. But there was no riddle for Alcest. What were you preparing for him, eh? Knowing what you did, perhaps you'd leave him to the King's Justices. After all, he did wear spurs. Chapler had probably told you that he kept the money for his friends, which might be discovered. He would die last: it would not only complete your riddle but suit your desire for revenge. Alcest would have suffered horrid execution.'

Benedicta, who had sat shocked, listening to it all, leaned forward to touch Athelstan's hand. 'But Alison told me that a man fitting the description of the killer had been seen round the tavern at which she'd been staying.'

'Oh, she told me the same,' Athelstan replied. 'That would make matters even more mysterious, wouldn't it? Deflect suspicions from her. No, no, somewhere in this city Mistress Alison has a chamber either in a house or a tavern, the same place she used to meet Edwin. There she could change from dress to hose, cloak, hat, riding boots and spurs. Dressed in such, she visited the Silver Lute to be seen, so never would anyone think she and this mysterious stranger were one and the same.'

Athelstan glanced at Alison, who had put both hands on the table. 'Sir John has enough evidence to arrest you and put you into prison. The King's serjeants at law will have sufficient to lay before the Justices at Westminster.' Athelstan ticked the points off his fingers. 'We can prove that you are not Alison Chapler. We will discover who you really are, and why you are hiding under another name and identity. We will search the city for your secret chamber. We will prove that you left Epping much earlier than you claim.'

'And there's more,' Cranston declared, coming round to stand beside Athelstan. 'We'll probably find other evidence in our searches. Perhaps a pair of spurs, a piece of string? The lawyers of the Crown will ask how you knew so much about Peslep's death. They will make inquiries about the caltrop amongst the armourers of the city.' Cranston spread his hands. 'Why go to such bother?'

Alison smiled so sweetly that Athelstan doubted for a moment whether she could kill a fly.

'What does it matter?' she asked. 'Edwin is dead. They are all dead.' Her face hardened. 'They with their big bellies, their codpieces, their swagger and their gold. Why didn't they just leave Edwin alone?' She glanced at Benedicta. 'I begged him, you know. I begged him just to ignore them: to do his task and leave them be, but Edwin wasn't like that. He was a good man, a truly decent soul.' She glanced at Athelstan. 'Isn't it strange, Father, being brought down by good men? First Edwin and now you. Perhaps it shows you can't escape your fate.'

'What do you mean?' Cranston asked.

'My father was a good man, a travelling player. He was also influenced by the teachings of Wycliffe and the Lollards.'

'I have heard of them,' Athelstan replied. 'They attack the corruption of the Church.'

'My father taught me to read and write,' Alison continued. 'When he began teaching, he was arrested in Cambridge. The Justices sentenced him to be branded, a red-hot iron slit through his tongue. My father died in prison. I was only twelve. God knows what would have happened to me, but Edwin used to visit the prisoners there.' She took a deep breath, fighting back the tears. 'He took pity on me, stood as guarantor for my good behaviour. When I was released, he secured employment for me in his hall. Afterwards he gained a position with a merchant, rented chambers and I became his housekeeper. He was very brave. The ecclesiastical authorities were suspicious, so we moved; first to Ely and then to Epping. I fell in love with Edwin. We became handfast as husband and wife. A hedge priest performed the ceremony but, to the world, we were brother and sister.'

She clasped her hands together, weaving her fingers in and out. 'The rest is as you know it. Edwin secured employment in the Chancery of the Green Wax. He hated what they did and believed he should reveal such corruption to the authorities. Of course they retaliated: first they killed his horse, then they tried to poison him. I used to come to London dressed as a man to our private chambers near the Abbot of St Alban's inn. I was frightened for Edwin. I was in London the night he died. He wanted to go to pray by himself in the chapel of St Thomas à Becket. When he didn't come back, I knew what had happened.'

She pushed her hair away from her face. 'I am glad I carried out justice. I sent them riddles. I made them frightened. Let them taste a little of the medicine they served out to poor Edwin.' She smiled at Athelstan. 'As soon as I met you, I wondered how it might go: that's why I struck so swiftly. All it took was a little cunning.'

Alison sipped from her tankard. 'Of course I was in London when Edwin died. Even before it happened, I had a premonition. When Edwin was taken ill after the attempted poisoning and sent me that letter, I came to London and wondered what I should do. Edwin never stayed away from me when I was in the city. I heard about the other clerks carousing at the Dancing Pig. Somehow I knew they were responsible for his death.'

'And so you decided to be two people?' Athelstan asked.

'Yes, Brother. When I was with my father, I had experience dressing as a youth. And again whenever I travelled into London to meet Edwin. It was a subtle disguise. On the morning I killed Peslep, I visited Edwin's garret once more, just to make sure. After that it was simply making sure that Alison Chapler was elsewhere whenever this young man was seen. When Ollerton died, I was in Southwark. After I killed Elflain I crossed the river, whilst I placed the caltrop in Napham's chamber very early in the day.'

'Did you hope to escape?' Cranston asked.

'Sir John,' Alison smiled, 'I didn't really care. I didn't disguise myself because I was frightened. I just wanted the time, the means to carry out my revenge. If I hadn't been caught,' she shrugged, 'I would have travelled back to Epping, perhaps sold my goods and entered some comfortable nunnery. Men like Edwin are rare: I would not meet his like again.'

'You were clever,' Athelstan broke in, 'deliberately being seen round the Silver Lute, asking the landlord to keep an eye out for a mysterious young man, although that did intrigue me. When we met William the Weasel,' he continued, 'you were not at all frightened. Yet you acted as if your life depended on leaving the Silver Lute.'

'I wasn't going to leave London,' Alison replied, 'until I saw the end of the game: the destruction of all those evil men.'

'And Alcest? Why didn't you take care of the leader?'

'It suited my purposes, Brother. His name was at the end of *Poena*. I actually planned that he take the blame for all the murders.' She glanced at Cranston. 'Have you found where they hid the profits of their wickedness?'

'No, we haven't,' the coroner replied. 'But I know our Regent. He'll search all the goldsmiths and bankers in the city for that gold.'

Alison got to her feet. 'And I suppose that is it, is it not?'

'Yes,' Athelstan answered softly. 'I suppose it is. Alcest killed Chapler. You carried out those murders.'

'I have to arrest you.' Cranston came round the table.

Alison dug into her wallet and brought out a purse of coins. She dropped these on the table in front of Athelstan. 'The game is finished,' she said. 'Brother, take care of poor Edwin's grave. I have left a will with the priest in Epping. Everything is to be sold and given to the poor. God will understand.'

'I'll go with you,' Benedicta volunteered.

'God forgive me,' Cranston whispered, beckoning Flaxwith forward, 'but you are to be lodged in Newgate.'

'Am I now?' Alison smiled.

Athelstan also rose. On the one hand this young woman had committed terrible murder but, on the other, she had loved deeply and, in her own eyes, carried out justice.

'Is there anything we can do, Sir John?'

'No, Father, there isn't,' Alison interrupted. 'I don't want Sir John making false promises. These clerks come from powerful families. If I sought sanctuary, they would track me down and, when I face the Justices, money will exchange hands.' She walked towards Athelstan and kissed him gently on each cheek. 'Don't worry,' she whispered. 'Look after Edwin's grave. Say masses for him and me.'

She joined Cranston, Flaxwith and Benedicta at the door.

'I'd best go, Brother.'

Benedicta, who was dabbing at her eyes, pointed across at the small writing desk under the window. 'Oh, I'm sorry. Whilst you were across at the Tower, Brother Niall came. He left a letter for you.'

'He probably wants a book back,' Athelstan replied quickly before Cranston could demand what the letter might contain. He walked to the door.

Alison smiled again, Cranston bade goodnight and they left.

Once they were gone, Athelstan sat down on the stool, face in his hands, and said a short prayer for Alison Chapler. 'I didn't even get to know her real name,' he murmured.

Bonaventure, as if he knew that Samson had gone, slipped through the window, tail erect, head stiff. He walked in and, as if disgusted at the fact that his master had dared to have a dog in the house, jumped on to the writing desk, curled up and went to sleep.

Athelstan walked across, picked up Brother Niall's letter, undid the seals and began to read it.

—

Cranston and his party walked on to London Bridge, along the narrow thoroughfare between the shops and houses. The coroner walked in front and Benedicta, one arm linked through Alison's, came next, Flaxwith and

Samson trailed behind. At the chapel of St Thomas, Alison stopped.

'Sir John!' she called out.

The coroner turned.

'I'll never be given the opportunity again,' she said and pointed to the narrow passageway which ran along the side of the chapel. 'I'd like to go there,' she said. 'I really would: say a short prayer where poor Edwin died.' She held the coroner's gaze. 'Please,' she whispered, gently pushing Benedicta's arm away. She walked up and tugged at Cranston's jerkin. 'Please,' she repeated. 'You know what is going to happen to me, no mercy will be shown. Just a few moments. Please!'

Cranston glanced at Benedicta. She looked away. Flaxwith crouched as if closely studying the leather collar round Samson's neck. Even the dog turned its head away. Cranston looked up at the sky.

'Go,' he said. 'Go and say your prayers, then I'll come for you.'

Alison walked away, the patter of her sandals echoing along the passageway.

'Sir John! Sir John!'

The coroner turned. Athelstan was running towards them, hood pulled back, one hand clutching his robe. He slipped and slithered in the mud. A window casement opened and someone shouted out.

'The riddle!' Athelstan gasped. 'The very first one.' He looked round. 'Where's Alison?'

'I let her go to the bridge rails,' Cranston replied. He pointed to the passageway, refusing to meet Athelstan's eyes. 'She said she wanted to pray where Edwin's corpse was thrown over.'

Athelstan ran down the passageway, Cranston and the others following. There was no one there, nothing, only a piece of silk Alison had wrapped round her waist; this was tied to one of the rails of the bridge, flapping forlornly in the evening breeze. Athelstan looked over at the water frothing below. He closed his eyes and said the Requiem.

'It's better that way,' Cranston said. 'Better that way, Athelstan. She had suffered enough. I didn't want to see her burnt at Smithfield or struggling at Tyburn. God knows what horrors would have happened to her in Newgate.'

'God rest her!' Benedicta whispered.

'She said she'd do it,' Athelstan declared. 'That first riddle, about a king conquering his enemy but, in the end, victor and vanquished lying in the same place, like chess pieces, gathered up and placed in their box. They've all gone now: Alcest, Ollerton, Elflain, Napham, Peslep. Good Lord, Sir John, what tangled lives we lead.' He turned. 'And for what? A little more gold, a little more silver? A pair of pretty breasts? Or the best food and wine to fill the stomach? The lust of money is surely a great sin. Because of that those clerks are dead. Alison is dead. Drayton is dead. Stablegate and Flinstead condemned to wander the face of the earth like the sons of Cain they are.' He rubbed his face. 'Sir John, tell the Fisher of Men to search for her corpse. Tell him to treat her gently. Bring it back to St Erconwald's. She can lie next to the man she loved and whom she so ruthlessly avenged.'

'I'll walk back with you,' Cranston declared. 'Darkness is falling.'

They went back to the Southwark side. Athelstan refused any offer of refreshment from Sir John.

'Take Benedicta home,' he said. 'Make sure she's safe. Oh, Sir John…?' Athelstan went up and gripped his hand. 'You are big in every way, Jack the lad,' he murmured. 'Big of body, big of mind, big of soul. God bless you, Sir John Cranston!'

The coroner looked at him strangely, but Athelstan just shook his head. He squeezed the coroner's podgy hand and strode off up an alleyway.

Once he was back in his house, Athelstan bolted and locked the doors. He filled his blackjack full of ale. He lit a candle and picked up Father Prior's letter, rereading it carefully, then put it down. For a short while he cried. Bonaventure came and jumped into his lap. Athelstan stroked the great tom cat. He picked up the letter again. One paragraph caught his eye:

> On your oath of obedience to me, you are to leave
> St Erconwald's quietly and as quickly as possible.
> Take those few possessions you have and proceed
> immediately to our house in Oxford. There you
> will receive fresh instructions.

Athelstan put Bonaventure down on the floor. 'Ah well!' he sighed. 'Now is as good a time as any.'

For the next hour Athelstan packed, pushing manuscripts and his other paltry possessions into battered leather saddlebags. He cleared the table and cleaned the scullery, leaving out any food for his parishioners to take. He then went out to the yard and surprised Philomel, leading him out and throwing the tattered saddle across him. He secured the saddlebags with a piece of twine and went back into the house. He checked that all was well, blew out the candles and walked to the door. Behind him Bonaventure miaowed. Athelstan stared down at him.

'It's up to you,' he said quietly. 'It's entirely up to you. Father Prior has said that I have got to go.'

Crouching down, he scratched the tom cat on the back of the neck. 'I can't stand any upset. I don't want to see old Jack cry or, worse, have Watkin try and bar me in the church. I'm going, not because I want to, but because I have to.'

The old cat looked up at him, studying him carefully with his one good eye.

'I'm sorry I can't write,' Athelstan continued. 'What on earth could I say? Maybe old Jack will come to Oxford, bring the Lady Maude and the poppets? Or Watkin? He and Pike could organise a pilgrimage to some shrine, call in and see me. Philomel's coming and, if you want, so can you.'

The cat padded back into the darkness. Athelstan shrugged and closed the door. He went and gathered Philomel's reins.

'Come on, old friend,' he murmured. 'We'll strike east and find a place to cross the Thames.' He looked up at the sky. 'Sleep out in the fields perhaps. Anyway, come on!'

Athelstan led Philomel down the alleyway. He turned and looked back at St Erconwald's and then jumped as something soft brushed his ankle. Bonaventure stared up at him expectantly.

'Oh, very well,' the friar whispered. 'You can come.'

And Brother Athelstan, friar in the Order of St Dominic, formerly secretarius to Sir John Cranston, coroner in the city of London, and parish priest of St Erconwald's, walked out of Southwark accompanied by his old warhorse and the faithful cat Bonaventure.